S0-DVC-460

Land
Tumbling
Backwards

Land
Tumbling
Backwards

Jonathan S. Coalson

ANTEDILUVIAN PRESS

LAND TUMBLING BACKWARDS
© Jonathan S. Coalson, 2011

This is a work of fiction. Names, characters, places, and
incidents either are the product of the author's imagination
or are used ficticiously. Any resemblance to actual persons,
living or dead, events, or locales is entirely coincidental.

All rights reserved. No part of this book may be reproduced
in any form, except for reviews or educational purposes,
without written permission.

antediluvianbooks.com

ISBN–13: 978-0-9828508-0-0

Library of Congress Control Number: 2011907253

Printed in the United States of America

For my parents

nd then one morning long ago I woke up and knew my self. It was a spring morning, I think. Maybe early autumn. But I woke up knowing things. Like the right amount of coffee grounds to put in the coffee maker to brew a perfect pot. I could never get it right (either too bitter or too weak) until that morning. I was old then, I am sure, because I knew things it takes a lifetime to learn, like knowing when to listen, like knowing one's own name.

I credit the success of this morning to Mister Rogers. His farewell song had been rattling around in my head for weeks.

It's such a good feeling, a very good feeling to know you're alive.

I stepped outside into sweatshirt weather and, not surprisingly on this day of knowledge, I had dressed appropriately. I wore an old green sweatshirt with rust-colored stains on the collar and cuffs. It held a faint floral scent. The sun was just up, breaking the darkness, purple-grey dawns of memory.

It's such a happy feeling, you're growing inside.

I was walking somewhere. It could have been school, either elementary or college, but I knew things—like how to tie my shoes. (Rabbit ear one. Rabbit ear two. Twist around, down and through. Pull both ears, I tied my shoe.) I knew all the U.S. state capitals and all the words to the Gettysburg address. I do not know how I knew these things, but I did. I knew the coffee thing, and I knew the Spanish word for Sunday. *Domingo.* But that one is easy. I just imagine flamingos attending church. I knew my name.

And then you wake up ready to say,

There was power in knowing myself, and I certainly felt powerful on that day. There is great potential in a dawn—the world unfolding. I held a tacit understanding of my dreams; hope was a tangible thing to hold and rub between my fingers like a flower petal or polished rock. As I walked, I sang lightly Mister Roger's song.

"I think I'll make a snappy new day."

I stopped singing for a moment, so I could listen to the sounds of morning: the echo and repeat of mockingbirds, the whistle-trill of the thrush, the tussle of leaves, wind in the trees, the whippoorwill in an unseen thicket—the chorus of day breaking anew.

It's such a happy feeling to know
that I'll be back when the day is new

The sun rose, and my memories changed hue in the growing light from purple-grey to tangerine to sky open blue.

and I'll have more ideas for you.

Memories rushed over me. I remembered a time in little league baseball, with the game on the line, the tying run on third base; I was at bat with a full count. My coach was shouting encouragements, my teammates lined the dugout, cheering wildly, their little fingers gripping chain-link fence. The pitcher spit and nodded and launched the ball toward the plate. I watched the pitch go by. The ump boomed, "Steeerriiiike Three! You're Out!" The bat felt heavy in my hands as I scanned the downcast faces of my teammates. In remembering, I was reminded of more things I knew, like how you should always swing on a full count.

I remembered returning late to my house, the pale orange glow of the porch light, moths clinging to the screen-door as I eased it open an hour past curfew, with the taste of Anna still in my mouth. Trembling and afire, she had said she would love me forever, and I had said I would spend my life devoted only to her, and I knew with complete certainty that these things were true.

I remembered sitting on top of a mountain in the Sangre de Cristos. Jack and I sat with our knees pulled to our chests and talked loud above the wind. He wore a blue fishing hat that had been his grandfather's, and we spoke of things that were not yet. We spoke of things to come. And I knew I was made for college and that I was ready for the changes ahead.

And you'll have things you want to talk about...I will too.

And that day, that morning, walking somewhere was the forgetting. I cannot tell you why or how. Nothing traumatic. I was either fifteen or forty, but I know for sure that I was ancient. And I am not sure whether the forgetting was like a snap or a wave or the setting in of fog, but the sun disappeared behind clouds like a shadow thrown across a window. And with it all of my clarity blurred. (I have known great beauty, and in knowing could not share.) Everything I knew that morning obscured—my shoelaces, the coffee, even my name. The only line I could remember from that old man's song was,

You'll have things you'll want to talk about...

And it kept playing over and over, amplifying in the growing day. *You'll have things you'll want to talk about...* but I could not remember when I would want to talk, or why, or to whom. Mainly I could not remember what the things were I wanted to talk about. And so on some unseasonably warm winter morning I forgot who I was.

I did not forget everything. I could still remember how the front porch looked on a late summer night, but I could not remember why it was relevant. It suggested only a door to a house that I once knew. Memories were there, surely, but their significance was gone. Why do I swing on a full count? *You'll have things you'll want to talk about...* And there was something about the sound of glass breaking, the curve of stone, the fall of hair, something about the combination of blood and water. Why was the cliff side important?

I was a drowning man. Water got into my memories. The pieces of my past were still there; they were still with me, but they did not fit anymore. Sure, I still remembered everything. In the forgetting I did not really forget anything except why any of it mattered. (Were there things I wanted to talk about?) Sure I still had a name, but it was only syllables, and when I spoke them my mouth filled with water.

Waves pounded me (and again), as a painful thought does, unwanted and unyielding, and each to each. I dove deep. I was ripped from sunlight and breath, down, into dark, into seas. And the darkness was full and complete. Water poured over me and through, cold and relentless, until I could only gasp for breath, until I became heavy with the weight of water, forcing me under and down, far beneath the surface, alone in utter darkness, enveloped by night pregnant with sound, a ceaseless vacuous seashell-roar in my ears. Impenetrable black, heavy with noise—that is all I knew. There are no reminders in the forgetting. I could eventually remember no state but that of blindness, could recall no sound but the loud shouting rumble-rush of my insecurity, as though I had escaped memory and time, born from womb directly to grave—simultaneously fetus and corpse. I floundered in the mud, wallowed in the dark mists, meandered in emptiness, resided below the surface alternately shallow and deep for months and years. I descended gradually but surely continuously for weeks and never came to rest on any firmament, sinking steadily as stone. Then, while in the grips of abyss, there came again (as though from sirens on a lonely shore or mermaids from the unreachable ocean floor) the song. It filled my nothingness yet reaffirmed my forgetting.

And you'll have things you'll want to talk about...

If you have ever awakened in the morning/afternoon after a long night of heavy drinking with a feeling of remorse that you cannot quite place, then you understand my waking in those dark days. There was a continual lingering notion of shame, as though

I had done something humiliating the night before, though I could not quite remember. I could not place what I had done to make me feel as such, but I had a vague uneasy feeling that there would be an e-mail or answering machine message chastising me for my indiscretions. But it was not simply one drunken mistake that could be sorted out through communal memory-recovery with friends, it was months and years of guilt built through repeated apathy, inaction and selfishness. I awoke every day with an undefined sense of my feckless existence. I was not the person I was supposed to be—had not been for a long time and that embarrassed me. I could not have articulated it that way then, of course. I only knew I had a desire to apologize, that there were things I needed to correct, (*you'll have things you'll want to talk about…*) but my mind was cloudy and confused. Shame besieged all hope of clarity. And so I pulled the sheets up over my head and hid from the world.

There is a nothingness that does not really exist, a void that irrationally aches to be filled. There is sometimes a need when you have just finished smoking to light another cigarette, the urge to eat when you have just finished a big meal, the gap you believe can be filled by another drink after you have already had enough. There is a yearning that blinds us to what we have. What is that hole in us? Is it addiction? Chemical imbalance? Is it forgetting? What do we have after we have indulged and still have nothing? What are the things we will say if we ever remember?

II

What I remember, before I forgot, is this.

American Pie was up, loud, windows down; we were driving mountain roads in the fluid blue of pre-dawn. We were singing. Both knowing every word to that seemingly endless song. It was a brisk morning, even in August. It was a mountain morning, and it poured into the down-rolled windows, rushing blue and cold. The day stretched before us. Jack and I were going to hike a mountain.

We had spent the last two weeks together at my grandparents' Colorado cabin. It was the summer of 1997, after our senior year of high school, and this was our last trip together before college. We had been whitewater rafting with my extended family the week before, but largely spent our time chopping firewood, playing gin rummy, and trying to feed the local wildlife. We had, nearly motionless, held bits of pecan between our fingers for hours, in hopes of gaining the trust of a chipmunk or chickadee. In those rare moments of success, there was a thrill, intimate and profound, nature deigning to pay us notice, to make contact, the whole mystery and power of the forest held in our hands.

Around the dinner table my family nightly related their memories of the cabin. I had heard all of these stories before, of course; they were a part of our family lore, but they felt more important this time. Maybe because I was finally old enough to appreciate them, maybe because I was preparing to leave for college and begin my own life and so sought history to ground myself.

Maybe they felt magical because Jack was with me, he hearing them for the first time.

The stories that slayed Jack were the hiking stories, tales of peril and adventure. My uncle had once been lost without a compass in the wilderness and had relied on a sort of Harriet Tubman-type resourcefulness, using moss and shadows to navigate his way home. As a boy, my father, hiking with his puppy, Scout, had descended an unfamiliar slope which subsequently terminated in river. He had been forced to forge the fast rushing water up to his neck, holding Scout above his head. Jack and I were captivated. There was an opportunity here in the mountains to not just lure nature reluctantly into our outreached palms with pecans, but to challenge it, to stare it in the eye, to flex our strength and conquer it, so that we, too, might be worthy of tale. Today was our last chance. Tomorrow we were to board an airplane for home.

Half off-key, belting out *American Pie*, I looked over at Jack. He was singing loud and staring out the open window. Trees lined our path, standing armies deep. The two sides facing off, divided by road. I could feel them in that morning, growing. All that life growing, the way a tree grows. Pine tall and strong, ever worn and broken strong. The way a tree grows, into the clouds, quiet nobility of wind-rocked wood, swinging in the air and climbing up the sky. Jack turned and faced me, wind ruffled his thin brown hair, as we screamed the final chorus with reckless abandon.

"Them good old boys were drinking whiskey and rye, singing, 'This'll be the day that I die!'"

"Great song," Jack said.

"God, I miss driving with the music up. What about you? You miss anything from back home?"

"I miss sex," he said.

I laughed, forced and loud. He laughed a little until I said, "With who?"

"Shut up. You know what I mean."

It was the one thing I had ever beaten him at. With us every-thing was a competition, even things that should not be, like sex. Anna had been my steady girlfriend for two years. Jack was always popular with the ladies, but had yet to have a girlfriend longer than three months. I constantly reminded him of this.

"I know you don't mean sex."

"Yeah," he said, half said it. He was quiet this morning.

Driving too fast, dirt and dust bellowed up behind the jeep until the rearview mirror reflected only a red cloud, as though Jack and I were exploding from some earthy haze, hurtling forward from an obscurity that we could not outrun. Pinned by pine on those narrow mountain roads and chased by a pluming history, we bar-reled upward, following broken, hand-painted signs, turning in and back upon ourselves until Jack spotted our trailhead and I parked. There must have been laughing. There must have been silence. A too small sign, wooden against a background forest, read Venable Lakes Trail. We were there.

We wandered around to the back of the jeep, opened the hatch and retrieved our backpacks. Jack got his first. I deferred to him often like this, simple small gestures, certain patterns that had emerged between us which on the whole defined our relationship. He had an ease of movement and singularity of mind. A natural leader. He was tall and handsome, the body of an athlete, skin dark golden brown from hours of yard work. His eyes, and I think prob-ably his eyes are what wooed the girls, were small and soft. Sad almost, but not really. They were more quiet than sad, so that they blended and faded, nearly unnoticeable, into his face. Yet his gaze was unwavering, steady. His eyes said, "If you trust me, I will never leave you."

The continual close proximity to my parents had severely shackled our smoking habits, and we both eagerly lit up cigarettes.

I took my first deep audible inhale. "Jesus, this is good."

Jack looked at me and grinned. "You're so addicted," he said, not in spite or in jest, just matter-of-factly.

"What can I say, I'm an addictive personality."

"Everything in moderation, or whatever," Jack said, kicking at the gravel. We still stood next to the jeep as though we had not been permitted to leave, as though we did not know how to begin.

I pulled another deep drag from my cigarette.

"Moderation is a great theory, but it doesn't work when you're as obsessive as I am."

"No shit, Waylan. You really got to cool it with the mastur-bation." He opened his mouth in a sort of half laugh. "What are you up to now? Six, seven times a day?"

I grinned, focused on ashing my cigarette while working on a response. "What else am I supposed to do when you keep turn-ing me down?"

"Come on, ass-wipe," Jack said. "Let's go."

Each sporting a backpack and a fishing hat, we started the hike. The first steep push consisted of well traveled horse trails. The sun was breaking open the dawn. Soft light penetrated the tall aspen and pine, lemon-washed shades of forest. Bark and rock, mud and moss, highlighted here by warm sun, there muted and deep cool in shadow, but always earth tones, everywhere brown and green.

One last day, I thought, breathing hard. The air itself seem-ingly hued green and brown, smell of pine and earth filled my nose with each inhale. Dampness and spice. Sap stuck in my sinuses, loam lodged in my lungs. Tomorrow we were heading back to In-diana, but it was no longer really like heading home. In just three weeks I would pack up the car and travel north to Macalester Col-lege in St. Paul, Minnesota. Jack was to attend Purdue. One last day, I thought, as we walked in stride, perpetually up, the earth inclining to meet our steps. His presence was familiar and soothing, his nearness to me had my whole life been a continual comfort.

"You know what pisses me off?" I continued on without a response. That was the way with Jack and me. "How schools ban books. Like Huck Finn. Great book. Okay, okay, the word nigger is in there. But come on, did the bastards actually read the book? It's a statement against racism"

"Yeah," Jack said, kind of half said it. "Look."

We had walked two miles up before I realized it. The trail had come to an opening, and we looked out. Trees spread endlessly over uneven, sloping mountain earth. They called it the Sangre de Cristo Mountain Range—the blood of Christ. Seventy-five miles of alpine range in southwest Colorado with no less than eight mountains reaching 14,000 feet. Our trailhead started us at 9,000 feet; it was to end just short of 13,000. Venable Peak rose to 13,334. I looked at Jack. That whole vast fall at our feet was in his eyes.

My shoulder. I am not sure why I thought of it then, but during my junior year of high school I had surgery for a tumor in my shoulder. People came to see me in the hospital: friends from school and camp and church. But when I went home, two weeks confined to bed, the people stopped visiting. Jack came to see me every day of those two weeks, after soccer practice, about seven in the evening. We watched Wheel of Fortune and Jeopardy together. He came every day.

After a while in silence, Jack spoke, and maybe just to prove he had been listening to me earlier, he said, "Hey, do you think Mark Twain would've made a good President?"

"I don't know. He was real cool. And smart. But I don't think he would have wanted to be."

"Yeah. And he was pretty messed up, wasn't he? Blew his head off with a shotgun or something."

"That was Hemingway."

"Oh," he said.

"Did you ever read that *Old Man and the Sea* book I gave you?"

"Great fuckin' book."

"Cool. I'm glad you liked it. But what do you think it was talking about?" I asked.

"I don't know. I'm not big on breaking books down. Just the way they feel. They have lots of stuff to say, but nothing you can describe, ya know?"

I understood quite well that there were things words could not describe. There were times when words were not appropriate. Especially between Jack and me. We did not have much to say to each other, I suppose. We had not been more than two weeks apart for most of our eighteen years. In those eighteen years we had seen each other's souls, gone through mistakes and triumphs and girls, and none could come between us. He was all I had. And that was enough. When we were little, we always had to be doing something active—whether it was basketball or water-balloon wars, we could not sit still. But after losing our way and each other a thousand times, we grew older and more relaxed. We found ourselves comfortable around coffee tables and conversation. We told each other everything. But somehow, with us, it was all in passing. As though it did not quite matter. As though that was how we dealt with the fact that sometimes there are not words enough. We shared important things off handedly in order to articulate them. "Hey, Jack, guess who lost their virginity last night. I'll give you a hint. It's not you." And "You know, I don't think I believe in God anymore." Or "Can you believe it? We're going to college."

We hiked upward all morning, our trail edged by boulders and trees, seldom encountering other people now, the world uninhabited save for us. We talked about nothing because there was nothing to say. We looked everywhere, because there was everywhere to see. We once spotted a doe just off the path. For a split second she stood, stock still, her nose to the wind, muscles quivering, poised to bound but not yet gone, and then she was lost to the underbrush with two powerful kicks. Occasionally Jack and I glimpsed light from a meandering creek, sun sparkling off jumping water. While the creek was rarely in sight, its rush and babble found our ears always.

And there at the trail's end, a silent empty world, our private realm, we came upon a ring of ancient trees. We settled there, dropping our bags, and sprawled in the shade. From there we gazed up at the final steep ascent to the mountain's top.

"Let's do it, Jack. I think we can make it. That's what we're here for. To climb a mountain."

The mountain rose before us, an ancient bulwark of weathered rock. In its presence, cool and rough to the touch, musty metallic smell of damp stone, it was as though we had entered into some timeless pact—here is nature before you at its most magnificent and daunting; test your strength. I grinned, pulled my fishing hat snug onto my head, and Jack and I began our ascent of Venable Peak.

The ragged rock under our soft palms chalked our fingertips with the grey dust of erosion, making us primal and powerful. Kicking footholds in slate and stretching and flexing our muscles with each pull, we were grand, raging youthful bodies defying mighty nature. With a surge of desire and ignorance to meet the challenge before us, we pushed the edge of caution and breath, and it wasn't long before we were aware that our steep incline had turned to straight climb. By then we were hundreds of feet above our start and well beyond the point at which the mountain still revealed an accommodating way down.

That was about the same time that the strength of youth left us.

"Waylan, I can't go any further!" The wind blew hard, and he had to shout.

"I'm tired too, but we're almost there."

I could see a ledge not fifty yards above our heads. If we could muster one last push, we could rest for as long as we needed.

"No, man. There's no where else to go!"

I looked up again. What had appeared to be a ledge was in fact a smooth rock that jutted out above Jack's head. It shot out into sky only a few feet, but it was for all the world something that dared be tackled only by an experienced climber with rope and gear. Jack and I were positioned precariously on the underside of a sheer rock shelf. We were stuck, clinging to mountainside, with no way up, and the only way down falling hundreds of feet.

III

A thrill of expectation took hold of me, which I later identified as the joy of independence, as I checked the door knob. To my dismay it turned. The excitement shrank from me. I had wanted to be the first to move in to my dorm room, or at least find it empty. I did not care about getting priority on bed choice or anything so territorial. It was instead about my emotional capacity.

I was a spent man. I had just yesterday left the only home I had ever known. The family car was crammed, my possessions forced and pressed into every available space, each item carefully selected and discussed, then puzzle-packed into position. Department stores had convinced me of a few college "necessities," of course. "If the bathroom is the down the hall, how will you carry all of your toiletries?" the display of shower buckets seemed to ask. "Public showers?" The flip-flop rack had answered.

All of this newness, this wrapped and boxed preparation, rode next to me on the drive from Indianapolis to Macalester College in St. Paul. These worldly possessions—new sheets, old clothes, hand-me-down dishes, the latest model computer, high school love letters from Anna and the mandatory Einstein poster—these things put me on edge. Yes, they reassured me. Armed with parts of my old life and supplies for my new, I had some sense of readiness. But there was something else, too. I was genuinely worried about whether I had brought the right things.

In elementary school I had learned quickly that what I liked was entirely different from what was cool. I can still remember the smell of those early scholastic years, some muted co-mingling of chalk dust, sanitizer, and vomit. Just a whiff of it inspires fear. Kids are cruel. Do not fool yourself into believing they are pure and innocent. They are brutal and ruthless. My Care Bear lunch box was my first real lesson. My parents could not justify throwing out a brand new lunch box, so I was stuck with it for half a school year. I was stuck with the moniker Sissy Boy for much longer. Elementary kids may not be all that clever with name calling, but they make up for it with persistence. Later I righted myself with the Transformer lunch box; I used it for four years, by the end duck-taped and bearing the strong scent of spoiled milk, because I dreaded going through the process again. One year, fresh off back-to-school shopping, I walked proudly onto the cheap green industrial carpeting of Mrs. Anderson's second grade classroom with new shoes. I had thought my decision for Velcro straps was inspired. I was, in fact, monumentally mistaken.

That is how I felt about my things the day I moved into college—the things that comforted me equally mortified me. I guess the first day of school is always the first day of school.

This dichotomy of emotion was also how I felt about my parents. I am aware that this is how almost all children feel about their parents, but that never seemed to be any consolation. I did not want the added anxiety of trudging along with my embarrassing parents, each charged with a box of my humiliating stuff, not while navigating a new campus, finding my new room, entering my new home.

"No, stay with the car. I'll find the room before we wander around with heavy stuff." And I rushed off without giving my parents time to respond. I was rushing to disassociate myself from the life I knew. I lingered between two worlds, caught between the old and the new. I could envision neither one as mine. I needed a foothold desperately and believed seeing my room would be that—that I might begin to see where at least I would be stationed in this new world. With all this in my heart I approached room 319. And so when the doorknob turned, I felt my knees slightly give. I was too weak to meet someone, let alone find some reserve for my new roommate. I took a breath to collect myself for a first impression, or at least for a smile.

If I had thought to knock, it might have given both of us time to prepare, but I just opened the door. Nathan stood on his bed, facing the wall. He was bouncing. He was not jumping, but the bed gave and returned to his bending knees and the wood frame creaked and the metal whined. He did not hear the door open, and I stood for a moment and watched him. And then suddenly he thrust his legs out from under him and crashed to the mattress onto his back. With this he saw me.

I blushed and stammered with embarrassment for him. "Hi, I..."

But he did not seem to share my feeling of discomfort. "Hey, buddy. You must be Waylan. HA!"

Nathan rolled off the bed onto his feet, and in one stride stood before me with his hand extended. He towered above me but was thin and lanky; I probably outweighed him. His clothes seemed too small. Angular, all bones and height. His ears shot out from a red shock of hair like fresh shoots from a flower searching for sunlight.

"I'm Nathan."

My nervousness about beginning college abated in his presence and I felt briefly an enormous sense of relief.

The grass was littered with carcasses of dead leaves. It was a cold, crisp afternoon, wind cutting through my sweatshirt and whipping about the browned leaves. They tumbled across ill-kempt yards. There in the street, the man and woman who had reared me and loved me, the man and woman whose attributes—some of which I was proud and others unwanted—I also possess, through genetics and sheer osmosis, that couple, my parents (I theirs and they mine), walked to the car. As they did, I felt the whole world being pulled; they seemed to drag the very landscape with them. Everything I knew and understood, they carried. And it was drained from me the further they walked. They walked away in a storm of leaves. They stopped, turned to wave as the leaves rained down, and as my father closed the driver-side door, the old world was severed. My last connection to the life I had known fell away.

As I made my way back toward my dorm room, I heard a vaguely familiar high-pitched whine, a kind of happy hum. Rounding the corner something bit at my ankle and I tripped forward. Looking down, I discovered the culprit to be a remote controlled car.

The hallway was littered with impromptu obstacles: textbook walls, notebook ramps, crumpled towel terrains.

Nathan beamed, standing outside our door. "I traded some guy. This thing for our TV."

"What?" I responded, surprise clearly affecting my voice.

"I know. I can't believe it either."

Nathan worked the remote until the car circled me repeatedly at ever growing speeds.

"I mean, between studying and parties and all the ladies, who's got time for TV?"

He had a point. But the TV? For a remote controlled car?

"Sort of feel bad for the guy," Nathan frowned. "But a deal's a deal."

The car shot off from it's track around me, sped down the hall, caught one of the homemade ramps and leaped a short distance into a pyramid of red and blue plastic cups. Nathan celebrated with a fist in the air.

His skyward-extended arm came down onto my shoulder. "So you got plans tonight?"

"Well, I..." I had hoped to call Anna, to tell her my first impressions of college. I longed to hear her reassuring voice.

"Didn't think so," he said. "You got some now."

Before long, I was sliding into the backseat of a rusted out Camaro.

"Waylan, this is Bret." As he settled into the passenger's seat, Nathan introduced me to the driver. "Bret, Waylan."

Bret's navy pea coat stretched over the broad thick shoulders of one who lifts weights, and the popped collar hid his neck, exposing only his shaved head. He eyed me through the rear view mirror, but did not turn around.

Nerves gripped my gut. I felt out of control there in the dark of the backseat, my direction now dictated by men I did not know. The city passing outside the window was unfamiliar. I was lost and alone. My isolation grew as the drive continued. Street lamps became sparse and the night profited.

Nathan began to fidget in the seat in front of me. He drummed the dashboard with open palms.

"So Bret, I get you're into this girl and her 'rents are out of town, but damn where does she live? Canada? Waylan, did you bring a passport? Christ, I mean, Columbus would have turned back by now."

"Cool it, man. We're almost there," Bret mumbled.

"My ex always said that, and it was never true," Nathan laughed and turned his gaze out the passenger window.

When we finally arrived, it was to a small house aglow on a dark country road. The door opened to a short squat brunette with an infectious smile. She waved us into a living room thick with smoke. On the couch, sitting sardine-style, were four girls, all smoking cigarettes. They glanced up at us as we entered, but quickly returned their attention to the television.

"So these are my friends..." Our hostess introduced each girl on the couch in order from left to right, but I did not listen. Just names I would soon surely forget.

"You got anything to drink?" Nathan said.

"Yeah, the girls brought some," she answered distractedly, her gaze solely on Bret.

Nathan and I looked over at the girls. I wished immediately that I had listened to their names. A heavily made-up girl with dyed red hair sat slouched, using a cooler as an ottoman.

"Perfect," Nathan groaned.

Just then, the phone rang. An odd voice from the dining room squawked, "Hello."

"Maybe *that* girl will give us the time of day," Nathan muttered to me, glaring at the four girls on the couch.

The phone rang again. Again came the answer, "Hello."

"Somebody getting that?" Nathan asked the brunette.

"No," she said. "I'll let the machine get it."

Ring. "Hello."

"What the hell?"

"Oh," the brunette giggled, grabbing Bret's hand and leading us all into the dining room. "That's my mom's parakeet."

The four of us stood around an enormous cage, comically large for the small green parakeet. The bird whistled and buzzed, between short bursts of recognizable phrases. "Hello. Pretty bird. Time to go." It was like listening to an old radio off dial—pop, whistle, hum, snippet of voice, then back to static.

"That's Francis. Mom's pride and joy," the brunette rolled her eyes. "Super pampered. Fancy food and bottled water."

The wide cage was cluttered with a collection of mirrors and an assortment of bird toys. The parakeet cocked it's head sideways, shuffled its feet in a sort of dance, and began whistling *We're in the Money.*

"Does your mom wipe it's ass when it shits?" Nathan quipped.

"Pretty bird."

"Thing's annoying as piss," the brunette said, dragging Bret out of the room and down a darkened hallway.

"So ladies," Nathan said, sauntering into the living room. "Mind if we snag a couple beers?"

The redheaded girl did not answer, but removed her feet from the cooler and produced two bottles.

"Thanks," Nathan said. "I guess."

He sat next to me on the floor against the far wall and handed me a wine cooler.

"I'm sorry, man," he said. "This sucks."

Cigarette smoke billowed up and out, creating a haze that separated us from the girls, us from the rest of the house. The smoke seemed to bear silence, or the silence bore smoke. We sat for a while, not speaking, sipping our wine coolers. I could feel Nathan's anger growing.

"How 'bout that crazy-ass bird?" I said eventually.

"Come on," he answered, standing up.

I followed him closely as he headed down the hallway.

"What's up? What are we…"

Nathan silenced me with a finger to his lips. He checked the doorknob. It did not turn. From behind the door we heard the faint squeaking of a bed frame. Nathan contorted his face and thrust his hips violently back and forth, a sort of perverse game of charades, then motioned me further down the hall.

The next door was slightly ajar, and Nathan pushed it open revealing the master bedroom. He tiptoed in, and I followed. I sat on the bed and watched him cross the still dark room. He slid open a dresser drawer and rummaged through it. Fear bear-hugged my chest, and I inhaled deeply to catch my breath.

"Just crappy costume jewelery," Nathan whispered loudly.

"What?"

Perusing a shelf, he muttered, "Here we go." He was scanning CD's. "Yanni? Really? Friggin' Yanni? Doesn't matter, it'll sell."

"Ah shit," I groaned.

"Come on. Harmless fun. They probably don't even listen to this light rock crap."

"I cannot be here, man," I said, standing, but remained in the middle of the room, unsure of where to go, feeling strangely bound to Nathan, needing his proximity.

"Jackpot!" he said, too loud for my comfort level. "Found the sex toys."

"No way!"

"Yup. And I mean, it's a stash." He held up an assortment of dildos and vibrators. His expression was so genuinely proud that I couldn't help but smile. "Believe this? So sweet! I mean, stealing sex toys. It's low, I know, but come on. Hilarious."

Though caught up in Nathan's delight, stealing still didn't strike me as hilarious; it struck me as illegal.

"Can we just go?" I asked.

Nathan clumsily stuffed the loot into his backpack, and we sneaked back to the living room.

And it was like walking into a fog, the smoke thick, as though something was on fire. The four girls just sat lethargically on the couch smoking away. Immediately I felt better, my mood lightened by leaving the scene of the crime. Nathan grabbed me around the neck and ruffled my hair. He and I sat on the floor in the haze, and I inexplicably began to laugh. Nathan laughed with me. Part of me then even appreciated a little the audacity of his theft.

After a while, Bret and the brunette emerged from the hallway.

"Need a beer?" Nathan asked.

Bret grinned, his face and body loose. "Sure."

"Sorry, all out. But you might be able to grab a wine cooler from the Cooler Nazi over there," Nathan laughed, pointing to the couch. There was no venom in his voice, as though all of his bitterness had evaporated via his petty larceny.

Headlights from the driveway flooded in the window, alighting swirls of smoke.

The brunette spun and shouted, "Shit! It's my dad!"

"What?" My stomach sank. "I thought they were out of town."

"Divorced," Bret answered briefly.

I thought I heard Francis the parakeet say, "Time to go."

And suddenly the room was chaos. The brunette was in motion, waving frantically in the air to disperse the smoke, then ran to the kitchen and returned with air freshener. I guessed then, it was a non-smoking house. The four girls, stirred from hibernation, snatched up their overflowing ashtray and dashed down the hallway, dragging the cooler with them.

Nathan stood tall and thin and red, unmoving in the middle of the room, commotion all around. "Our cars are in the driveway. It doesn't matter. We're busted."

By then Bret had exploded out of the room, pushing fast through the kitchen side door. Seeing his retreat spurred me to action. My loyalty to Nathan was trumped by fear, and I jumped into the front room's coat closet.

Dark and cramped. For a moment I heard nothing but my own rapid heartbeat and labored breath. Then came the sound of a door slamming, followed by angry shouting. Nathan's rational analysis returned to me. We were caught. I might as well accept the consequences. Yet anxiety paralyzed me. The yelling crescendoed, and I began to tremble uncontrollably. I shut my eyes and tried to wish myself away. But there was no escape; I was trapped. I stood there in the dark, balancing on boots and tennis rackets, hiding my face, cocooned in a thick placenta of coats, having not the courage to open the door.

"So this bitch..." Nathan pointed at me from across the room. "Yup, this one right here, hides in the closet. Don't know if he thought it was the door or what, but..."

My face reddened with embarrassment at my recent past. There were several people in our dorm room listening to Nathan's rendition of our adventure. The guys from down the hall were there. Dave and Mara were there, too.

Mara sat with her legs crossed in the middle of my dorm room. Her shoulder-length dark hair was thrown casually into a ponytail, and she wore her glasses, as opposed to her contacts, which always signified either too much study, too little sleep, or low-key hanging out. This evening, it probably represented all three.

In a sense, I never *met* Mara. I had known her since the beginning. She lived across the hall, and I saw her every day. I am sure there had been introductions, but whatever the moment or scenario in which we met, we had both agreed beyond words or gesture or even introduction that we were infinitely comfortable with each other. Mara was seamlessly connected to college life. She just always was.

She wore no shoes that night in my room, but rather big, wooly grey socks which she picked at and pulled on while she listened intently to Nathan's story. I was more than a little disturbed by this depiction of me, Nathan carefully crafting a yarn in which I was the goat. I hoped that Mara would understand.

My real concern about this public humiliation was focused on Dave. He grinned and laughed at each twist in Nathan's story. He kept looking in my direction, as though he were learning about me, assessing, coming to certain conclusions.

I had met Dave the night before in the way one meets people

in college. The party had spilled into the hallway, people and music burgeoning from an open door in a communal, inviting way
that beckoned me with the potential for free beer.

I judged that it had been going awhile by the noise level.
People were talking, drunk and loud, over the hip hop music blar-
ing from a stereo. Two beds and two matching desk/chair sets were
the only furniture. By design, or by happenstance, one bed seemed
to be for sitting and the other exclusively for dancing. The room
moved with the rhythm of energy and youth, alcohol and hormones.
Amidst the pulsating bodies a hand grabbed my shoulder.

"Hey, man," Dave screamed, although I did not yet know it
was Dave. "Do a shot with me."

"All right." I yelled back.

I followed him through the thick crowd to a desk. It was populated by empty beer cans and an assortment of half consumed liquor bottles.

"What are we shootin'?" I was next to him now and spoke
loud in his ear.

He turned toward me and smiled. "Whiskey. Always whiskey."

He set up two shot glasses and then grabbed up from the
array of bottles a fifth of Jim Beam. As he measured out the shots
with an aptness of the practiced, I shouted, "So whose room is this
anyway?"

He handed me my drink. "I've got no idea."

I grinned.

He clinked my glass with his in a toast and said, "Here's to
college."

I opened my throat and tossed back my shot in synchrony
with him. The whiskey stung my lips, warm and sweet on the way
down.

He wiped his mouth with his right hand, then wiping it on his
jeans, offered it to me. I grabbed it firmly, and he pulled me in close.

"Dave Carter."

"Waylan Gray," I said. "Pleased to meet you."

I felt I had in Dave, met a friend. It had been my idea to invite him over to our room on this night, and now Nathan had compromised any chance at friend-building. I was being exposed as gutless in front of all of these people. I grew hot with anger, but more than angry, I was ashamed.

"So while Waylan was in the closet having an incredibly difficult time finding our coats, the dad comes in and goes ballistic. I mean, he's pissed. And he's berating me. Thinks I've been smoking. Thinks I'm there to screw his daughter. I mean, I am the only one in sight." Nathan paused and glared at me, but then broke the gaze with a wink.

"So, of course, after he's flipped out for what seems like forever, he tells me to get out. Everybody sort of emerges, and we cut fast, you know? And I was fire pissed. Getting thrashed by this dad. And no beer, and I wasn't even there to get sex, and now I had this long-ass ride home. But I still had my backpack with the CDs and the sex toys. So it wasn't a total loss. I'm not even feeling bad at all for stealing it."

Nathan was all revved up. And still bitter. It added an edge, an intensity, to the story that kept everyone breathless. All recognized the injustices Nathan had suffered. Everyone there, like I had the night of the party, began to feel his theft nearly legitimate

.

"So a couple days later I get this call, right? It's my buddy, Bret, the one who dragged us to the girl's house. And he's like, 'Man, the girl called, and her mom is going psycho apparently. Figured out her stuff was missing. Says she'll call the cops unless we return it. Says she'll press charges. She wants her shit back.'"

"All of it?" Dave said.

"All of it.

"So then my buddy says he's not coming with me! Says he figured he didn't steal nothin'. Says he wants no part of it. That cocksucker."

And all of us there felt betrayed by Bret. Stabbed in the back. What about the drive and the wretched girls and the thrashing by the dad, all so this guy could get his rocks off? What about loyalty? What about justice? That cocksucker.

"So I show up at the door, right? I'm standing there outside this woman's house with a bag full of her sex toys. Well, she answers the door and, you know, she's kinda cute, for a mom. But she kind of just looks at me funny, doesn't say anything. I hand her the bag and she takes it. And she looks very sad. Embarrassed, I guessed. I start to feel kind of stupid. Or mean. And so I start to leave."

Nathan pounded his feet on the floor. Smiled wide. There was a glint in his eye.

"That's when she starts crying."

"What?"

"Yeah, I mean, like she turned on a damn faucet or something. Mascara running and sobbing and mumbling stuff. And I'm scared, you know? She's a bit unstable, maybe. But I'm fascinated, too. I mean, over sex toys? And she's talking to me. Yelling really. And sobbing. Saying something about how I should know better than to smoke at other people's houses. Well, I'm thinking, I don't even smoke. Then I get it. The bitch told her mom we were smoking. Or the dad did. Or both. So I'm gonna say something. Ya know, rat on the girl. But then I'm thinking, 'Who cares? I don't know this lady. Who cares? It's just smoke.'

"Then she says, 'It's all your fault!'

"And I'm going, sex toys and smoking? Who cares?

"She's like sobbing and screaming, 'Damn it, it's your fault!'

"So I'm having like an out of body experience, you know? It's all rushing around—the party, the boy-scared girls, the dad, the sex toys, being all this way out here by myself, and standing in this doorway while this woman breaks down. And I'm truly like, 'This is fucking unbelievable.'"

And we were all there with Nathan as he stood there and looked at himself in the doorway. Confused. In awe. Staring at this seemingly shattered woman. We all began to shake our heads in disbelief.

"So this woman leans inside the doorway, like reaching for something, right? And she pulls out this little plastic baggy. She's really sobbing now, and she thrusts it in my face."

He waited. We held our collective breaths.

"It's the parakeet. In a fucking plastic bag!" Nathan jumped up. Screaming almost.

"And she's yelling, 'You killed him! It's your fault! He can't handle smoke! You killed my precious bird!' And the whole while waving this goddamn parakeet in my face."

Nathan, smiling wide, loosened his arms and legs at each joint, and flailed them about as if he was a marionette manipulated by strings. To the crowd's delight, he danced a brief jig in this manner and then finished with a deep swivel-hip bow and stayed with his torso parallel to the floor, swaying slightly, his arms dangling, as though his unseen puppeteer had retired.

To my particular amusement, Nathan stayed like that until the entire room became uneasily quiet. My anger and shame abated. It was a good story, despite my role in it. I popped out of my seat, stood next to Nathan and used my fingers as scissors, saying "snip, snip" to cut his invisible strings. He immediately collapsed in a heap onto the floor.

"Much obliged," Nathan said from his crumpled position.

"Hey," I said, "that's what roommates are for."

IV

"You heard of antimatter?" Dave asked me one Friday evening.

"Yeah, sure, I guess," I said.

"So did you know it was real?"

I had found Dave sitting alone at the appointed time at one of our preferred tables in the Kagin dining hall. In a certain way, the people I hung out with was completely based on meal times. There were the students who went to breakfast. It was a group of students I never met. Lunchtime was determined by class schedule, and I ate with those who had the same breaks, so it changed every day, but dinner was a consistent event. Kagin opened at five for dinner and was a breezy three hour affair. Occasionally the dinner scene was an opportune platform for some student to read from a new manifesto or the arena for a food fight, but most often it was about bland food and decompressing from a day of study. My friends and I always went right at five o'clock because, even though it meant waiting in line, in general we had eaten an early lunch to cover for our missed breakfast, or equally probable, dinner was the first meal of the day. The tables were long and picnic-style so we could usually sit together.

As I sat down across from Dave that Friday, he gave me no greeting. He appeared deep in thought as he ate his curry and rice before unexpectedly breaking the silence with his discussion of antimatter.

"You see, it's antimatter because the electrons move in the opposite direction of electrons in matter," Dave said, demonstrating his point distractedly by rearranging food on his plate, swirling it clockwise, then counter-clockwise.

It was a typical conversation. Dave and I were continually sharing new discoveries, delving into the possibilities.

"And when matter interacts with antimatter, it results in a massive explosion."

"Sweet," I said.

"So if you ever meet anti-you on the street," Dave paused and directed his fork at me to drive home the seriousness of his point, "do not shake his hand."

"Yeah, well, I suppose anti-Waylan would be a smoke-free sober jock with good grades and a small dick."

Dave grinned yellow teeth. "I didn't say you'd want to meet him, just saying it's not a good idea."

"Good. Mara, I'm glad you're here," I said spying Mara on her way to the table. She took a seat next to me.

"Well thanks. It's nice to be missed."

"I don't mean it like that. I need your opinion."

"Excellent start," Mara said, her eyes widening in disapproval.

"So I'm in my Intro to Novel class…" I began.

"Here we go," Dave groaned.

"No, really," I said.

"Seriously. You're going to bring this up to Mara?"

"I need a female perspective."

"You need a beating," Dave said.

Mara smiled. "Aren't you two a cute couple."

"Okay, no really," I said, anxious to get her opinion. "So we just finished Jane Austen's *Emma* and spent the whole class talking about Austen as an early feminist writer, who, while taking great strides in strengthening the female voice, was too restricted by her era to fully realize her main characters."

"And…" Mara stared blankly at me.

"Just make him stop," Dave said.

"So here's what I don't understand. I don't understand why Emma fails in the end."

Mara nodded. "Okay, well, she spent the whole book in the process of self-actualization and then she gives in and marries Knightly."

"But why is that a failure? Why can't she get married and be happy? Do all women have to walk into the ocean like in *The Awakening*?"

"See. I can't be here for this. I'm getting dessert." Dave stood up carrying his tray of empty dishes and meandered into the milling crowd.

"Waylan, you're missing the point."

I suspected I was. "I really want to understand," I said and then, abandoning tact, asked, "Does being a feminist require a complete rejection of men?"

Mara smiled, but her tone was serious. "It's not a rejection of men; it's about female empowerment. *Feminist* has become a dirty word. Society belittles the idea of it by labeling strong women feminazis as though they were an extremist group." She leaned back in her chair and examined her butter knife for a moment without speaking. I waited for her to continue. "Look, we are on the verge of the twenty-first century, and women still are not on equal footing with men in any arena. Why can't a woman be outraged by these things without being demonized?" she asked, but did not wait for an answer, her voice getting louder, her speech faster. "We get pigeonholed into these categories of virgin-mother, mistress-temptress or bitch-lesbian, characterized as emotionally unstable or incompetent. We are objectified and encouraged to starve ourselves to meet some unattainable goal of beauty established by marketing groups. It's got to change, and everyone—women, men, the media, government, corporations, you and me—we all have to step up and be part of that change."

"You're right. Sure," I said, "but none of that explains why Emma can't get married?"

"She can. She just shouldn't have to."

"I didn't read it that way.""That is why you don't get it, Waylan. You read it the way you wanted to. You wanted the order and structure provided by her marriage. 'Emma is safe in the arms of a man, so now I can close the book and not worry about her anymore.' It didn't upset you, and that is exactly why it should have."

I had not thought of it in those terms. I felt equally ashamed and energized. This was a world of thought that refused to accept even something as seemingly benign as the end of an eighteenth century novel. College was a place where things I could not see were being revealed, like the existence of anti-universes. Mara and I were quiet for a while, and I thought about what might be a better ending for *Emma*.

Dave soon returned to the table with two massive pieces of chocolate cake.

"Whoa, that is not going to sit well with your whiskey later tonight." Mara said.

"Well, my theory on whiskey is that it's like a woman," Dave said staring at his cake. "Sometimes she makes me angry. Sometimes she disagrees with me. Occasionally she makes me sick. But in the end she makes me feel warm, and that's worth all the other bullshit."

"You're quite the romantic," Mara snickered. "Honestly, between you and Waylan I can't decide who is the bigger jackass right now."

"Never claimed it was a *good* theory."

"You know, Dave, Mara's probably right," I said. "You might want to show a little self-restraint."

Dave licked icing from his fork. "Self-restraint is for people without cake."

"Hey kids," Nathan said as he arrived. He sat down next to Dave, sliding his orange plastic food tray onto the table. "What did I miss?"

"Only my realization that I need to start hanging out with more women," Mara said.

"Cool. Bring 'em around. I do love the ladies."

Mara blew bangs out of her eyes. "That pretty much makes my point."

Nathan began to shovel mashed potatoes into his mouth, but continued to talk. "I wouldn't introduce them to Waylan though. I heard he was confused by his class's reaction to the end of *Emma*."

"Unbelievable," I said, feeling my face flush.

"No one but yourself to blame," Dave grinned.

"Sure. This from the guy that thinks women are like whiskey," Mara retorted.

"No. I said whiskey is like a woman. There's a distinct difference," Dave said.

"I think that's a distinction we need to test," Nathan said and then took a long and probably intentional dramatic pause as he sipped his milk. "What is it? Six o'clock on a Friday? Happy hour in 319 is awaitin'."

Back in the room, Mara played bartender. She handed me a whiskey drink as I sat on my bed. Nathan turned on the stereo, and *De La Sol* thumped out beats and shouts. Dave slipped off his tennis shoes and stepped onto the bed, it giving to his weight, before he sat cross-legged to face me. His over-sized jeans swallowed his socked feet.

"Chess?" He asked, the box already in his hand.

"Sure," I answered. "It's still early."

As we set up our small wooden pieces, Mara handed Dave his drink. He winked at her—a simple act I had always felt awkward pulling off. It took a certain amount of confidence, something Dave did not lack. He was good looking, I suppose: sky blue eyes, close-cropped hair, a charming smile he did not give freely. But his attire was always sloppy, his severe jaw never properly shaved. There was a hardness to his features. He was more rugged than handsome, more marine than movie star.

"Mac rules," he said when the board was set. Traditionally the player with the white chess pieces initiates the action, but we had decided, in a token protest against four hundred years of American institutionalized slavery, segregation, and racism, that at Macalester, black pieces assumed the honor of proceeding first.

I cautiously slid out my pawn. I could see it in Dave's eyes, the board was immediately a sea of movement. He was studying, calculating. Already he was three, maybe six moves deep, predicting and countering. It was math fused with imagination, a dance of extrapolated equations in his mind.

"What's up, troops?" The guys from down the hall popped in through the open door.

Nathan and Mara welcomed them. Dave shot his chin up in greeting, but hurried his attention back to the chess board. He scanned the field, maneuvering within speculation, counter-attacking my potential, though certainly not yet plotted, sortie. Chess is a game of things not yet, things that might yet still be.

I tried to see the board the way Dave saw it, attempted to project my pieces into the future—the squares, diagonals and L's invisibly amassing in the possible, all colliding, overlapping, staccato lines hovering in the realm of improv. More jazz than math, I thought, while unwittingly sacrificing a knight.

A few more regulars joined the party. Dave turned up the music slightly.

"You know, they did a study," he said, glancing around the room. "Music level affects social inhibition."

"I thought that's what alcohol was for."

"That's the main one, no doubt. But the louder the music, the more comfortable people become."

I quickly observed our guests. There were a handful of freshmen chatting quietly, a few were even watching us play chess.

"Why not just blast it then?" I asked in a sudden urge to entertain.

"Just wait. Just watch," Dave said, increasing the volume another notch.

Before I knew it, half of my chess ranks had been decimated. I did not mind losing. It was something to which I had become accustomed after long hours playing a superior opponent. To his credit, Dave never threw a game, in our minds an act of condescension, although he definitely went easy on me. Some of my more unorthodox (Dave's nice way of saying stupid) moves were not fully exploited, not out of pity so much as out his love of playing. The longer the game, the better.

Unprompted, Nathan brought me a drink, exchanging it for my empty glass. I thanked him, and he smiled, not a polite response but rather a mischievous grin. I knew instantly what to expect next. He turned and spoke loudly to no one in particular.

"So I'm on this road trip, right. And it's like five in the morning, so I stop in this diner for some coffee."

Immediately he had an audience.

"Well, I don't know about the whole volume thing," I said to Dave, "but Nathan is damn sure good for a party."

Dave brought his queen down heavily onto my rook.

"Don't bring your queen out too early," I said.

"They're not patzers," he responded.

They were both lines from Dave's favorite movie, *Searching for Bobby Fischer*, about a young chess prodigy. We had already watched it together several times. Quotes from the movie abounded when we played chess.

One pivotal scene in the movie shows the prodigy during a chess lesson being asked to visualize the outcome of numerous moves into the future. The kid says, "I can't see it." The mentor, played by Ben Kingsley, responds, "Here, let me make it easier for you," and sweeps all of the pieces off the board—they crashing violently to the floor. My imitation of this scene one afternoon came as a great amusement to Dave until we couldn't find one of the scattered pieces. The white king was now a bottle cap, and the "let me make it easier" quote was strictly off limits.

I noticed Mara's roommate Jane wander in with a girl I had not seen before. My chest tightened. The girl was short, petite, her hair sandy blond, and at a glance she looked for all the world like Anna. My shock transformed into a strange ease. Somehow having the girl in the room brought me unexpected comfort.

Dave leaned over and upped the music volume. With it Nathan's voice grew louder as he continued his story.

"How are we going to distinguish between inhibition levels altered by the volume or by alcohol?" I asked Dave.

"Good call. This ain't exactly a control group."

"Not exactly," I mumbled and surveyed the crowd. There were a dozen or so revelers, most listening to Nathan, most with drinks in their hands. Jane and the girl who reminded me of Anna were chatting near the doorway.

I looked back to find Dave staring at the ceiling as though counting stars.

"You've lost," he said. "You just don't know it yet."

It was a line straight out of *Bobby Fischer*, but I was surprised to hear it just the same.

"Really?"

"No. I'm just fucking with you. I got no idea," Dave laughed.

His laugh, like his features, was hard and fierce. There was great strength in his laughter.

"Hey," Jane said, approaching us, the blonde still next to her. "Guess we missed the beginning of the story."

She gestured to Nathan as he paced the length of the room, listeners making space for his long strides.

"And it's working," Nathan's words clarifying with my focus. "Brilliant, ya know. I've got him convinced that I'm the Regional Manager. But what I don't realize is that a waitress overheard the whole thing. By the time I sit down, the whole staff is busting ass. Cook's putting on his hairnet, waitresses rushing to clear dirty tables..."

"It sounds like a good one," I said.

"So can we hang with you guys?" Jane asked.

As she spoke, both girls looked to Dave. It was a common occurrence. People were instinctively drawn to Dave's dominance, deferred to his authority. By his side I was an afterthought; in his company no one sought my approval. But I did not begrudge this dynamic. I understood. Dave, in his assuredness of movement and explosive laughter, possessed a devastating allure.

"Whatever," Dave said, as though inconvenienced, flexing his uncanny ability to legitimize things, like playing chess in the middle of a party.

I felt Dave's invitation rather cold, so I smiled reassuringly at the girls.

"So what you ladies been into tonight?" I said in an attempt to engage them.

"You're looking at it," the blonde said, her hair half wet, not yet dry, dampening the shoulders of her thin grey T-shirt. Up close the lack of similarities between her and Anna were obvious: her nose longer, eyebrows thicker, her lips more full. The differences seemed to disconcert me, my feeling of calm slipped away. My acne burned, my hair felt itchy and wild. I lit a cigarette to ease my nerves and tried to think of something clever to say, as the girls glanced nonchalantly around the room.

"You playing, or what?" Dave asked, still studying the board.

"Yeah, 'course," I answered.

As we played, Dave had the girls' attention. They looked to him: watched him lean back to adjust the music level, observed him as he smoked while contemplating his next move, followed the precision of his nimble fingers as he navigated his pieces ever closer to my king. He joked and laughed. The girls smiled and laughed with him, but he spoke solely to me. Yes, near his radiance, I appeared dim. Certainly, on occasion, I felt awkward, our juxtaposition exposing my inadequacies, my countenance comparably grim. Yet always, his devotion to me, his focused attention, ultimately unburdened me of embarrassment. In his presence I was perhaps graceless but still esteemed, simultaneously condemned and redeemed.

Nathan's voice rose among the din. "Yep. That's how I got banned from every Waffle House in the continental United States."

There was a smattering of applause and someone called for shots all around. The room stirred and shifted as guests began to mingle. Dave took the opportunity to increase the music volume several levels. The bass of *Wu Tang* vibrated my bed, the percussive beats suddenly orchestrating the rhythms of my body. I bobbed my head, bounced slightly against the springs of my mattress, and let the music take me.

Mara appeared behind Dave and slung her arm around his neck. "You boys still playing chess?"

"No," Dave answered back. "We're done."

"What?" I said, looking at him, then the board.

With his index finger, Dave inched his queen two spaces. The hidden angles and secret portals evaporated, the trajectories extending from each remaining piece extinguished. The invisible passageways of possibility staggered to a halt.

"Checkmate."

"I definitely need another drink," I said.

"Speaking of drinks," Mara spoke to Dave, her arm still around his neck, and nodded toward her roommate. "Have you told Jane and Sara your whiskey theory?"

"It's a working theory," he answered. "I'm still collecting data."

"Do tell," Jane leaned in close.

"Well, it's less survey and more clinical trial." Dave said, and with that they were lost to me, consumed by one another.

The blonde, recognizing her new situation, looked at me and forced a smile.

"Can I get you a drink?" I asked.

"Sure. That'd be nice."

I stood and the previous drinks rushed to my head. I swayed slightly. The blonde pretended not to notice, but instead of embarrassment, I felt a sort of empowerment. I wanted to ask Dave whether he would have attributed this to music or alcohol.

When I returned, the blonde was talking with a guy from down the hall. She thanked me as I delivered her drink. I sat down on my bed next to her, but as she was engaged in conversation there was no pressure for me to speak. I surrendered again to the music, the loud pounding beat, I pulled smoke deep into my lungs, I let the cacophony of raised voices fill my mind, I took long swigs of whiskey coke in silence. The more I drank, the more I gave myself to the hip hop, the more I closed my eyes and tried to feel the room more than see it, the more my increasingly impression-istic cognizance of the blonde's slight build reminded me of Anna.

"They're not patzers," I shouted in Dave's direction. His sky blue eyes found me, and he raised his glass in toast.

Thunderous bass thumped, my head throbbed knowledge. I knew my body in sound, the smoke from my lungs bore truth. The warm sun of Anna's presence blazed in the blue sky of Dave's eyes. Unseen paths extended from each person in the room, chess pieces in hypothetical flux, their futures intertwined and jumbled, moving around and through me. Our potential was interconnected, jointly propelled from this moment, this dark, loud, surging dorm room. Things not yet, things still to be.

"Anna," I yelled, throwing my hand on the blonde's knee. "The future is all right here, in this room, ya know?"

She jumped at my touch. "Sara," she said back. "I'm Sara."

"Right, I knew that. Sorry. It's just, you remind me of my girlfriend...I mean my ex...well, it's complicated."

"I'm sure," she said and turned away.

Checkmate. Patzers. Sound. Beat. I fell back onto my bed, squeezing between bodies, people sitting on all sides, and tried to project us all into an unseen future. We there together were the new minds, the young blood. We were going to change the world. Trajectories. Jazz. I thought too of Anna. She wore a white cotton nightgown, and she leaned over the bed to me, her straight hair made wavy, her face flush and warm. Beat. Pulse. Smoke. Sky. Angles. Anna. I lay there on the bed, surrounded by people and stared at the ceiling as though counting stars.

V

"Come on. Come up with something," I shouted into the wind.

"There's nowhere to go!" The words spat from Jack.

Jack and I found ourselves stuck beneath an unassailable geological obstacle—the rock face protruded out as if a ceiling above our heads.

"You've got to go down!" Jack yelled.

"You're kidding, right?"

"Waylan!"

This is an excellent way to get ourselves killed was all I could think, but did not say. Jack was in no mood for debate.

I was able to find a few steps downward, but it took several minutes. We were in no condition for such a time consuming journey, but we had no other options. I looked down. Some hundred feet below we must have climbed over a lip in the cliff face because beyond that point I could see nothing of the mountain, only the valley below.

"This ain't gonna work, Jack. No going down."

I imagined myself losing my tiring grip and sliding down the steep craggy surface, grabbing, clawing desperately for some hold before hitting that edge and tumbling off into the void. I could no longer see the path of our ascent or the ancient tree circle that grew at the base of the rock face. But the lush green of Venable's mountain basin at trail's end spread out dotted by pine and shrub, and it all looked small and muted green from so high up. I had the momentary sensation that such a ground would comfortably break my now inevitable fall, deceived myself into believing that the wild scrub grass of the mountain floor might be cool and soft against my face, between my fingers, like watching the moon at night, lying on my back in the backyard. We were above sparse clouds, and though the day was cool and bright it was moving quickly to late afternoon. I could see the peaks of competing mountains, all breathtaking and close, as though they were a simple hike away, an easy trip to the top. Like this peak had seemed so close, so accessible.

I began to gauge my strength. How long could I hold onto this rock face? How long until my muscles failed? Could I sleep and still hang on? How long would it take until my parents missed us? Dark, at least. We had said we would be gone all day. And even after they began to worry, they would come out and have a look, drive up to the trailhead, but when would they call out the search party? Maybe when they saw the Jeep, or maybe they would still wait for a while. How long until they know it has been too long? And then do they call the police? Is there a waiting period on missing persons? How long to organize a search party? They could not drive the trail we took. It had taken us over five hours to reach the trail's end. And it would take them longer in the dark, even if they had big flashlights. The darkness is so complete in the mountains. Surely when they made it to the basin we would see their lights, but would they be able to hear our shouts all the way down there? Us all the way up here in the blind darkness. Did we bring a flare or a flashlight? I could not remember.

Roughly six hours to nightfall. Another few hours before my folks called for help. Two hours or so to organize a search party. Five hours up the trail. An hour until a climber could reach us and strap us into harnesses to lower us down. Seventeen hours. Can a body endure? Is the instinct to survive strong enough?

Something akin to sobs choked my throat. I hugged the mountain, pressed the side of my face against the cold unforgiving surface of stone, as though it might embrace me back, take me up, wrap me in warmth, bear me away to safer heights. I thought of my family back at the cabin, seated around the fireplace, mesmerized by the crackle and dance of flame. And, too, of Anna, her lips, my nose lost in the fruit scent of her shoulder-length hair. It cannot end like this. Not this way, I cursed to myself. Not splayed, exposed, clinging helplessly to unrepentant rock, slowly succumbing to exhaustion and ultimately gravity.

What about helicopters? Do they use helicopters? With big flood lights? That could save hours. If we were lucky, twelve hours until our rescue with helicopters. I could do it if they bring helicopters.

But what about Jack? What if Jack cannot? What if one of us falls? What if one can endure, but not the other?

I thought, then, of the old nursery rhyme, and it began to unfold in my mind.

Jack and Way went up the hill
To see what they could master.
Jack fell down and broke his crown
And Way went tumbling after.

I made myself smile, and being proud of the small license I had taken with the rhyme, I looked up to share it with Jack. His long body was sprawled and clung to the face of the mountain. Suddenly I was aware that the rock beneath his right foot was cracking, dislodging under the vibrating weight of Jack's body. Gravel and crumbled rock rained down on my upturned face. I shut my eyes and ducked my head, spitting and gagging. The image of the loose stone that had showered me with debris was all I could see in the darkness of my closed eyes. My stomach knotted. There was no time.

"Jack!" I screamed, between coughs. "Move!"

"Damn it, Waylan, I can't."

I rubbed my eyes free of dust on the shoulder of my jacket and looked up. The rock was crumbling, spewing shards of slate.

"Move your right foot. Now!"

He heard the urgency in my voice, but there was no where to go. All he could do was shift his weight to his left foot. And as he did the rock broke free beneath his right foot and careened into my forearm, then caromed off down the steep to the ledge and disappeared just as I imagined it would be when I fell.

"Jesus," I said.

But Jack was silent. He now hugged the cliff with a hold for only one foot. Seventeen hours, I thought again, as a fierce gust of wind lashed us. Twelve if they use helicopters. But now all of Jack's weight was on one leg, and my calculations of how long we might last seemed naïve. How long in fact can he sustain? After a moment he kicked at the hole left by the fallen rock a few times until his toes carved out space to settle. My fear eased slightly. Jack was a warrior; he would be fine.

I had observed firsthand his grit and guts, had cataloged his strengths during our near constant togetherness growing up. He had, our whole lives, bested me at every competitive undertaking. He possessed a physical superiority, but it was his keen mind and interminable will that had continually awed me. These attributes added up to the likelihood that he would fare better in our current circumstances. But for me, the sum of his gifts did not equate to his survival. Irrationally, it was his dependability that reassured me. He had never not been at my side.

For all my belief in Jack's strength, he had yet to speak since the rock had released beneath his foot. I suddenly, innately, understood that while Jack had just averted death he was now on borrowed time. He clung to the mountainside, his body visibly shaking, his face ghost white. Waiting for rescue was no longer an option and leading us to safety was solely up to me. I did not, by any means, feel stronger than Jack at that moment, but I knew that I must fake it for his sake. It was my duty as his best friend.

To our right was empty space; the rock face cut away into air. I ran my hand along the unseen surface for holds, but it was relatively smooth. Engaged now, determined now, I inched my body over, muscles taut and strained, and craned my neck to peek around the edge. The smooth surface I had explored was in fact one side of a large V-shaped fissure, whose point terminated maybe five feet below. The fissure was wide and deep enough to accommodate me and Jack, yet it was at a right angle from our position and allowed for no place to hold or settle except the point far below. My mind surged, my eyes scanning, gauging distance and probability. If I could jump, maybe fling myself out and around, down and in and catch the far side of the fissure, I could theoretically land with my back against the inclining rock wall. Maybe. I looked again down to the valley. Felt the fall in my bones again. This was my only plan.

"Jack. We're getting outta here."

I carefully pulled my left foot next to my right on the same narrow ledge. I slid my hands until both were on the inside of the fissure's polished left face. I do not think I thought of Anna then, or my family, did not try to imagine college or any future that I might now never experience. Trembling and breathless I managed to shout. "Watch this!"

And with that I thrust myself across the void, down and into the V to the far rock face, my back pack crushed and forced against the wide flat surface by my momentum. I lay there pressed against the rock wall that separated me and the fall, feeling as though I had cheated death. Feeling as though death knew my name now, knew my fear now, and it would not be long. My temporary reprieve was exquisite in my nose and on my tongue.

"All right, Jack, if I can do it, I know you can," I said, trying to sound upbeat. I was aware that I had lost some part of Jack when the rock had fallen from underneath his foothold. It gave me a wild courage, needing to be his strength. It had pushed me to this jump and it took hold of my voice, loud and reassuring, like some sort of camp counselor.

"Yeah. All right. One more step. Right about there. You got it. Got it? All right."

Jack cleared the gap with a push of his superior arm strength and met the distance with his long legs making the jump seem far less a feat than I had thought it. But he had the contorted ashen look that I surely must have had as his back crashed against the rock.

"Ya got it!" I said, grabbing his arm.

Jack smiled a small and crooked grin. "Yeah, I got it. You crazy bastard."

"Ha-haa! Whoo! Do you believe that shit?"

"All right. What's your plan now, Indiana Jones?" Jack and I loved Harrison Ford.

"Well, you see. I hadn't really gotten that far."

To our delight and luck the back wall of the fissure was rough and easily climbed. We found new rock holds and made our way up and out and over to the rock we had been stuck under. And there the mountain changed. Scrub grass covered a steady incline to the top, of the kind we could scramble up. My arms and legs were jelly, but were finally grounded. The wind was cold and sharp, yet unlike my experience on the cliff in which it had felt cruel and dangerous, it was now invigorating. I shuddered with a chill and smiled. Rugged purple flowers, a variety I could not identify, grew from the rock. The clouds were low and fast moving. Life was still ours, the world churning and vast and, at that moment, for us. We could see the peak now. On all fours we hurried our weary limbs up and up, but as we rounded our way to the top, I pulled myself to my feet and walked the final few steps to the summit.

We had done it. Jack and I had climbed a mountain. We had together made our way to the very pinnacle of creation. No, it was not Everest or K-2. Hell, it was not even the highest peak in the Sangre de Cristos. But it was our Everest. Beaming, I turned to Jack to hug him, but he was not looking at me. He was looking out, and I followed his gaze. Our rolling grassy top descended beyond us to the south then rose up again, turning into a rock peak yet another hundred feet into the air.

I looked back at Jack. "Does this count?"

"This counts."

I dropped my pack and collapsed in exhaustion. But Jack was still up, surveying our mountain top with long confident strides.

"What do you think my chances of lighting a cigarette up here are?" I shouted.

"Well," Jack said, "with this wind and this little oxygen, I'd say about as much chance as me sucking your dick."

"So 'bout 50-50, then, huh?"

As an answer Jack walked over, grabbed my fishing hat off my head and threw it a few yards away. I got up and stumbled to retrieve it. Below me and to the west, Venable Peak descended rapidly into spectacular unmolested mountainside. The wind rushed and swirled in my ears as I looked out on the roaring green infinity of the craggy pined Sangre de Cristo Wilderness.

"Hey, we gotta get a picture of this. Of us, I mean. Up here. Proof, you know. That we did it. Or almost. No one has to know."

"Like I said, Waylan. This counts."

That made me smile. A minor bending of the truth recast the story of our adventure. Reaching the mountain top is a more compelling tale than almost reaching it. Jack understood this. I knew that such a secret would be safe with my friend. I knew too that he would not really consider this altered detail a lie. For him, this was enough.

But not for me. I had a sense that I had missed something important. We had been hiking and hiking, moving further upward, up and up toward our destination at the top, that we might conquer and stand arms up and out, shouting, declaring victory over some peak. Our endeavor in some ways had helped us avoid another, less tactile, more daunting obstacle. The future loomed as large as any mountain.

"College, man! That's big shit," I shouted above the wind.

"Friggin' sweet, dude," Jack returned emphatically, but then smiled in his measured way.

"You ready?" I asked.

"Aren't you?"

"Yeah, sure, I think so. It's just..." I could not find words. "Ya know, this..." I motioned out at our view. Beyond the rolling green of Spring Mountain, Horn Peak jutted, jagged and fierce, into the white sky. "Us, I mean...it's almost over."

"We're getting old, buddy. All growed up."

"But Jack," I said. "How am I supposed to know who I am without being your best friend?"

He did not answer at first. So much silence between us. I realized that even though I knew everything about him, I really knew nothing.

"You will," he said.

I was frustrated and left flat. "How?"

He sat staring out at mountains and valleys, unfazed by my concern. "It's starting over, you know, but it's not. I'm always your best friend. What we've been doesn't change."

He was right, of course. Our years of friendship would always be a part of who we were, both together and as individuals. But suddenly it was not enough anymore; the words were true, but not enough. I was terrified of not having him with me for the next phase of my life and it seemed to me that he was not comprehending the enormity of change that was to come. His words seemed trite, too simple, even foolish. "You're so full of shit."

He did not laugh. I did not say it to be funny. He looked at me as though I had struck him. He turned away and did not speak, while the wind roared in our ears. It should have been enough just to be there—the two of us, alone, on the edge of rock and life and college, the end and the beginning. It should have been. But instead I had tried to make it more.

I felt like crying. Knowing that Jack was right, and knowing too that there was nothing I could say to stop time, no words to give me courage, no words for the death of me or for the life of someone new. No, not for that. But something within me still wanted to push forward, needed to break our rushing silence, feeling as though if I did not, I might become like Jack's loose rock, careening down, breaking against mountainside, exploding open into pebbles and dust, my being scattered and swept away by unforgiving winds.

I wanted to sing to him then. Maybe because there was something about song that could finally voice what for nearly eighteen years had needed no discussion. I needed somehow to articulate the power of our consistency, the beauty of daily devotion. If I could sing it, create a clear note, sound from nothingness, than perhaps I could elucidate our joint evolution, itself forged in silence, long steady years cultivating the bonds of our connection. I had grown up with Jack. I had grown strong through Jack. I suddenly desperately needed for him to understand how much he was a part of who I was and that everything was about to change. I knew things were going to be different, I knew he and I would never be the same. Yet I could not comprehend my life without Jack. I could not envision a world that existed without his unfailing presence.

I wanted to sing to him so that he might know all of that. I wanted to sing to him like Anna had sung for me. When Anna and

I were still just friends, I had gone to see her in a few musicals and choral concerts and had been beguiled by her. She would sway slowly in a floor-length dress and too much make-up, and the notes would pour from her lips, her sound enveloping me. In singing she revealed her beauty, and weak-kneed I had fallen in love. I often wished I could be her songs, (how the notes must feel on her lips,) that she might sing me, and I might rise up over the crowd and through the open windows into the night air, soaring as sound. I wanted to sing to Jack like that. I wanted to sing him over the mountain. "I will lose him," I thought, "and he will never know this thing I would sing if I could." But I had no voice for it—for all that he was, for all that we were. No voice of a woman. No song of a bird.

"All I've built up is gone," I said

"I guess so."

"I'm scared, Jack."

"Waylan, you and I were born for college. You're going to find your answers on your own."

VI

Something changed. At least that is what Anna had said. But that would have been near the beginning of college, I think. We were sitting on her front steps perhaps, hunched against a winter wind. (She smelled of lilacs.) She knew somehow before we knew anything, and she said something about the change she saw in me.

I had left Indianapolis with vastness caught in my throat, had journeyed north to Minnesota chasing freedom. I believed unfalteringly in every part of my being, that I was going to reside at the top of the nation, to reign over it like a king. Not as a master of others, not as a ruler over lands, but as dictator of my own destiny. And from my high throne, seated there alongside the inchoate trickle that would become the Mississippi River, I believed I would scan my infinite realm and plot out my path. My choices appeared limitless—that I might blaze trails of new thought, pioneer unexplored facets of social change, or perhaps merely amble happily along certain garden walks lined by tall grass and irises. My first weeks of college were exactly what I had hoped, what I had expected. The land itself seemed to rise up and meet each new uncharted step I took. Schoolwork was light and stimulating. My mind was blown wide open—Marx and Foucault, Kant and Whitman, Marcus Garvey and Virginia Woolf, Imperialism and Feminism, Universalism, Post-modernism, Post-structuralism. The world was so much bigger and stronger, so much smaller and more fragile, than I could have ever possibly imagined. And it was all before me, that whole beautiful, complex, roaring, rushing world, on every page, in every lecture, on every tongue. It seemed each new dorm room was populated with bright, interesting people deconstructing the constructs and saving the world with fevered breath.

Often the afternoons were warm, and I could walk Macalester's small, attractive campus. With the sun out, the open grassy square hemmed by Kagin dining hall, dorms, and Grand Avenue, was populated by students reading on blankets. Guys in knit hats and baggy cargo pants tossed frisbees. A stiff breeze often carried the pungent scent of marijuana. On the other side of Grand, the Student Union, Library, and Old Main hugged manicured lawn, benches and trees where students gathered to eat and share and laugh. All around me women walked in pairs or groups, the necessity of coats not yet obscuring the healthy curves of youth. They chatted inaudibly, but I was certain they spoke of substantive things, like the plight of Palestine, or the politicization of pregnancy. Surely they spoke of Shakespeare, of Bach, of Michelangelo. Knowledge ballooned and took to the air, knowledge itself seemed carried by the halting staccato of bongo drum circles, or perhaps the resonant hum and winsome whine of Mac's bagpipers practicing on the campus's far end. The space was one of life, of liveliness, of scholarship and possibility.

My friendships with Mara and Nathan and Dave deepened. Our parties started early and ended late. It was not always drinking, of course, but college was a constant state of hanging out. If you had to study, you studied in the same room as someone else. The rules were clear and simple. After class, but before dinner, was free time. After dinner there was a digestion time—get on the internet, talk about your day, play chess or cards. Then it was time for serious study. The quiet was not broken except for the following exceptions: If the CD ended and needed to be changed. (This always prompted debate.) If someone came by for a visit. (There was a steady stream of faces in those first weeks.) If someone came across something particularly interesting in their studies and thought it ought be shared.

After a few "sustained" hours of study, however, all bets were off—around midnight the books were put away and bullshitting would begin. There was a rhythm to it that fostered a sense of autonomy; no one was looking over my shoulder asking why I was still up at three A.M. or why I had not started my homework yet. I felt so adult. So free.

But it faded. The days grew grey and cold. Papers and readings piled up. People divided up into cliques, and I realized I had forgotten to remember almost anyone's name. Jack and Anna were on my mind and in my heart at all times because I realized that while I was experimenting with my identity, no one in college had an opportunity to actually know me. And too, I found out there was no one to make sure I slept enough and got my assignments done. I began to feel unexpectedly afraid. My whole life had led me here. I had been told once that I was made for college, but I began to realize I was in many ways ill-prepared.

Perhaps it was Nathan who noticed first, maybe even before Anna. I stumbled into my dorm room from a late night session with Dave after having slept a few hours in his reading chair. It was mid-morning. Nathan was at his desk typing on his computer. I was still half asleep. My mouth was sticky, and my teeth felt furry from lack of brushing. I smelled of whiskey. I staggered straight into bed. I must have looked awful because he leaned back in his chair, a cup of coffee in one hand, and said, "You're a freaking train wreck, man!"

I recalled then what I always thought of when people mentioned train wrecks. It was one Memorial Day when my family and I had walked the graveyard to pay our respects. We came across the stones of three brothers, ages of five, nine and eleven, all inscribed with the same death date. What tragedy must have befallen to rob this family of three sons? A fire? A wreck? Some-one thought it might have been the school bus accident, thought that might have been in '62. A train had collided with a bus full of children. I remember walking away and finding a granite bench to sit on in silence, consumed by the thought of those last moments, how they must have hung there almost endlessly. Those last sec-onds—pulsating, staggered, fiercely loud. The long heavy sound of the train whistle, the whine of steel on steel, hiss and scrape of brakes that are too late to stop the weight of death. I wondered whether the children on the bus were all screaming and crying and scrambling. Surely they were. But perhaps there was finally calm as their minds raced and hummed in a vacuum of time. "It is hap-pening," perhaps they thought. "It is done," perhaps they knew.

"No, dude, not a train wreck. A mess maybe, but not a wreck." I said, my face half-covered by my pillow.

"Well, whatever. But I'm worried about you, man."

"Thanks, but I just need some sleep, that's all."

"You know my granddad used to say that his problem with beauty sleep is that it never made him pretty."

"I'm sorry your grandfather was ugly. Now let me sleep."

"What I mean is, sleep doesn't always do the trick. Are you sure it's just about being tired?"

For a moment I was not sure. For that brief instant I wanted to tell him about my growing sense of isolation, about how much I missed home and Anna and Jack, how I felt strange in my own skin, but then I thought of the train wreck again.

I wondered about the train conductor. Surely he survived. How must it have been, perhaps still is, to wake every morning to the reality of that inexplicable carnage? Surely he could not have stopped. But to live, to carry those deaths, must have meant his death as well. All those children. Mere children. And among them three brothers—a family's line, a mother's heart, a father's pride. Demolished parents, now barren, now ancient. A town brought to its knees. Their future stolen in a violent moment of metal and glass. How we spend our days, our minutes, our years is not worthy of that town, not worthy of those parents, that conductor, those boys. My pain is unworthy in the face of that pain.

"I'm okay, buddy."

Nathan stood and gazed out the window, his face bathed in light, the sun amplified by its reflection off of snow. He turned to pour himself more coffee and looked at me but did not speak.

"Really, I'm fine," I said. "But do you mind pulling the shade?"

But I was not fine. I did not know it then, but I was descending rapidly. The college, the learning and drinking, was my losing and sinking. College was the beginning of my new life, but it was tearing me apart. I had kissed Anna goodbye, watched her board her plane for New Orleans and walked away, and in so doing had walked away from high school, friends and family, and now pieces of me were pulled and scattered all across the country in different cities and different dorm rooms. Now that Jack was gone, now that Anna was gone, I had become separated from the life I knew, from the me I knew, from the place I understood as real and unified. There was a distance widening within me, a division of voices in my head—the span of ten bathroom floor tiles, the length of a green sweatshirt or the width of a blade. But I could not see the measure of these things yet. I was instead only conscious of the enormous length of the Mississippi River (that which tethered me to Anna). All else was lost to the sound of children's screams and then exploding glass and steel. This is when my memory begins to get hazy and fails.

VII

I was in the back seat of a car. I was not sure where we were going. Mara drove. I sat next to a woman I did not know, but I knew I loved her. I loved her for the way she sat erect and calm and did not look at me, the way her hair caromed thick and full down against and off her shoulders, for the fingerless mittens she wore and how she grabbed the head cushion of the driver's seat and pulled herself close when she spoke to Mara and Dave up front. Loved her for the way her breasts pushed out the heavy, too big sweater she wore. I did not know her name. She was a friend of Mara's. I am sure we had been introduced, but I did not want to push my memory. I loved her for not knowing her name.

They all made small talk, but I could not hear them. Could not focus, could only think about this nameless beauty. I began to overheat with my desire—thinking about touching her, not naked, but with her mittens on and wool sweater, for her to feel my hands through her jeans, her nipples hardening beneath her sweater. I wanted her to arch and ache and feel erotic and beautiful the way I saw her. I was hard off the vision of her holding my head in her lap there in the back seat, her stroking my hair with her mittens, cradling me gently. Knowing nothing but the warmth of her sweater, the softness of her body, the rhythm of night driving.

She glanced at me suspiciously, as though she could see my thoughts, feel my eyes. I grinned. It seemed to affirm something for her. She looked away.

I felt ugly and stupid. I hated myself for being shallow, being common, for being a man. I wanted to disappear. I squeezed into the corner against the door hoping I might be hidden in the darkness of the car. But we kept passing street lamps and bright signs, neon beer advertisements from bar windows. And I am sure that they illuminated me eerily, back lighting my outer wretchedness, my inner darkness—my face lighting up alternately blue and red and yellow, but always sickly.

I looked at her next to me. Her eyes were closed, and the lights were casting colored shadows against her skin. She must be alone, I thought, to feel the deep blue behind her neck. And there must be a place behind her eyes where green finds a home and orange a place to swim. I wondered how the purple felt on her lips. She sat there, the body of a dancer, the face of a soldier. And I wanted to take her away from all that was evil in the world. I wanted to protect her even from myself. If only we could get beyond the confinements of this tiny car and mounting snow, to a place where she and I could sit on a deck and drink lemonade, and be ourselves and free. Ice clinking in our glasses, on days when lawns smell hot summer mown, and old men sit with faces to the air conditioner. Cool. Like her shadows, touching lightly where her skin meets her sweater. She will not open her eyes. Not for me, not here, her back against the seat meeting blue, and me so goofy and in the light.

I was all pain and remorse for my fantasies, for my objectification of this woman. Knowing now, for sure, that she knew my thoughts, had seen it all and was repulsed. Mara and Dave continued to talk. But my now epic silence began to emit a tension that radiated out from me and steadily engulfed the space until everyone felt it. And the car fell silent.

My chin against my chest, I stared at the door handle. I was leaning against the door. All I would have to do is pull the handle. I could escape then. Pull the handle and push open the door. And fall. Free for an instant. In the cold air. Away from the stuffy, recycled heater air. Fall free from the oppressive silence and my exposed indiscretion. There would be a moment flying, refreshed and whole again before the cement. Before the violent tumble. Before my skin would be dragged open, before the crunch and shattering of bones. There would be utter disbelief in the car. Mara would swerve and slam the brakes. I would roll forward for a while with the momentum. But with any luck my neck would snap, or I would be mercifully hit by an oncoming car. The nameless girl would be shocked and crushed. Not knowing me would become meaningless, because she was *there*. And she would love me after my death, weep for me at the funeral, wish she had not rejected me, wish she had taken the time to understand the sensitive and passionate spirit I housed in my cruel and awkward body. She would wish she had held me that night in the back seat. Just pull the handle. *Now.* My friends and family would be devastated, regret all the pressure they had put on me, agonize over every harsh word. They would nostalgically remember my kindness and wisdom, all the good times and special moments. Each would have their own particular memories, and those would become precious, like family heirlooms, to be held close and then eventually passed down. They would forget about my recent descent into selfishness and pain. They would only remember the Waylan I wanted to be. Their love would sharpen with my sudden death, and they all would, through memory, codify the me I now struggled to find every morning when I woke up. With my death those that loved me would be capable of what I was not. They would remember who I was supposed to be. Pull the handle. Just pull the handle.

"You cool, dude?" Dave asked from the front seat.

I looked up. "Yeah. Fine."

"We're almost there."

"Cool." I said, trying to be nonchalant. Trying to remember I was still alive.

Mara pulled the car into the parking lot of an old, beat up building. Christmas lights framed the dark windows. A large, hand painted sign hanging above the door read, The Wildcat. A bar. I had never tried to get into a bar before.

"Our fakes aren't going to work, guys," I said.

"Relax," Mara returned. "You guys are my roadies." She grinned. "We're going in the back door. Just carry something. Nobody's going to care."

I felt like I was floating as I got out of the car. It was cold. Ice and snow crunched under my feet as I stood by the trunk waiting for my piece of equipment.

In the end we could hardly be considered roadies. We were each charged with something. Dave carried the guitar. The nameless beauty carried a mic stand, and I toted a duffle bag full of mics and cords. Of course, the bar had a sound system, so everything except the guitar was extraneous. That put me on edge. Several large men stood around outside the backdoor smoking. I shuffled awkwardly with my bag on the snow and tried to avoid eye contact with them. My gut ached. I just knew they would see my fear and ask for my ID, so I tried to be casual, tried to pretend I belonged there. Fortunately, the equipment we carried spoke for us, because I would not have been able to.

When the door finally closed behind me and we were inside, I turned to Dave. "Jesus, that was lucky."

"What're you talking about, dude. You think those guys really give a shit whether we're legal or not."

I could not decide if he was just trying to play it cool, or whether I was in fact overreacting.

"You never have to worry until you have to worry," he remarked as we shuffled down the short dark hallway in which we now found ourselves. The walls were plywood painted black. The hallway ended in two steps that led directly up onto the side of a stage. It was a small wooden platform, well worn. The stage opened onto a large cement-floored room. Metal folding chairs circled a dozen or so round tables in the dingy, smoke-filled room. Most of the tables had been leveled with napkins and matchbooks. The room was about half full. People talked loudly and sucked down beers. It was noisy and hot and dirty. It was glorious.

Mara turned to her roadies. "I need to go find the manager. Can you guys just hang here for a minute?"

We all nodded and then set our burdens at our feet. The three of us leaned our backs against the plywood as though synchronized, all in a line along the wall. I had nothing to say, my nameless beauty next to me, my throat dry, my timid soul now balled up in the fetal position. We all stared at our shoes.

Dave shifted his weight and broke the collective trance.

"So, Lindsay, how do you know Mara?"

Her name. Lindsay. Yes. Somehow I had known all along. Lindsay. The sound of it stirred something deep in my mind, as though a snippet of a nursery rhyme, a completion of some murky childhood memory. Like saying, like believing, "Of course. That's right. I should have remembered. It is so obvious. I really should have known all along."

"Same discussion group in Lit class," Lindsay answered. "You guys?"

"Oh," Dave began, "she lives across the hall from this guy." He pointed out and around Lindsay to me. She half turned her head toward me. I nodded, and then only belatedly, as she began to turn back to Dave and say something, I spoke, so that in its mistiming it sounded awkward and inappropriate. "She's great," I said.

Lindsay, caught off-guard, appeared annoyed, but managed some warmth in her voice as she answered. "Yeah, she is."

We all became quiet until, mercifully, Mara came back.

"Go ahead and get a table, guys. I'm just gonna get set up."

"Cool," I said. We walked up onto the stage, hopped down onto the bar floor, and sat at the nearest table.

Eventually a waitress came to our table. She was not chewing gum, but her jaw moved constantly as though she were accustomed to having some with her.

"Hey, kids," she said knowingly. "We've got whiskey, vodka, gin, tequila, and we've got beer. What'll it be?"

"What kind of beer do you have?" Dave asked.

"Like I said, we've got liquor or beer," she barked.

"I see. Beer sounds good then."

"Yeah, here too."

"I'll take a beer."

She slid a pen from behind her ear and pointed at each of us in succession. "Three beers?" she both asked and stated. I nodded reassuringly and completely unnecessarily. "Comin' up," she said and rushed off into the haze.

I looked at Lindsay. She was smiling at Dave. "You are clearly not a regular," she said.

Mara, up on stage, stepped to the mic. She was leaning over her guitar, her hair falling across her face.

"Hi there." And her voice came loud and unnatural out of large speakers on either side of her. As Mara's three groupies we did our best to make noise. A drunk guy somewhere in the back whooped, but the crowd largely went on talking.

"All right then. Here we go."

She strummed her guitar strings a few times, checking the key and preparing her fingers. It was almost sensual, as if she were caressing the face of a lover, reacquainting herself with the familiar feel—her chest tightening, her desire stirred again, as it once was, as it always is. And then she was off. The guitar hummed and vibrated as she partly played, partly pounded. Immediately she was lost in it, moving, bouncing, jumping, eyes closed. And I was with her. The world got dark and small on all sides, closing in, until it was her—her movement, her flooding, pulsing, crushing, rhythm. She began to sing. Untrained, unassuming, but a strong melodious timbre poured from the stage. Not above the guitar, not with the guitar, but of the guitar, her voice seemed to emit from the guitar itself, as if one sound. I wanted to stay there in her sound. I wanted my life to be that full, that warm and passionate.

Mara belted out her rock riff, then played a folk tune. She finished with a quiet ballad, simple soft picking of the strings, her voice naked and breathy. And I fought back tears *(weak fool)*, my eyes glassy, my spirit afire. She held me with those songs. She had played my uncertainty, revealing publicly the secrets of my soul.

When she finished, she took her guitar off her shoulder and said lightly into the microphone, "Thank you." With that she was done, and I was broken.

"Fucking unreal," I said as she came toward our table. "I had no idea."

"Thanks," she grinned. "I'm really glad you guys came."

"We are too," Lindsay said.

"Really great. Really," Dave said.

Mara grabbed an empty chair from a nearby table, dragging it next to mine. "You guys are sweet. Thanks."

"And that's your own stuff?" I asked.

"Shit yeah," she said, sitting down. "I only do covers when I've got a big set to fill, which is hardly ever. I don't know many."

"Like what?"

"Mostly Janis and Joni," Mara answered.

"You do Joplin?"

"Well, I don't do her justice. But I have very little shame."

Mara was wired, still drunk on adrenaline. Her energy was infectious. I began to talk with her about the meaning of her songs, and each question prompted a story of Mara's past. She was sharing difficult, personal experiences, and they seemed to tumble out of her, as though the music had freed her. And I was enthralled, rapt, almost in the same way I had been in her singing. I hardly noticed that Lindsay and Dave were not a part of our conversation, that they sat close together in intense discussion. I was too busy feeding off Mara's playful, vulnerable, energized state. And that is how we spent the rest of the evening, in separate conversations, until last call.

It was the next afternoon that Dave and I decided to play some basketball. Basketball was in my blood; it oozed from my pores. It was growing up in Indiana. Dave grew up in Chicago and, happily, he shared my obsession. He and I spent probably forty percent of our conversations on basketball (another forty percent on women and the last twenty percent divided between school and politics), and I loved him for it. Granted, we did not play much basketball, but we both grew up knowing how. We could occasionally get a jump-shot going. At the very least I could hit my free throws. Maybe I could not take anyone off the dribble, but if anything, a Hoosier boy can hit free throws. Even if you did not like him, or God forbid, did not pay attention to IU basketball, Bobby Knight's voice seemed to grumble through Indy's schoolyards and driveways. "You better hit your goddamn free throws, or you ain't gonna play!"

The new basketball season was fresh and underway, and though academia had made us lethargic and sleep deprived, the old calling stirred us from our beds on that cold Minnesota day. We began by walking around Macalester's neighborhood searching for a hoop. Our search was turning up little.

"That's the problem with Minnesota! Back home I'd go to the first garage I saw, and it'd have a backboard." Dave bemoaned.

"Too cold here," I said, shivering a bit as the north wind sliced through my sweatshirt.

"Did that ever stop you in Indy?"

I shook my head. It never had. We walked down every alley in sight because we both remembered alleys as havens for numerous hoops. Failing again and again, I finally pointed us toward a nearby church. In Indiana and Chicago, church parking lots almost always…but not in Minnesota.

"They do everything inside here," Dave said.

It was an obvious, yet excellent point. We entered the church and looked for its gymnasium or rec center. What rec center?

Our idea for a little exercise and light competition had become a fruitless odyssey. We had walked about at random for miles.

"This is ridiculous," I told Dave, in the way I said things to Dave—part jocular, part sarcastic, part pained. "Where are all the parks?"

Dave waited, sensing my coming tirade.

"If I ran a city, I'd put parks everywhere. Places for the community to gather, for kids to play. Parks reduce crime, they up property value. And the more trees and plants, I figure, the better. I mean, I would employ a bunch of people to build the parks and could pay unemployed people in the community to do the upkeep. That way they'd always look nice. It would be something the whole neighborhood could claim and take pride in."

I took a breath, pleased with myself. "I mean, stuff is not as hard as the government makes it."

Dave smiled, "So who is going to pay for all these parks?"

"Taxes," I answered.

"Why are taxpayers going to want to pay for your parks?"

"My parks? They're everybody's parks."

"But the rich have backyards. So they don't care. And the poor have no power."

I came to Dave often with things such as this. I had a curious mind and a willingness to push and talk for hours. I tapped my peers for information and ideas, and in so doing had surrounded myself with intelligent people my whole life. I valued ideas, and that was enough to keep the bright minds entertained and appreciative of my presence. That is how it had started with Dave and me. But now, of course, it was nothing so trite or contrived. We had become inseparable. College had a way of magnifying and compressing everything—experiences and days and emotions—into a tight knot of a conversation. I knew him after three months as a brother. And we kept finding out that there was really no one else. We were alone together. We had each other and not much else. That added a heavy precious stone of burden on the strands of our connection. It was a dark, desperate blessing—a sacred curse.

"Well, what if I get corporations to pay for *my* parks?" I asked.

"Again, why should they care? Parks don't generate revenue."

"But it would raise the corporations esteem in the community. That could indirectly generate revenue."

I dribbled the ball as we walked. The familiar sound of basketball against cement. Air and rubber encountering concrete. The way the smack reverberates inside the ball in a high-pitched stifled echo. The rhythm. The bounce.

"Sure. Okay, ideally," Dave responded. "But do you think corporations care what people think of them?"

"Well…"

Dave anticipated my indecision and continued immediately.

"You really think Wal-Mart gives a damn what people think about them as a corporation? No way. They provide cheap and convenient shit, and so people will always go there—even if that means losing independent businesses and mom and pop shops. Wal-Mart doesn't need people to like them because people will go anyway."

Meandering down a narrow alleyway, we eventually found a basketball goal fixed to someone's garage. Within moments we had shed our coats. They sat balled on the cement driveway, the sole witnesses as we worked on our rusty jump shots and embarrassed ourselves with slow awkward crossover dribbles. It was painfully clear that it had been a long time since either of us had played. Regardless, after a while we started up a game of twenty-one, sort of.

"I'm too old for that shit," Dave said, sucking air. "How 'bout ten, by ones?"

I nodded. He bounced me the ball.

"Check," he barked in the tradition of marking possession, and I returned him the ball with a bounce pass. This declaration reminded me of our nights of chess, and I had a distant feeling of pursuit, as though I was already losing before the game had begun. He dribbled casually for a moment, before cutting hard to his left and pulling up for an uncontested shot that fell softly into the frozen net.

"So Lindsay, eh?" I said, watching Dave retrieve the ball and return to the edge of the driveway.

"Yeah, whatever. She's cool." He bounced me the ball. "Check."

"Yeah, she is." I said, trailing him as he drove to the basket for a missed layup.

"You two hit it off, that's all," I pried. My hands were numb as I grabbed the ball.

"We'd had some beers and whatnot."

We both struggled from poor endurance, alternating between offense and defense, exchanging missed shots, but the physical exertion began to make me feel powerful and reckless. Our light workout escalated toward scrum.

"Check," I said, breathing hard, my lungs burning in the cold afternoon air. "So'd you fuck her?"

Dave looked down. "Yeah," he said, but he said it quietly, so that it almost got lost in the sound of rhythmic dribbling.

"Yeah?"

"Yeah, and I fucked up," he said, louder this time, almost laughing, almost angry.

"What do you mean?" I rose up and released a flat jumper that clanged off the front rim.

"She was a virgin."

"What?" I pushed him hard as he went for the rebound and he stumbled backwards. Grabbing the loose ball, I circled out to the top of the key. "And you did it anyway?"

"Well, you know," he said as though it was an answer, but I waited for him to continue. "By the time she mentioned it, I was all riled up. I'd been drinking. It didn't seem that big a deal at the time. I just really wanted to get laid."

"But Christ, Dave. I mean, the first time..." I had stopped dribbling the basketball. I was clutching it tightly. Though I felt Dave was being callous, I was not sure why I was so angry. I was increasingly hot despite the afternoon cold. My armpits began to perspire in my growing heat, and in my self-righteousness I reaped judgment. "She gave you that, ya know. That means something."

"Whatever. It's just sex," he said.

"I..." I started, then took a strong, slow breath through my nose.

Maybe he was right. It was difficult for me to comprehend, but perhaps my ideas about sex were so colored by some over-intellectualization based on society's pseudo-religious moral value system that I could not separate the carnal from the metaphysical. It is in the end natural—our most animal instinct. Sex. And rage.

"Yeah, I guess."

"5-2. Come on, check it," Dave said, motioning for the ball.

"Check," I obliged, and we exchanged bounce passes.

"Who knows," he said, "maybe she's over it. I know when I lost my virginity, I just wanted to get it out of the way."

"Maybe," I said quietly, not believing it, because it had been the opposite for me. It was not so much about my ideas or values, which might be naïve, as much as it was about my emotional truth. My virginity had been sacred, something to give, to share. That moment was so significant to me, so connected to my relationship with Anna.

I remember she commented on the black blue roundness of the too-warm autumn night sky. I had felt so bold and free that evening. And it was all there with us—every ice cream cone and cigarette, every campfire and movie screen—even the tears and harsh words were there. So full with us. Tight in my chest and shooting down my arms—us in its entirety seemed on my lips. I was half skipping, half prancing and humming, while holding her hand, damp and hot.

I had wanted to say things to her, about her shoulder length hair and its golden grey quality in the dim moonlight. I cannot remember exactly what I told her that night, but I meant it all. My labored speech, my fevered pitch, book-ending short, seemingly profound silences.

"And I think...I think we should start reading the same books sometimes...I mean outside of school. So we can talk about them." I said.

"Sounds like a homework assignment. Not your strong suit." She grinned and squeezed my palm.

"But no, 'cause I'll want to. Because I love talking to you. I love listening. Your opinions. You make things better, ya know? More important. I just..."

"Stop." She said, and simultaneously stopped walking.

"What? What is it?"

"It's you, silly. You're all wired tonight. All wound up."

"Sorry. I..."

And she kissed me hard. I stumbled backwards against a tree. Pressed against bark. Her quick breath. Indigo-skyness of my closed eyes. The night grew cool and late until our backs became dew dripping grass, our hands roots, probing deep.

I realized then that Dave was looking at me, and cool night slowly became cold afternoon, as I brought myself back from memory, back to Minnesota and basketball and Dave and Lindsay. I dribbled to the right, pump-faked, then pivoted into a short lefty jump hook.

"Nice move," Dave said. "6-4. You're catching up."

"So what are you going to do if it's not just sex for her?" I asked, still unable to fully shake my past, still reliving the bark and damp earth.

"I'll play it cool. See what she wants. I could stick with her, for a while, I mean. I like her, ya know? It could be nice."

My inexplicable anger became clear to me as he spoke. Because of my own experience of the power of sex, I believed that Dave, in one night, had made me obsolete to Lindsay.

He smiled. "Some regular ass would be nice."

I bounced him the basketball and forced a grin. "Check."

VIII

L indsay's face blanched when she opened the door to Dave's room. Dave and I sat together reading. Light classical music played in the background, something Dave usually insisted upon when he studied, as he sat digesting Foucault. I was working through Edward Said's theory of *otherization*. Late evening was quickly degrading into late night as she entered the room. She was surprised, I think, to see both of us together. That struck me as funny because Dave and I were always together.

"What's up?" Dave said.

"Not much," she answered as she stepped tentatively inside, her demeanor suggesting that she might yet turn back, until the heavy door shut abruptly behind her. She sat unceremoniously, flopping down, dropping her backpack at her feet, perhaps making an effort to be overlooked. I did not oblige. I studied her closely.

Lindsay's hair was up in a ponytail, casually but not haphazardly done. Her attire, too, seemed intentionally unconcerned; faded jeans that fit closely to her skin, a flower patch on her knee, probably her favorite pants. She wore a too-big sweatshirt that I recognized as Dave's. It seemed clear to me that she had carefully prepared to appear relaxed.

Initially I was confused by her uncertainty, and equally by her effort at informality. Until she unzipped her backpack. As she pulled out a hefty textbook, she re-stuffed clothes down to the bottom of the bag. I also recognized the bristles of a toothbrush. Dave had invited her here—their relationship still so new and undefined. She had prepared to stay, but perhaps did not want to give the impression that she was too eager. She had not expected me.

In all honesty, I was somewhat pleased by her discomfort. Perhaps, I thought, she feels exposed in what she had believed was a clandestine affair. Part of me desperately wanted her to feel as though she was in the wrong room, that she was with the wrong man. Feeling her embarrassment, I gained hope that she was not entirely sure of what she was doing with Dave. But I was equally crushed. She was here, she was here to see him. *Not me.* She had not felt their sleeping together a mistake.

Dave sat in his chair reading with a kind of cool indifference to the whole situation. Lindsay organized herself and began study-ing, as though the madness was not swirling unchecked between the three of us. She did not know me, but how could she not feel that I so desperately wanted her to know me. "Don't you see? Surely you must understand," I said silently in our uncomfortable silence. Of course, neither Lindsay nor Dave knew how I felt, so leaving abruptly would only create an unexplained scene, but nor could I speak. My mind rushed, my gut churned. I stared at my book and read nothing.

I awoke, my heart racing. Disoriented, eyes crusted with sleep, I shot up to a sitting position in bed. I knew instantly that I had slept through class. The phone was ringing. Was it a professor calling to chastise me? Unbalanced and groggy, I hopped to the floor, stunned to action by adrenaline, and grabbed the receiver of the phone, then stopped. Standing over the phone, my hand vibrated with the tremor of each successive ring, but something in me refused to answer. The phone rang and I waited and stared.

Every day hundreds of decisions manifest as hesitation and indecision. But that morning, though guilty and confused, I found the courage to lift the phone on its final torturous warble.

"Hello," I croaked, my voice still unused.

"Whatcha sayin', Waylan?" Anna's familiar greeting swept reassuringly through the receiver. "Did I wake you?"

"Not at all. Just studying," I lied. A small lie, but a lie all the same. It was unlike me to be dishonest with her. I had always prided myself on the nature of my relationship with Anna, one of trust and openness. She would not judge me for sleeping late, so why hide it? The clock read 2:34 PM. Well, maybe not judge, but she might worry at that.

"How you doing?" she asked.

"Great," I lied again.

To be honest, I was becoming an excellent liar. All the little lies were slowly adding up, until I had effectively changed reality for those around me—until my whole life was a lie. I had spent long nights studying with Dave and Lindsay and pretended to be comfortable. Mara would ask if I had finished a book, and my response of "almost" meant I had read the first few pages. I was always cheery and upbeat with my parents and Jack over the phone. I did not want people to worry or to pity me—I did not need their disapproval or guilt. I was too ashamed of the truth. The actual was pathetic, and so I created an alternative that was not for the people who loved me.

And so that afternoon, it began with Anna as well. We spoke of the usual and inconsequential, while I had something to share, murky and uncertain, but certainly in need of voice. I lied to Anna with my silence.

"I'm going to some guy's party tonight with the girls," she said.

I could see Anna there, in my mind, sitting on a couch at a New Orleans house party, surrounded by people having conversations. Leaning comfortably forward, her elbows on her knees, holding a beer bottle casually between both hands, she looks at the floor and then without moving her head, her eyes move up, watching him across the room. She is not quite staring, but almost, her blond hair down, her loose tank top exposing her bare collarbones to the room. He is telling a story to some guys, but he notices. Later, this boy checks on her. He is pleased by her intent listening, her exaggerated laughter. She stays until everyone at the party has left. The two of them talk. Trivially at first, then maybe more serious. Maybe he shares something personal. He loves how she touches his forearm occasionally while he talks. She likes his depth, his humor, his thick dark hair. Then they kiss. It is awkward at first, finding each other's lips, then matching their rhythms. She knocks over her half-full beer. She is humiliated. He laughs it off and grabs a towel, consoles her with a confident hand on her waist. And then it gets intense: alcohol-courage and pent up libidos. Soon they move to the bedroom. It is not a surprise. They had both hoped and planned from her first coquettish glance across the room. They do not have sex. No, not this time, but she spends the night. And the morning is not uncomfortable as it often is. Like it can be.

"I won't know anybody really, but it should be fun," I heard her say through the phone.

"Sounds good. Just don't go finding yourself a new man tonight," I said, attempting to sound flippant, knowing immediately that I had failed.

"You're not actually jealous are you?"

They will make breakfast together, I thought. I could see Anna and the boy in the kitchen as they feed each other pieces of fruit, maybe strawberries or cantaloupe. They laugh, more than they can remember having laughed in a long time. They are at ease, already teasing each other in a chummy way. Then she has to leave, she has to study. And they kiss long and deep on his front porch before she stumbles, lightheaded and exhilarated, to her bike. She unlocks it self-consciously. He still stands on the porch and watches her as she gets on her bike, pushes off, teeters, then pulls away. He stands there, until she is out of sight, loving that moment, not yet ready to reenter the house to the ribbing of his roommates. He stays there, his lips still tingling from their last kiss, never wanting that moment to end. That is how it would be. That is how I would lose her.

"No, no. We said we were free to date other people," I said quietly through the phone.

Anna giggled. "You *are* jealous!"

I wanted more than anything at that moment to get on a Greyhound bus and head to New Orleans. I could not be there before the party, could not stop her from meeting a man that she might someday soon love more than me. But I could be there all the same, be with her, make my case, hold her close, remind her of things she would surely forget in his presence. I wondered how long it would take Mara to drive me to the bus station. *There is no time.* I imagined myself in a short line of drifters and runaways at the downtown depot waiting to buy the next ticket to New Orleans. Pacing in the lobby, eating vending machine candy bars, I might periodically pull out my ticket and again check the time and wait more, while the day fades slowly to dark just outside the wall-sized windows. And then the bus—idling loud, choking, rumbling, as I step up and rise above the line of seats as though breaking the surface of water after a dive. Finding a seat, waiting. The teenage mother who sizes me up, then sits next to me, will smile as I help her put her diaper bag under the seat. Her name is Angie and her eighteen-month-old son is Trevor. At a stop somewhere in Wisconsin, Angie will ask me to pick up a milk or an orange juice from the store while I'm off the bus for a smoke break. Hours pass away during my reading and sleeping, great American cities pass away as well. Night will become day and then again night. At some point, I will hold Trevor, perhaps for an hour or so. He will chortle and sleep. Eventually, on the last day of our journey, the light will change in the sky. The sun will seem closer, stronger, malevolent almost. The bus then will be in southern states. Still hours away, I will be nearer her, with time yet to save us still.

"Nothing's changed for me," Anna's voice said, bringing me back from that southbound Greyhound to my Minnesotan dorm room.

"Nothing's changed," I repeated. "I know."

There was a soft rap at my door, immediately followed by the door easing open. Lindsay popped her head around and smiled. My chest tightened.

"Look, I gotta go," I said to the phone.

Lindsay put up a hand, gesturing that I take my time. She tiptoed in, exaggerating her ability to be quiet.

"What's wrong?" Anna responded.

Once inside my room Lindsay mimed blindness, arms out in front of her as though she could not see, groping comically for the light switch. I smiled. It had not occurred to me that I was stand-ing in the dark. I realized then in a flash of embarrassment that I was also still in nothing but my boxer shorts from last night's sleep.

"Nothing's wrong," I said. "Someone's here, that's all."

Lindsay mouthed "sorry" before casually scanning the con-tents of my bookshelf.

"Who?" Anna asked.

I was not willing to share even a hint of the existence of my desire for another woman to Anna. My feelings for Lindsay were my secret. A secret from Anna, from Dave, and yes, even from Lindsay herself. Yet I longed to have Lindsay know, and the reality of my having a girlfriend would certainly taint that confession. Suddenly I was caught in a three way conversation with two people I desperately ached to keep separate, not only in reality, but in my mind. My worlds were colliding. I was trapped and could see no sincere way out.

"It's Dave," I said.

Lindsay glanced at me, perceiving my indiscretion.

"Say hi for me," Anna chirped.

"I will," I said warmly, the end now at hand.

"I love you," Anna said.

I looked at Lindsay, she now sitting in my desk chair a mere arm's length away, swallowed hard and said, "You too."

Lindsay grinned. "Who was that? Some crazy possessive girl-friend?"

"No. My buddy Jack from back home."

"Why'd you say I was Dave then?"

"Isn't he with you?" I answered, clumsily completing my deception.

"No." She stood and wandered over to my closet. "We're going to the museum for an art history credit." She casually leafed through my hanging sweatshirts before pausing on my over-sized green one. The shirt released in response to her downward tug and the flimsy wire hanger spun and swayed with it's new freedom.

"And you're coming with us." Lindsay walked over to my dresser and on her second guess found the jeans drawer. Satisfied with her choice of outfit, she threw it at me. "So put some clothes on, for Christ's sake."

Dave and Lindsay meandered ten paces in front of me, talking quietly so that I could not hear them. Their hushed tones floated about indiscernibly, but her occasional light laughter pierced my ears with all clarity. *Neither of them would miss me if I were not here.*

The museum rooms were broad, precise, sterile. They seemed pretentiously sacred, an altar to high art. Paintings hanging at equal intervals against clean white walls bored me. I thought for a moment how different this outing would have been with Jack and Anna. How I would not have walked alone. I would have held Anna's hand, and Jack and I would have ogled the nudes just to make her angry. And we would have laughed loud and together. Jack might have taken his shoes off and slid across the waxed floors, and Anna and I would surely have found a hidden room to sneak a long kiss.

Dave and Lindsay mounted a flight of stairs, and I followed, they in front and above me. Finally at our floor, Lindsay stopped at a water fountain. She leaned forward, tucked her wavy auburn hair behind her ear, a big hoop earring swung down across her cheek, and she kissed the arc of water. I wondered if the water was cold or room temperature. I wondered what it would be like to kiss a woman other than Anna.

As we surveyed each successive room, Dave's hand periodically rested on the small of her back. Pausing at a painting, Lindsay tossed her head ever so slightly, coyly. Watching them, my mind was blank, save for jealousy. In a futile attempt to relax, I tried to focus on the art we passed. I fixed my gaze on a particular piece, but saw nothing, merely lengthened the time between stolen looks in their direction. I wanted to be him. I wanted to effortlessly flirt and banter. I wanted to feel handsome and strong. I wanted to be held.

Before I knew what I was doing, I approached them as they stood together examining a brass sculpture. They were speaking privately when I interjected.

"This is fine and all, but I mean, I guess I'm interested in grittier environments, in art that springs from the thicket of reality, ya know?"

Lindsay looked decidedly unimpressed, so I stammered on.

"The stuff in Mac's art building is maybe less polished, but it's got an edginess, a passion. You know. Raw. All this here just feels fake. False."

Her face softened with a half-smile. "Picasso once said something like, "Art is not truth. It is a lie that makes us realize the truth."

In multiple classes I had been reading about and discussing the subjectivity of truth. In history, it fell under terms of unreliable sources. In psychology, it was in regards to the malleable nature of memory. In study after study scientists had been able to alter and even plant memories through suggestion. Lies became memories. I wondered if compulsive liars eventually forgot what they believed, had no concept of what was actual, until falsehood was the only truth.

I thought then about the mountain hike with Jack and how even though we had not quite reached the peak, he had said, "this counts." It was a simple lie we would share to bolster the story of our travail—only Jack and I would remember any other reality. Yet it was, in fact, the emotional truth. We had triumphed over adversity and death. Victory was our truth. In an effort to translate that to the people we told, it was easier to lie.

I wanted to bring this point up to Lindsay, thought it might be pertinent, but it felt like more than I could explain. But I wanted to engage her. I decided to quote back to her, "Art is dead," although I wasn't sure who had said it, or if in fact anyone had said it, though I was pretty sure someone must have. So I said nothing. But suddenly I didn't believe it in any case. If art was a lie, it was not dead to me. It was instead a medium to which I could relate.

Art was merely protecting a world incapable of stomaching the heinous face of truth.

Without speaking, Lindsay glided nonchalantly toward another sculpture. My shoulders slouched in resignation. I had nothing intelligent to share that might keep her by my side. Anna would have stayed with me, I thought. But would she now? After all my drinking, my lies, after betraying her trust by lusting after another woman?

On the wall before me hung an impressionist's canvas, splashes of color twisting, intermingling—shapes with undefined lines, darks and lights of unfinished form. A background aflame. Amidst a raging fire of yellow and orange, lively spirals of green arched, spanning a stream of crimson and blue as though water carried the fire forward, out toward me. In the foreground, thick lines of mahogany, perhaps a tree, and there an emerald splash of bush. The painting's label read *Le pont japonais, The Japanese Bridge*.

Without knowing why really, I began to cry silent, hot tears.

Unannounced, Dave threw an arm around my neck and pulled me close to his side. "Definitely gotta love me some Monet."

IX

I am not sure when it all became a blur. Not sure when college became one long day of trauma and binge drinking and reading and paper writing. I did not sleep unless I passed out from too much whiskey. I rarely dreamed. My heart was in New Orleans. I sat many afternoons at the Broiler writing Anna love letters, hoping to keep her close through my pen. My soul was on my fingertips, and it reeked of cigarette smoke.

I am not sure when the voices started or when the rushing became too much and consumed me. It had not always been, nor was it new. It is frightening to me how easy it is to recall the voices. Frightening how much they are still my own. Overlapping voice on voice. Not always a raging, screaming, deafening crescendo, not always, but a constant, deep, soft, rumble-roar touched lightly by a high-pitched nearly cricket chirp—spectrum of frequency. Imperial purple and pumpkin orange. Distant moving water. Yes, the rushing of water in my ears. Like cars idling. Like crowd murmurs. Like the secrets of small children whispered too loud.

I am so tired. It is too much. Too heavy. There is no time, not enough time to get anything done. How can I begin, when I am so tired? If I get up I am already behind. How many papers due? I cannot go to class without my paper, without having read the assignment. The professor will ask me where I have been. How can I possibly explain? How can I lie? I could lie. There is no excuse. I am simply a failure. I cannot get out of bed. God, it's already noon. I slept twelve hours I am such an idiot No one needs twelve hours. I only let you stay up late because you prom-

ised to get up, get a fresh start. Now look at you! What about your parents, your professors? All the time and money they've invested inYou are so selfish. I'm trapped. You're trapped. You can't leave. I can try…it is too late. How many excuses until people get tired of your bullshit. You make them sick. Imakethemsick. Privileged, intelligent, talented, waste. What a fuckingwaste. God, I have lost already too much. Everything.Everyone.I'veFailed—there is no point in getting up. Why try? It is too late. Not enough time. Not enough strength. They do not pity me. They hate me. TheyHateYou. Life is too much. Only for you. Life is too much only for me. I am weak. You are shit.I cannot DO THIS. You're so pathetic. So selfish. Just get up. I cannot. Just do it. It is too-I cannot-much. I am always behind. There is no time. And I'm soJustsotired. Go back to sleep. I am so scared. You are weak. No one will miss me. They will all missyou and wonderwhat'swrong and won't understand and demand more andwon'tcare. I will sleep. I am tired. You are worthless. I am shit.

Such is the nature of the forgetting.

"You know, I feel like I've been here before."

"Déjà vu?"

"No, no. Not like that. Like I've *felt* this way before," Lindsay said.

"Felt like what?" I asked.

"Like, I don't know. Awake, I guess. Alive."

I smiled at that. She looked at me as I did.

"Come on." She frowned. "You know what I mean."

"Yes. I do." I had not been conscious of such feelings for some time. But I could remember. Her openness and enthusiasm beckoned me to remember. I had taken Lindsay to the St. Clair Broiler, a greasy diner within walking distance, for dinner. It had not been set up as a date. It could not be. But that was my silent intent and furtive hope. I know for certain that I had, at this point, lost all sense, because surely I must have understood that my hopes and intents could easily destroy the world as I knew it. But apparently I did not understand. Or perhaps I did not care. I do remember walking back to campus, wanting to hold her hand. I remember the dark leafless trees, old black limbs creaking in the wind, clawing, scratching at the grey sky.

"It's just hard to describe. Something about the night, something in my body. It reminds me of another time," Lindsay said.

"When?"

"I'm not sure. Maybe…God, I remember now."

"What? Tell me."

She smiled coyly and rolled her eyes. "I can't tell you. Sorry. It's too embarrassing."

"Embarrassing?"

She sighed heavily and playfully.

"Oh, come on," I said. "You brought it up."

"Okay, okay. I can't believe I'm going to tell you this. All right, I feel like, or, I mean, something about tonight makes me think of myself in eighth grade."

She swung her legs up on the cement bench and crossed them, her back straight, now positioned to face me. I took this to mean she expected my attention, but I also noted that her seat allowed her to see easily beyond me.

"It was the night Andy Kristopherson felt me up."

"Really?"

"He was so sweet. I mean, really sweet. And nervous. Shit, I was too." She smiled at this, to herself, at her past. "It was Rebecca

Hacker's birthday party. In the summer, right after eight grade graduation. And, God, we all felt so old. Pool party. All the girls were spending the night. Some of the boys figured out a way to stay late, I guess. There wasn't really any drinking. But there was a six pack. Coors Light bottles. We were just passing the bottles around, about ten of us. Nobody got more than a few sips. And I remember the beer tasting terrible, I mean just god-awful, but also how good it was, because it tasted like freedom, reckless and mature all at once, you know?"

Lindsay pulled her knees up close to her chin, looking out now totally at the night, as though she had forgotten I was there.

"Well, I had loved Andy as long as I could remember. Which in eighth grade meant all the way back to seventh. And I had spent two years pursuing him, meaning I had passed notes in class to my girlfriends about it, had filled pages upon pages of my first name coupled with his last name, and had largely been silent around him, or cruel. Putting him down or stealing his backpack passed for flirting then. But tonight, that night, it was grown-up. It was long glances and not-so-accidental touches. In the pool he asked me if he could kiss me. I told him no and dunked him. But it was out there, that was between us, all night after that. That tension between us felt adult."

She finally looked at me again and smiled. "Anyway, later that night he and I ended up on the yard swing, swinging, and he kissed me. It was my first real kiss. And we made out."

"And he felt you up," I interjected.

"And, yes, he felt me up," she retorted, incredulous.

"Hey, that's how you advertised the story. Just trying to get my money's worth."

"Satisfied?"

"Not yet. So were you still wearing your bathing suit?"

"When?"

"What do you mean when?"

"Okay, pervert."

I put my hands up in self-defense. "Just trying to get the details straight. It's your story."

"No, I'd changed to a sweatshirt and jeans."

"So he felt you over the sweatshirt."

She grinned.

"Under?"

Lindsay laughed. "Surprised the hell out of him when I wasn't wearing a bra."

I feigned indignation. "You are such a hooker."

"It was perfect. So innocent and scandalous. We didn't know what we were doing. We were figuring it out as we went. Incredibly awkward and exciting."

"So what ever happened to this Andy guy?"

"Don't know. He went to a different high school than I did. That was the last time I ever saw him."

"Ah ha, Lindsay's lost love. The unfulfilled romance."

"There was some of that, sure. That summer, of course, constantly. Yeah, I pined, but then it was high school. It was a whole new world. I let it go. There were other things to keep me occupied."

"You mean other boys."

"Yes. But just partly. I saw that night as a beginning. Not something to dwell on, but to jump off from."

"So this feeling then, this night that reminds you of how you feel tonight, is about discovering yourself as a sexual being."

"You wish," she laughed and pushed me. But I was being serious. She saw this, paused, and grew pensive before speaking again.

"That was part of it, sure. But it was more than that. After making out with someone for the first time ever, I went and hung out with everybody. We were all sitting around, feet in the pool, hair wet, drinking beer. And being graduated. Meaning we were high school kids. But we weren't. We were nervous and awkward, but it didn't feel like it that night. I felt almost comfortable in my own skin. But for all the acne, the braces, the lanky legs, none of it mattered that night. I felt, and maybe for the first time, I felt beautiful. That's what it was." She looked at me. "That's what it is."

I met her eyes, then turned my gaze out at the campus. *You are not enough.* Across Grand Avenue two women, one with a long rainbow-colored scarf that nearly dragged along the ground, walked from the library toward the Student Union. Perhaps going for a late dinner, I thought, distractedly. I was quiet for a while. I wanted to focus and fully appreciate what she was trying to tell me.

"But surely this isn't the first time you've felt beautiful since eighth grade."

"No, that's not what I'm saying. There is something pure about that night—something in the newness of it all, something to being that open."

She moved over and put her arm around my shoulder. "And I lost that. I don't know, life beats it out of you. But tonight I was reminded of being that open and innocent and awake. It's nice, that's all."

"So, what is this, like a date or something?" I asked, telling my secret. And in so doing began to realize that I was way out of my depth.

"I don't know." She smiled. "And that's not even what I mean. Oh Christ, come on, walk me back."

Back, she had said, as though that had some meaning. As though back was a place to which we could just get up and go. As though we could return.

Something was lost that I cannot yet articulate. It has something to do with Anna's front steps and how we spoke in hushed tones of the change she saw in me. Careful words. Soft quality of her sharp words. It has something to do with the nape of her neck, draw of her shoulders, the small of her back.

Anna was always a serious person. That is not a comment on her capacity for joy. It is instead an attempt to describe her in a way that might shed light on our connection. In our inception, we were high school kids, caught up in the devastating, exhilarating, effusiveness of first love. Yet for her, or more accurately, what I saw in her, there was an ability to keep perspective. She seemed to be able to slow us down in her mind, to step back from the hysteria. She was infinitely practical—but not in a way that made me feel insecure or foolish. She inspired deep trust with her calm. The cruel, humiliating euphoria of adolescent love was somehow a safe secret, a quiet personal elation that only we shared. She was not the type to tell her girlfriends every detail. She did not log my moronic confessions or asinine comments to build a future case against me. She took me for who I was. And loved me for all of it.

She always had a deep sense of purpose, of direction. Her life was on a path which she understood not just in the present but years into the future. And I was a part of that plan. It was so comforting being a constant. I remember so clearly the discussion we had about college.

"You love me," Anna said. It was not a question. "And I love you. And that means we can't go to the same school."

"Okay," I said, trying to understand her logic, knowing she would explain it to me.

"Because we will not be one of those high school couples that goes to the same college and stays together and misses out on opportunities, and then they resent each other for it and have a messy breakup in the middle of finals. We're better than that."

It did not matter whether I believed in that scenario, because for her it was a possibility. It sat looming on her probability radar. In her mind we could not shackle ourselves to a childhood reality when we had no idea what the wide world held.

"We're supposed to be together. College isn't going to change that," I said, being hokey and utterly in love.

"It will be hard, changing," she said cryptically.

That was before I had been accepted to Macalester, before she committed to Tulane. And perhaps as I relate this story, it sounds as though Anna in fact broke up with me then. Poor fool that I did not see it. But that idea never crossed my mind. Anna, in everything she did and said, expressed her commitment. We were a solid entity. At eighteen years old we had become so engrained in each others' young identities that all else sprang from our connection. We were together, and would be, despite feigning practicality. We talked about marriage in a concrete way, but always as though it came after we had accomplished some indeterminate goals and navigated certain vaguely-conceived obstacles.

I, however, had no goals and saw no obstacles. I think she loved me for that. We depended on each other for balance. She clarified my dreams while I broadened hers. If there is a place where passion and duty coalesce, it was our relationship. Her gravity, her sincerity, her loyalty, were gifts to me that buoyed me through the chaos of high school. Perhaps in my innocence I believed that the world was full of such benevolence. Perhaps in my ignorance I believed it was I who possessed such gifts.

One night near Christmas, home from college on winter break, I sat with Anna on the front steps of her parent's house. I was supposed to be leaving. It was late, the air cold and crisp. We were not talking, just sitting. But something kept us both there, silently bound there.

Finally she said, "You've changed."

It was not a compliment. And it struck deep. I did not know why, but I was wounded, ripped apart almost. My face got hot. My eyes teared up. I wanted to rage in response. "It's college. New people, new knowledge. Of course I've changed! Should I not? How can I not?"

But before I spoke, I could see myself for a moment through her eyes. She was not talking about distance created by space or time or about different slang and gestures one picks up from new friends, or even about how minds change and expand with new information. No, she was seeing in me a fundamental shift. And though perhaps she could not put her finger on it, it occurred to me that what she noticed was a new and integral grief. I was mourning the loss of hope. Turned down and around and through, I found myself now on the other side of what I believed. In high school I had believed in people, in the power of love and community, in the evolution of mind and the rise of the humane. But now, here, I knew that it had all been a lie—my education, my religion, my life. Some small yet basic piece was mourning the death of the me I loved best.

"Yeah, maybe so," I finally answered.

"What is it, ya think? The change."

I could not tell her, not so that she could understand.

"I don't know, Anna," I whispered. But I felt betrayed, on trial somehow. She was blaming me for our alienation—as though I should fix it, like I was responsible for her not feeling comfortable.

"Maybe we've both changed," I accused, quickly and too loud.

She closed her eyes then, suddenly looking exhausted.

"Goodnight, Waylan."

"Ah, Anna, don't do that. I'm sorry."

But already she stood and held the door half open.

"I'll talk to you tomorrow, Waylan. Go home."

She closed the door. I sat there on the steps shivering, but did not feel the cold.

One night, like a hundred other nights, Dave sat in his chair, a heavy glass mug of Beam and Coke in one hand, a cigarette in the other. Lindsay lay on his bed, propped on her elbows so that her body was open before me. I kept looking at her, staring at her really. It was inappropriate and surely too obvious, but that night I could not gauge my indiscretion. I remember feeling dizzy, my body almost outside of itself, as though my actions were not my own. I could stare at Lindsay while a stand-in me could pretend to carry on a conversation with Dave. The real me could impress upon Lindsay my desire for her. I could even go to her and hold her and be held, all the while my shell would sit on the floor cross-legged and smoke and laugh and debate. But I was in fact constrained by my physical being, and so in my daze the two me's did battle. The stalemate left me sitting on the floor and staring at Lindsay unabashedly.

She stirred and shifted to a sitting position.

"All right," I heard Dave say as from a great distance.

Lindsay stood up, smiled at me and left the room. When the door closed behind her, Dave put out his cigarette in the ashtray balanced on the arm of his chair. He breathed out his last drag of smoke through his nose as a dragon might and leaned forward.

"So what the fuck's up," he said. There was no anger in his voice, but neither was it inquisitive. It held in it hints of accusation. Perhaps he knows, I thought. Perhaps I have revealed myself in my daze.

"What?" I said.

"Did you just mix that strong as shit or what?" he said, referring to my half-consumed drink.

"Not really."

"You seem out of it."

"I'm in love with your girlfriend." Just say it. That would be enough. If I could start there. No, that's too much. I need to start with something more casual. I need to prepare him for my confession, my demand.

"So how you two doin'?" I asked.

"What? Me and Lindsay?"

"Yeah."

"It's cool. I mean slow, you know. She's new at it and all that."

"But it's good?"

"Yeah. Beats whacking off."

"Let me love her." I could almost say it. "I mean, since you're just fucking her." That is how he spoke of it, but it was not true. I knew that this was machismo man-talk, the posturing of emotional defense mechanisms. She was more to him than just object. But I did not want to see it that way. I wanted to take his word at face value.

"I took her on a date last night." I almost said. "She shared with me. Told me about her junior high boyfriend. I bet you haven't heard that story." I felt as though he might comprehend my unspoken words, because these thoughts were pouring from my eyes as I looked at him. He knew me so well. He could surely discern the enormity of emotion in my face.

"I don't know," he continued. "I'm getting used to having her around. I mean this works, right?" He lazily gestured to the room, putting question to the dynamics of our current evening.

"Yeah, no. Great." I assured him. It was not true though. If I were more in control, perhaps. But my obsession with Lindsay clearly had been felt, if not understood, that evening by Dave. He seemed uneasy. *He knows.* And Lindsay had left. Perhaps she had felt it too. My God, I thought, it is all about to become clear, to be out in the open, and I do not know what he will do. I had no idea how he would react.

"Dave…" I started. My voice sounded tired to me. His name formed and then fell to the floor. There was more than I knew how to say.

The door opened without warning and Lindsay walked in with her overnight bag.

"Did I miss anything?"

"Nope. Waylan and I here were just discussing whether it can ever be too cold to snow."

"Really?" she said, half knowing we had been talking about her.

"Yeah, I was saying to Nathan tonight, 'I wonder if it'll snow.' And he says, 'No, it's too cold.' You know, you hear that all the time around here."

"And we were just wondering if it has any scientific merit." Dave finished.

"I see." Lindsay sat down on the bed and smiled. She seemed pleased, either by the game or by yet another topic with which to waste away the night hours. "Well, it's always snowing in the arctic circle. And it's cold as shit there."

"I made you feel beautiful. You told me you felt alive. Lindsay, don't you see me. I am for you," I thought, my mouth half open as though, if I could create a sound it would all pour out to her, to both of them there. But instead there was silence, and Dave filled it with conversation.

"True," he said. "But isn't the blizzard season in the summer months when it's a bit warmer?"

"Got me," I responded to Dave's prompting. "But I swear this is something someone should know."

"You're talking to a psychology major over here." Lindsay said and shrugged.

"You got any science texts, Dave?" I asked.

He laughed explosively, and the surprise of its intensity made us all laugh. Dave's strength was in his laughter.

"What about Nathan?" Lindsay said. "I mean it was his theory. And he's a science guy, right?"

I looked at Lindsay and then at Dave. They were both looking to me for a response as Nathan's roommate.

"Not exactly sure," I said, and we all laughed. "Does that guy even go to school here?"

"No, dude," Dave started, "the guy across the hall is a chem major. He'll know."

"We are definitely not waking anybody up for this," Lindsay said. "It can wait until tomorrow."

"You're right," I said. "That's a little too embarrassing. Even for us. And I should probably be getting to bed."

"Well, man, it's been a pleasure," Dave said, with his usual nighttime farewell, holding his hand out to me.

"As always," I said, grabbing his hand and releasing it with a snap as per our custom.

"Lindsay," I said. "Come with me. Walk me to my dorm and put me to bed and lay with me. Be with me. I am all alone. Make me whole," my mind screamed.

"Goodnight," I said instead.

X

Haptic memory, that's what it's called. I crammed my hand into my jeans' pocket to find my lighter. My fingers distinguished between my pen and chapstick and dorm keys to know my lighter without seeing it. I knew the difference between the objects without thinking about how I knew them. I created a mental picture of each merely by feel. Tactile knowledge. Haptic memory. Later, in my darkest, when all other memory failed me, my fingers still remembered the touch of the side of her face.

The snow fell and did not stop. It snowed and continued to snow, sometimes as fat fluffy crystals floating in jagged trajectories down, but more often as tiny gnat-sized flakes descending in swaths, almost imperceptibly but steadily amassing on roofs and tree limbs and blanketing every inch of earth.

"You know, at first this was cute," Mara said, bundled in a puffy Gore-Tex coat. She stood with a plastic shovel, staring at the icy berm that half-buried her car. "How do people live like this?" The heat of her question vaporized and rose as a billow of steam.

"Come on," I said. "Let's walk. I'm meeting Dave and Lindsay at the Grand."

"This snow isn't gonna shovel itself, Waylan."

"It's bound to melt sometime."

"Yeah, come spring," she said, adjusting her knit cap.

I held out my hand in invitation. "First round's on me. We'll get something to warm you up."

The Grand was a small bar right off campus. They made their money on college kids, so they never checked ID's and only rarely cut anyone off from drinking. It was always surprisingly bright inside for a bar, awash in florescent light, and so as Mara and I arrived, we spotted Dave and Lindsay right away. Banging the snow from our boots, unwinding our scarves, we took Dave up on his offer to grab a couple of pint glasses and share in their pitcher of Leinenkugel.

Finally seated around the well-worn Formica table, our reception was warm as we lamented the cold and the snow. From there the conversation escalated and careened in all directions. The pitchers kept coming and were often accompanied by shots of whiskey.

"So what I've gathered is that Neitzsche believes deep self-awareness perfected through solitary thought and creativity is the only way to achieve the next level of consciousness—his superman or *ubermensch*," Dave rattled on about his recent studies.

"Wasn't he a Nazi?" I asked.

"Co-opted by them, apparently. The idea of supermen fit nicely enough, but he was actually rejecting 'isms,' socialism, universalism, moralism, religion—these are forms of intellectual laziness. He's saying even human connection is a weakness, that we seek closeness in an attempt to satisfy our own inadequacies. That the only way to have a true friend is to regard him as an enemy, to honor him as a worthy adversary."

Dave glanced in my direction then, and I tried to gauge if it was intentional or not, wondered whether he was speculating on our connection. Maybe he understood our relationship as adversarial and therefore healthy. Or perhaps this new revelation exposed my devotion to him as weakness. I made an effort to nonchalantly divert my eyes.

"That doesn't make any sense to me," Lindsay interjected.

"Well," Dave said, "his take is that love is exploitation, and therefore undercuts our attempts at wholeness."

"Sounds like Neitzsche probably threw some killer parties," Mara quipped.

Dave smiled and lit a cigarette. "I'm not saying I get it all, or that he's right, but he was one of the most influential thinkers of the nineteenth century. And really, when you think about it, he's saying some pretty thought-provoking shit."

"It sounds like bullshit," Lindsay said.

A strangely inflated quiet followed her comment. Sudden tension churned in my stomach, buzzed in my ears. No one spoke. It felt to me like psychological warfare, as though Lindsay's fierce, albeit undefined, statement was being met with disdain. Why were my friends so contentious?

"I think what Lindsay means," I said, breaking the interminable silence, "is that you have to buy into Neitzsche's premise of power through self-will being the ultimate goal, before you can discount the power of love."

Lindsay shot me a glare. "No. I know exactly what I mean. I mean its bullshit. To run away, to make yourself alone in order to avoid the trappings of relationships sounds to me more like fear than enlightenment."

"That's right, I forgot," Dave said. "You adhere to the philosophy of rock-n-roll." He pulled his hands together, as though holding an unseen microphone. "All you need is love!"

Lindsay stood, pulling her coat from the back of her chair. "Don't worry, you'll have plenty of time in your superman fortress of solitude tonight."

"Ouch," Mara said, eyebrows raised.

As Lindsay fumbled with wadded up cash from her pocket and threw it on the table, Dave sang, "Money can't buy you love."

"Why do have to be such a prick?" Lindsay said and kissed the top of his head. "Anyway, I'm done. Good night you guys."

"I'm outta here, too. It's late," I said. "Lindsay, wait up, I'll walk you back."

"Sure. Whatever."

Once outside, Lindsay stopped and faced me.

"Why do you do that?"

"What?"

The night was alight, moon and lamp reflecting off the white laden earth, the air sharp cold, hard almost, like a plate-glass window. The snow had slowed, so now each falling flake seemed fragile by nature of its lonely descent.

"Why do you always feel the need to protect him?" She asked.

"What do you mean? I don't."

"Yes you do. Just because you never challenge him on anything, doesn't mean he's always right."

"That's not fair."

"You were just in there," Lindsay threw out both arms at the bar door, "explaining my position to him, translating almost so I wouldn't hurt his feelings."

"I wasn't trying to protect him," I said, stunned. Had she not felt the judgment levied upon her in that protracted silence? "You know Dave, he can be difficult. I was trying...I thought I was helping you."

"Why? Are you afraid I'm gonna look stupid in front of your precious genius boyfriend?"

The comment stung, her rancor pierced a festering truth. "Let's go. It's cold," I said and began walking back toward campus, Lindsay followed a half-step behind.

"You don't get it do you?" she said.

"Get what?"

"Me and him."

"I don't want to. I want to understand only us," I thought but stifled it out of habit. Yet something in me questioned my self-censorship. Surely fueled by alcohol I could feel my confession propelled from my quivering gut up to the rostrum of my throat.

"Lindsay," I said, turning, grabbing for her hand, but my balance was betrayed by both ice and drink. I fell backwards into a bank of shoveled snow.

"Waylan!" Lindsay shouted in surprise, but quickly snorted an affectionate rebuke. "Come on, you drunk. Get up." She offered me her hands.

Seized by my new and reckless boldness, I impulsively pulled her down on top of me.

"Waylan," she giggled. "You are not helping."

"Kiss me," I said, my head swimming.

"What? No." Her tone was still lightened by laughter, her face inches from mine.

"Why not?"

"You're serious?" She sighed heavy clouds. "How about Dave, for one? And Anna? You're either drunk or you've lost your mind. Now let me up."

But I did not let her up. I held her there, our chests together. To my surprise she made no attempt to rise. We no longer spoke. I stared at her and she back, our chilled-red noses nearly touching.

"Get a room!" The shout broke our trance.

Lindsay struggled to her feet, stamping and brushing herself free of snow.

"I'd definitely wrap your shit up, dude. She looks like she's been around," the voice said.

"Excuse me?" Lindsay was looking at someone standing at the front door of the Grand.

"Come on, man. That's not necessary," I said, laboring to my feet. I recognized the figure by the entryway—a fellow student, a football player, a year or two ahead of us. He had been sitting at the bar most of the night.

"Relax guys," he slurred, swaying. "I'm just busting your balls."

Behind him Dave emerged through the doorway. He walked straight to Lindsay and put an arm around her.

"What's going on," Dave said, eyeing our verbal assailant instinctively.

"Nothing. No worries. We were just headed back."

"Wait, I'm confused," the drunk said, releasing a tired, forced laugh. "You guys take turns with her, or you do her at the same time?"

"What's he talking about," Dave asked Lindsay.

"Who knows," she said. "He's drunk."

"Surprised you're getting pussy at all. Always assumed you boys were faggots."

Lindsay brushed Dave's arm off her shoulder and stepped forward, pointing her mittened hand. "You need to stop talking shit and go do something you're good at, like losing football games."

"What, bitch?"

"What did you call her?"

"Dave, I can take care of myself."

"You heard me," the drunk yelled, followed by all too typical rhetoric like, "What you gonna do about it?" splitting the crisp night air with a slew of foul language.

Dave in short order was no longer returning the threats and barbs. Instead, in a eerie reserved silence, he calmly removed his gloves and took off his coat. He stood stock still, his white T-shirt wrinkled and untucked, reflected the light of the street lamp directly above. Steam poured upward from his exposed skin. The drunk was pacing in abrupt tracts, agitatedly pulling at his gloves and spewing nonsensical vitriol.

I stepped in front of Dave and put my hand firmly on the center of his chest. "Come on, let's go. He's just drunk."

"I don't give a shit." He was not looking at me, but over my shoulder. His eyes were wild. I could feel his heart beating rapidly against the palm of my hand.

"Dave." I said his name in an attempt to bring him back. "It's not worth it."

Dave had been in a number of fights during our first year and a half of college. Nothing serious, usually more posturing than punching. He knew how to handle himself and never backed down from a challenge. In fact, he initiated confrontation far too often for my liking. I never approved, abhorred violence, and early on had taken the stance of pacifism.

"Where's the line?" Dave had asked one late night. "At some point you have to at least protect yourself."

"Not really. That's what I got you for."

"I figured that much."

"Look, I just don't want to give in to rage. It's only destructive." I searched the carpet for some better explanation. I was concerned by my growing capacity for hate. I was terrified of my own strength. "Ultimately I guess, I'd prefer to limit suffering."

"So there's your line," Dave smiled. "You'd use force to stop suffering."

"I suppose, yes. It would depend on the situation."

"You are aware that's not pacifism, right?"

"There's already too much pain and hurt, ya know," I said. *Sentimental drivel.*

"So if I'm absolutely getting my ass kicked, I can count on you?"

"Depends. Did you start it?"

Dave shook his head. "I guess as a code of ethics, I can respect it. But coming from you as a friend, I gotta say that's pretty shitty."

This philosophical divide led to a number of tense moments between us, and almost without exception eventually became fodder for Dave's good natured ridicule. One of his favorite face-offs came when I had rushed into the fray, the two challengers stalking in a tight circle. I pushed Dave and shouted at him with an apparently comic amount of theatrics, "If you're going to hit anyone, it's gonna be me. Not him. ME! Hit me, dammit! Hit me first!"

Dave used this line to great effect, particularly during late night blackjack games, as his turn came around, saying, "Okay, hit me." He would occasionally unleash in a deranged high-pitched voice, "Hit me, dammit! Hit me first!" making himself laugh whether he went bust or not. In such ways we traversed our differences, both remaining amenable and steadfast.

But this time, the night outside of the Grand felt different. I was tired of the games, exhausted by the relentlessness of our maddening accord.

"Dave," I said again, this time with force, clasping my hand to grip his shirt. I pulled him to me with a violent tug, but my voice softened to just above a whisper. "If you do this, I'm leaving."

He looked at me then, finally. His anger abating briefly, his contorted face relaxed at the intimacy of my tone. His eyes searched mine in disbelief. We had been in this situation before. I had protested, defused, disapproved, but I had never left.

"Do what you need to do," he said and focused his attention again beyond me, to the drunk, to the seemingly inevitable task at hand.

I released his shirt, my shoulders falling in resignation. Walking passed Lindsay I said quietly, "I'm sorry." I said it for her and for him, yet to neither.

I was half a block away when I heard the door creak open and then Mara's voice. "What's going on?" And after a moment. "Waylan!"

I turned at Mara's plea.

Dave and the drunk were chest to chest, noses nearly touching, as Lindsay and I had been moments before.

"Where are you going?" Mara implored.

Clear beneath the street lamp I could see the two men grappling, dancing almost, before the drunk pushed off and the two were separated. Dave swung with this fresh distance. His fist landed against the side of the drunk's head, but with the force of his momentum he tumbled forward. As I turned away, I saw Dave fall into banked snow and the drunk descending on him in a hail of punches.

"Jesus! Dave!" Lindsay screamed.

The terrified shouts of Lindsay and Mara filled my ears as I walked down the icy sidewalk toward campus, but I did not turn around.

I followed the blood trail, drops of fresh blood on the hall carpet, maroon finger smears on the wall. I felt as though I was wading through thick air and moving too slowly. Time itself slowed. Mara had told me that security was looking for him. I remember being afraid time had slowed only for me, not for anyone else, and it would not be long before men in shiny boots with many jangling keys would pass me in my search.

I found Dave in the first floor men's restroom. He was stooped over the sink, water running. He was shirtless. His white T-shirt hung ripped and blood soaked over the edge of the trash can. He looked up at me through the mirror and grinned, teeth thick and red.

"I scared the hell outta the guy that was in here when I came in."

I half laughed. "I bet." Pushing my voice loud to steady it.

I looked around the tiled bathroom. All was red on white. Blood streaks on the wall and distinguishable handprints on the paper towel dispenser. The basin was splattered with watered down blood. So much blood. I studied Dave's reflection uneasily. Gash above his brow, busted lip. But so much blood. It fell freely from his nose into the sink, diluted by the running water.

He saw me examining him in the mirror.

"Broken, probably," he said, grabbing a paper towel to his nose.

"Fuck!" He shouted and releasing the towel, pounded his fist against the wall. Then again. And again.

"Fuck!"

He hit the towel dispenser, and it popped open. A stack of brown paper towels dropped, sliding haphazardly across the tile floor to my feet.

My tremors became visible with my growing fear. I was scared. I was scared by the lurid brutality of it all. Scared by the blood and hate. I hunched my shoulders and put my hands in my pockets to conceal their trembling.

"I should have...if only...but I fucking side armed it." He continued to rage.

"Look, Dave, security's asking questions. There's so much blood."

"It's all about the first swing and...Fuck!"

"They'll be here soon."

With that, he swung his fist at the mirror, hitting level with the reflection of his face. He will break his hand, was all I could think. He bent to the sink again and looked at me through the mirror. I realized then that he had not looked at me directly since I entered the room.

"Dave."

He spit blood and watched it disappear down the drain. "Yeah?"

I had tried to think the whole miserable walk to the bathroom, following his blood, what I would say at this moment. I felt I had to say something, but I had no idea what. Even as I opened my mouth I was unsure of what I was saying. My voice was weak and flat.

"I can't do this. I can't go here." Immediately, I felt small and cruel. I believe Dave understood my stilted words, despite the fact that I did not have precise language for what I meant. I could not follow him down this dark path. I did not know this man in the mirror. I did not want to know him.

My head cleared briefly. "Here, man." I took off my coat and pulled off my sweatshirt. "Put this on."

I held the sweatshirt out across the room, and it became obvious to me what a distance I had kept from Dave the whole time. I was pressed against a stall door. The sweatshirt hung green and loose in my grip, held out, bridging our divide. If only he would take it, that we might be connected again, through fabric, if only for a moment.

Finally he took it. And a burden was lifted from me, as though the sweatshirt had held in its keeping boulders or earth.

"And try not to get blood on it," I joked, smiling, feeling light.

"No prob," he said, but did not smile back.

"Now get out of here. I'll clean this up."

"Screw you. It's my mess." He was staring at the sink, as though answers were held in the combination of blood and water.

I understood this was, to some extent, about my unspoken, though surely guessed at, desire for Lindsay. But that was not all of it. There is part of me which thinks that night, Dave and I both realized I could not take his pain and heal it. I wanted to. I wanted to make him whole and had been trying. As though by soothing his wounds I could save us both. But staring at him in the mirror with his wounds so obvious, so tacit as opposed to metaphorical, so actual and open and bleeding real blood, I realized I was not up to the task. I was too weak. That was the fear I felt. The fear of meeting his pain unveiled, and knowing I could not defeat it. But at that moment I attributed my fear to the inevitable arrival of campus security.

"Dave, they're coming." But as I said it, I realized I did not believe it. The bathroom was dreamlike. The towel strewn floor, blood-covered surfaces, a haven not yet disturbed. Even though I was drunk and terrified, I felt held there. Dave's mood-swings drew me more than repelled me. I was suspended in a fluorescent-lit tile illusion, as he and I struggled between connection and loss, rage and love.

"Fuck them. And fuck you!" He said loudly. And the last with intention. I did not understand how to help him, did not understand anything except that it was time for me to go. *It's too late.* I fumbled the door open and stepped into the hallway, into carpeted reality. My mind rushed thoughts so quick and loud, it was like having no thoughts at all as I found my way out of the building and staggered into the night.

XI

Mara found me on a bench in the middle of campus beneath flag poles, surrounded by a barren flower bed, long past midnight. By then I had smoked all of my cigarettes, my skin like ice, I no longer felt my body. There was much to discuss, but we did not speak. She took me back to her room, covered me in wool blankets, and I promptly fell asleep in her chair. She woke me late morning and made coffee.

"You have to go see him," Mara said. "He needs you."

I lacked Mara's certainty, but consented. By early-afternoon I opened Dave's door after receiving no response from my knock. He still lay in bed, his body turned from me, facing the wall. As I walked toward him, I noticed my green sweatshirt balled up on the floor.

"How ya feeling?" I said.

"How ya think?" he answered and sat up. His face was purple and blue, blood crusted his right eyebrow and lower lip. A cut spanned the bridge of his nose.

"You need to get that looked at."

"Why? Think I'm gonna pay for an X-ray so they can tell me what I already know? Besides they can't do shit for a broken nose 'cept a splint."

"Dave..."

"Don't." He pulled off his sheets. He was shirtless, but wore jeans from the previous night, denim spattered with droplets of crimson.

"How about dinner?"

"'Preciate what you're trying to do here, but I'm fine. Just gonna lay low for a bit."

He rose and strode barefooted across the room to his mini-fridge. He poured himself a pint glass of whiskey, splashing it with Pepsi for color.

I declined his offer of whiskey and opted for beer.

"Suit yourself," he said, taking a dramatic gulp of his drink and then of the one he had prepared for me. He sat now with the two pint glasses, both half-consumed, alternating between sips.

"You okay, Dave?" He looked at me, but instead of answering, he took another deep swig of his drink. I should have asked, "Are *we* okay?" but that question was too loaded. The cuts and bruises, his discolored face, screamed to me of my ineptitude. Something that I could not yet comprehend had transpired between us. It was too much to ask at that moment. "There will be time," I thought. "There will be time."

"Got the cure for what ails me right here." Dave eased his swollen lips into a crooked smile and raised one of his glasses, toasting the nothingness before him.

He and I talked for several hours, largely about the inconsequential. But I needed to be there. Just to be with him, to be present, that we might start to bridge the short gap of ten bathroom tiles. But I was angry—angry at him for getting into a fight, for his decision to get drunk in response to his defeat. I was angry, too, that he believed we could drink ourselves beyond our current estrangement.

Unspoken even to myself, my anger stemmed, too, from a deeper issue at work. I had begun to resent Dave and his ability to make college seem effortless. I no longer could comprehend how to sustain the world I inhabited. At first, I had pulled all-nighters, crammed for tests and devoured entire books in a coffee-propelled vigor, slamming out papers that in the morning I would have little or no recollection of composing. Yet as time passed, the ideas became jumbled, the words I read and the sentences I attempted to construct were lost to the low constant rumble of anxiety and self-doubt in my mind. Recently, I had begun more often than not to sleep instead. Sleep through classes and all day until dinner. My friends, Dave chief among them, seemed able to accomplish what I could not, to remain focused, to complete tasks and still interact. We had parties four nights a week; to me they seemed now all squandered hours. Socializing was part of our education, I understood, but having regularly slept away daylight, there was no time for my studies. And in the evenings when study turned to conversation, I rarely had anything to add. My mind felt as if it overflowed with muddy water—no coherent thoughts, no room for knowledge. All I had was ugly and mistimed, vague and awkward. I was dull, my mind a rusted blade, so I stayed increasingly quiet and often alone. I had no idea if Dave had even noticed.

"Do you ever feel like something's not right?" I asked him.

"Yeah, it ain't right I got my ass beat," he barked. Though his tone was harsh, it did not feel like an attack on my decision to leave the night before. I was reassured by the fact that his eyes were glassy with consumption, figuring subtlety was not currently in his repertoire. But being there with Dave, he half-drunk, everything was irreconcilably connected to the previous night. His face itself a purple bruised reminder of how I had abandoned him, a violet allusion to my attempt at kissing Lindsay.

"You ever feel like something's gotta change?" I said, but it was almost as if I had not said it. Some force within me, sad and hidden, spoke words I did not yet understand. "Ya ever feel it so much that it aches inside you, until it's everything? And you don't know how exactly, but you know change is coming, because it has to, because it must?"

I stared at him. I wanted him to feel what I felt, I wanted him to agree, or disagree, at the very least engage me. I needed to know

I wasn't crazy. Instead he picked at crusted blood on his too-big jeans with a ragged fingernail.

"Come on," he said eventually, and stood to open his door.

"Where we going?" I asked, following his lead.

"For a walk," he answered as the door slammed behind us. We stood now in the hallway outside his dorm room.

"First of all," I said. "You can't just carry those around."

In response he chugged the remainder of his recently refreshed two drinks and set them on the window sill. "What else you got?"

"It's like ten below out. Let's just go back inside."

As I grabbed for the doorknob, he shoved me. He pushed me hard in the back and my body crashed against the unopened door. Sparks exploded behind my closed eyes, accompanied by a brief blast of pain as my forehead hit wood. The door smelled of campfires, tasted like peanut shells.

"Quit being a pussy," he yelled.

Stunned and a bit dazed, I turned, raising my hands in a sign of passivity as well as resignation. "I'm done. I'm fucking done."

"Look, I'm sorry," Dave said. "I know you're trying, man. Know you're worried, but I'm okay. In fact, I'm really happy. Why aren't you? This is college, for chrissake. The best years of our lives." He leaned against the wall for stability. "I mean, all that change talk. What is it? What do you want?"

I took a swig of beer and watched him. I felt tired and false. Me, soft and lying, "I'm happy, too. I don't know what I want."

I had not spent much time on such concerns before, I had instead proceeded on without evaluation. College was always an inevitability. Jack had said something about how I was made for college. I existed now in a world that had been all but preordained. Despite the ever growing chaos in my mind, and a sense that something had perhaps gone awry and needed to change, this was my life—it had not occurred to me that I had any choice. ("Every choice is a chance," Jack would have said, in the way he said things, casual, yet steady.)

Lindsay came to me that night. We did not make love. We did not even kiss. But I held her close as she cried. As we slept. Not much was said. I understood somehow. The phone rang endlessly until we finally took it off the hook. Then the ceaseless knocking at my dorm-room door. Pounding really. Violent pounding. I remember being afraid. Dave was so drunk. Trying the locked doorknob over and over, like it might give way. I began to believe it might. The wood of the door seemed to crack, the knob rattled and whined. The door will open, I thought, and I do not know what will happen in his rage. Us here like this, together. And she cried, and I stroked her hair and held her close. Lying there in bed, heart racing, I ached for sleep, silently begging for peace as the pounding continued with stubborn, drunken persistence. I was terrified, but felt compelled to be strong for her. Her coming to me made me feel like a man.

Nathan regularly attended shows in downtown Minneapolis, had numerous friends off campus, and I was accustomed to him not coming home some nights. When he returned he often found me still asleep and rarely woke me. It must have been a shock to find Lindsay and me together in my bed that next morning. Lindsay, to my surprise, reacted without embarrassment to what I felt was an awkward situation. She greeted Nathan warmly, gathered her things, hugged me at length and promised to return after class, saying that it would make her feel more comfortable to stay with me for awhile.

"It's not what you think," I said, a few drawn out minutes after she left.

"Who said I was thinking anything?" Nathan responded.

"Despite what this looks like, I was wondering if you had somewhere to crash the next couple of nights?"

"Ya see, now I'm thinking things."

"Honestly, I was going to offer her your bed," I said, staring at the floor, hoping in some way my gaze might ground me, with the world I knew so suddenly on it's head.

Nathan stayed quiet, unmoving, as though waiting, but I did not continue. He turned to the window, and as he did I felt uneasy, adrift without his attention, needing his advice, his ear, his comfort, to share the new burden of the last forty-eight hours.

"You think we drink too much?" I asked.

"Do bears wear funny hats?" He answered.

"What?"

"Does the pope shit in the woods?" Nathan sat and began twirling a pen in his hand.

"No. But I think you're mixing your metaphors."

The pen spun to the floor. He reached down to retrieve it and still bent to the ground, looked up. "How about this then? Do walruses have regrets?"

"I don't know."

"Does it matter?" He smiled, his pen awhirl.

"Maybe. I mean I guess it should matter, right?"

"That's my point." Nathan tossed his pen in the air, focusing on its flight, his voice distracted, distant almost, as if with the pen. "If you say 'I don't know' then you have already decided that it doesn't matter to you."

"You're not making any sense."

The motion of the pen stopped. "What matters to you, Waylan? What do you want?"

The question had legs. What do you want? And the repetition of it, first from Dave, then from Nathan, seemed to reinforce its importance. It sat upright and alert at the base of my skull, checking the air, scanning, probing, until it began to dominate my mind. It became the *only* question. It crept into every conversation that weekend. So to me the exchanges began to overlap, enfolded together, as if one contiguous conversation.

A few days later Mara and I sat on the front steps of my dorm. The sun was out, melting snow. She had come by to see me, and I knew what it was about, but we both watched the street and the pale sun for a long while in silence. I smoked to fill the stillness. She kicked at the snow.

"I'm worried about Dave," she said finally. "Something's really wrong."

"He's just drunk," I returned.

"But for three days? I mean, Christ, what's going on?"

"He's angry. Embarrassed. He got his ass kicked."

"And you left," she said.

I nodded, but did not speak for a time. I stared and thought of Lindsay, the warmth of her body next to mine that first night, feeling her tremble, holding her as she shook.

"It'll snow again, ya know. It's only March," I said.

"Waylan..."

"Lindsay spent the last two nights in my room."

"What?"

"Nothing happened, Mara."

"Does Dave know?"

I closed my eyes and could hear the pounding on the door again. Felt the fear again.

"He definitely knows she spent the night," I said.

When I opened the door, Lindsay, normally tall and proud, seemed small, her body shrunken, caving in on itself. Tears stained her face. I had spent the evening with Dave, had watched his quick descent into drunkenness, had felt his rage grow and expand until it consumed his room. Immediately I knew she had fled from him.

Without words I took her into my arms, us standing there in the doorway's threshold, and she began to cry anew. Violent sobs. That's when the phone rang. I did not answer as it rang the customary four times before the voicemail picked up, but I closed the door, instinctively locked it, and led Lindsay to my bed. The four ring cycle began again, then repeated, and again.

I imagined Dave in his room dialing over and over, pacing like a lion, golden, singular, with a sort of regal knowledge of his own physicality, an easy faith in the strength of his jaw as it flexed, teeth grinding together. His massive hands holding the phone, his left dwarfing the receiver, his right gripping the cradle, as he took long determined strides, the cord curling in his wake, following dutifully as if a tail. Instinct possessed him now, the hunt afoot, prowling a restless tract. He, savage and powerful. If I answered the rings, I feared I would hear only roar.

Soon after, a knock came at the door, slow, drawn out, hard. My heart began thumping hard like the knock. What was happening? Had Dave lost his mind? None of it felt real, and I squeezed my eyes closed, trying to wish him gone. Increasing in volume and frequency, raps escalated to thumps, thunderous and vehement. The door shuttered wildly. Lindsay accepted my offered tissue as I shouted, "I'm asleep! Go away!" Instantly, I regretted speaking. If I had said nothing, the next day I could have said I'd not been home, maybe studying late at the diner, or out with Nathan in Minneapolis. At the sound of my voice, Dave knew for certain what he already suspected, and intensified his battering. By not answering, I had all but admitted I was harboring Lindsay. I had sealed our fate. The abuse of the door evolved to periodic kicks. It was relentless and I began to assume it would go on all night. I believed at that moment that Dave was capable of anything. *You are weak, too weak to open the door and face him. Sit here instead, trapped in your own room. Pathetic. Why of all people did she choose you?* But she chose me. My only modicum of courage came from Lindsay's presence, the task of comforting and protecting her afforded me some strength.

"He did not hurt me," Lindsay said. "He's just so drunk. And angry."

And I, there that first night in my room, listening to the endless banging and holding her, felt foolish for all my drinking and all my hate. Amidst the din of phone rings, Lindsay's tearful sniffles, and incessant door pounding, "the question" was already there, pulsating, a reverberant hum. Even though I had for so long wanted her next to me, I suddenly felt that she had been wrong for choosing me. But she felt my apprehension and touched my arm.

"Tonight you're sober," she said. "Tonight you're safe."

I said none of this to Mara, however. Sitting with her on the front steps, she looked at me and sighed, disappointed perhaps, perhaps exasperated. "You have to know that Dave assumes the worst. Don't you think he deserves to know..."

"I'm not sure what he deserves," I cut her off, louder than I should have perhaps, too forced, too cold. The door was being hammered and kicked repeatedly in my mind. "He's out of control."

"And you don't see any connection?"

"Mara, you're acting like he hasn't brought this on himself."

"Maybe," she said. "But you're acting like you haven't played a big part in it."

The second night she stayed, Lindsay stayed in Nathan's empty bed. As I lay there, staring at her prone silhouette across the room in the low light, I could hear her crying. I went to her then and sat on the edge of the bed. Fully clothed beneath the sheets, even though I had left earlier to give her time to change, she did not turn to me. I looked at the side of her face, stroked her hair, untangling it from the big silver hoop earrings she still wore.

Her rapid sharp breaths slowed, but neither of us spoke. So many things to share—but words seemed too weighty, like bricked earth, muting sound. I relished those long hours, caressing her auburn hair, watching her succumb to sleep. In spite of the horrific circumstances that had forced her here, part of me wished it would never end. I wanted her to be there always, asleep beneath my gaze, trusting me, eased by my touch.

"What do you want, Mara?" I asked then, in my guilt, hoping she too might want things within her reach, beyond reason.

"I want you to be his friend."

"I am his friend, dammit," I said, my voice beginning to crack. "He's...we're..."

"Okay," Mara stopped me, her tone gentle, but firm. She put a hand on my back. "I get it, I do, but he's hurting...

"Hurting her. And me. And you." I spat. "And now I'm supposed to feel sorry for him?"

She did not answer. The pale sun sat low on the horizon, stark sky accruing color. There is no sky quite like a Minnesota sky, crisp with clouds red pulling from the north.

"So what is it? That you want, I mean? Not about this, just anything. It's a question I've been thinking about. I wondered, I guess, about you, what you want." I said.

Mara seemed shocked and lost at the abrupt turn of our conversation. "I don't know what I want. Not this. I can't..."

Dave's bender continued, certainly fueled by Lindsay's and my seclusion, until my room became our only haven. And so, night after night Lindsay and I holed up there, sharing and crying, our lives in stasis. Not stasis exactly, re-formed, more accurately, those first nights disfigured by pain and fear, then fired in the kiln of our joint isolation.

My daytime patterns altered as well. I no longer met Dave to share a cigarette after Astronomy. In fact I went out of my way to avoid our familiar spot. Lindsay and I thought it best not to join the regular crew in Kagin at five o'clock, but instead ate at the Broiler every night that week. I do not know if Dave attended dinner as usual, or his classes for that matter. My vision of him continued to be pacing like a caged lion alone in his room. I am not even sure when he stopped drinking.

It felt strange, days without Dave. I had up to that point never spent two consecutive college days without some interaction with my friend. But I was unwilling to face him. More than worried about the awkwardness of bumping into him accidentally, I was, in short, afraid. My afternoons on campus were excruciating, constantly wary, peering over my shoulder, as though he might blindside me, emerge from behind the hackberry bushes or around the corner of Old Main, and lay me out with one punch.

The anxiety of navigating each day, however, was balanced by the new stability I experienced at night. A routine arose with Lindsay. Every evening commenced at the Broiler. We habitually sat in the booth by the front window. I always ordered the tuna melt on wheat, Lindsay the club with a side of cheese grits. We talked about our day, and inevitably we spoke of Dave. We shared our thoughts, she spoke to me of ferris wheels and tortoise shells, we ate, we studied.

And then back to my room. Nathan came by daily, but left us alone at night. How sacred those nights became. I was soothed by our rhythm as customs quickly sprouted. We nightly played a running game of gin rummy, she sitting cross-legged in her flannel pajama pants. There was comfort in watching her brush her teeth, the way she grabbed and pulled back her long wavy hair as she gargled and rinsed. Slowly my anxiety dissipated. Soon enough our common fear had faded, our crying morphed into laughter.

Battened down together against the storm, Lindsay suddenly had become closer to me than anyone.

And then the night came when I turned on the music, and she lit the candles. We sat together for hours in the low flickering orange-grey light and did not speak. Nothing was said before I kissed her. As if in a dream I kissed her. I kissed her, because what I wanted was to return mountains to ash and sand to sea. Turn again to the age before the clock, perhaps then there was no pain, no shoulders heavy with the world's weight. Without time, there can be no late, no aging, no date, perhaps then there was no shame. I ached to return again to only place, to forget the day, the hour, enter only space, our bodies neither young nor old. And death may not know our names. Forget the tick-tock of the when and the now, that we might begin to understand who and how. I wanted Lindsay to take me beneath all thought, tired, angry, tormented thought, under into dark rushing light, timeless, we.

"I don't know what I want. Not this. I can't..." Mara paused, kicked at the snow, then leaned her head back and spoke, as if to me but also out and up to the pale sun. "Time moves so fast, you know? We're going to wake up one morning and we'll be 50. And before we know it, before we have any idea what happened, we'll be dead."

Lindsay said, "I've never spent a night like this before."

"Never," I thought, our bodies intertwined, but still fully clothed, hardly kissing, just touching. I explored her face, the softness of her skin, observing the way her body reacted to pressures and movements, finding the ticklish and sensitive spots. Allowing my tongue to familiarize itself with the elasticity of her earlobes, learning the shape of her lips with my thumb and forefinger. "Never," I thought, "Never anything so sweet and simple, this most basic of romantic physical contact." And I felt first, how tragic for her, but then quickly the responsibility to do right by her. I studied her: impish grin, bashful eyes, thick wavy hair falling across her face. I had wanted her from the first moment that I sat next to her in the back seat of Mara's car. I had secretly pined and obsessed over her, and now suddenly it was a shared secret.

Night after night she stayed with me. My room awash in candlelight became a dreamlike sanctuary, a place significant and hidden from reality. But the outside world crept in occasionally, shattering our delusion. Interestingly enough such disenchantments were normally self-imposed.

"It's different with him," Lindsay said one evening.

"Do we have to talk about him?" I asked.

"You telling me you aren't thinking about him."

"I'm trying not to."

She kissed my bare chest. "We both love him for the same reasons."

"Lindsay, please."

"I mean, how hard it is to earn his trust, so that when you do, after all that work, you feel special then, lucky."

"I get it," I said sitting up, concentrating on the door, as though Dave might be listening. Part of me wanted him to be there, like that first night, still hammering at the door, twisting the knob, and that this time the door might give. That this new chaos might splinter with the shattered wood.

"No, you don't get it," she said, grinning wide in the orange-grey light. My face felt to me in comparison, somber, pensive. "You have no idea how amazing you are, do you?"

"Well...I..." I stammered.

"We'll work on that," she said with finality and laughing kissed me hard, a long passionate closed mouth kiss like something from a black and white movie.

I remember the guilt that consumed me in those first tentative, glorious, agonizing nights, knowing that I was hurting Dave, but I could not think, could only feel Lindsay near me, waking me gently like a dream, comfortable kissing, lightly touching, her eyes burning, reflecting flame.

"I'm not sure what I want," Lindsay, soft and half-undressed in the candle half-light, whispered, "but this feels right."

And there with Mara again on the front steps, our pale sun descended, our sky blue fading pink and yellow in hue. She spoke to me, her voice warming, combating cold.

"At thirty it's all going to be laid out for us. And it's going to fly by in a blur of birthdays and anniversaries and work days. And then we'll wake up and wonder where it all went. And God forbid, one day we wake up and wonder where it all went wrong. And then we'll be dead. I don't want to live an ordinary life. The expected. I'm afraid of that. I'm scared shitless of that. I want...something more."

And Nathan, tall and red, sat eating an apple and turned, "What about you?"

I looked down and around and pretended to smoke. "I want Anna, the one I can't have, the one down river."

"No," he shouted back, "What do you *want*?"

I was lost and whispered, "Maybe this. *This*, I thought. I've changed though. Anna was right, I have changed. It all has. Everything's a mess now. I've betrayed Dave."

"You betray him if you leave him." Red, tall, always in motion, Nathan banged his feet on the floor.

"But not if I take her? Her, who he doesn't even know he needs?"

"Just don't leave," he said. Lindsay said the same too, in the half light.

"I won't leave," I said.

"You already have," they said, and I wondered what they meant and knew they were right.

What I wanted was to live strong and scream at Dave, "What happened man? What happened to you? What went wrong?"

"You tell me, Waylan," he said coolly. We had not talked in well over a week. His drunkenness had kept us apart, and then, too, Dave had sobered up to the reality of my betrayal with Lindsay in a steady silence. I had eventually mustered up the courage to go to him, to knock on his dorm room door. He answered my knock and upon seeing me, said nothing and sat down in his reading chair, but left the door ajar. I padded into the room with precise steps, careful not to disturb, as though I had entered a funeral parlor or arrived late to church during prayer. Easing onto the edge of his bed, I looked at him across the room, and we sat that way for a long while in quiet before I asked him what had happened between us. I can still see him there, uncertain, trying to be truthful, as close to vulnerable as he could be. I had never seen him like that before. Wounded but not full of rage. He looked at me sheepishly, spoke carefully. I had left him, and he knew it. So we talked of nothing. We were suspended there, and neither knew how to proceed. Yet I was caught in some strange calm that I hoped might save us both. "This is the moment, what it has all been leading toward," I thought. Yet the only thing I could find in my heart to say was drenched in judgment.

"You know," my head heavy and low, "I remember when drinking was fun." Needing to say somehow that he had crossed the line with his violent bender, knowing he knew already.

"I can't remember the last time anything was fun," he said.

Mara, on the front steps, looked far off. "I look forward to sleeping at night."

I almost laughed, then realized she was serious. So unable to share she. I could see it tearing her up inside to say it.

"I'll tell you what I want." I smiled and tried not to cry. "I want to chain smoke."

"You are things I never knew I wanted. Things I never knew I could ask for even," Lindsay said. "Things I didn't even know existed."

I let the statement sit, because some part within me ached. Her openness, her devotion, soothed it. Something felt heavy on my chest, something irrationally weighty taking my breath. All at once in a gasp, in a breath lost, in a cry strangled, I understood how much I needed her. Her presence enlivened me, fought the rigor that had seized me. And lying there in bed, sticking to Lindsay's sweaty skin, I began to say things that I did not censor— things that scared me, things I believed.

"This is what I wanted," I said to her. "To be here, with you."

"What do you want?" Dave, that first night in the hallway, pushed drunk and loud.

"Not this. I mean…I want more coffee and less whiskey," I said back, "and a house."

"A house with a big kitchen," Lindsay said, her eyes aflame. Alone with her again, I could feel it, could almost see us there, the two of us together in a home.

"And a porch." I said. She smiled.

I stopped then so I could listen to the radio playing *American Pie* and not lose the past. Because what I really wanted…what I wanted desperately, was the past. Cumulative memories intertwining like the strands of color in Monet's painting, a bridge that might span fiery currents. My past, a scalable mountain, wild and pristine, holding unknown adventure and promise. My past, days of togetherness and porch lit evenings of white cotton nightgowns, nights of no hiding or shame. It was too much—too much to desecrate, too seminal to abandon, perhaps because I was afraid of the reordering of all I knew. But once up on a mountain, a friend said I was made for college, and there was something in me that believed him still.

I was afraid of Lindsay. Of loving her perhaps, of giving myself over to this new life. Because of the way Monet painted and the way it would taste if I ever stopped smoking. Because there was a life that I once lived with confidence and joy. Something about the smell of pine. Or something about soil beneath my fingernails. Perhaps Lindsay would sense it. Knowing somehow outside of knowing that I was closed and frightened. A boy merely. And for a body rivers away.

XII

Anna said something had changed in me, or would have said it if she didn't. The voices, too, understood this. They told me as much. *You are empty now. Hollow.* I had lost something, *you have nothing*, lost the part that made me recognizable to myself. I lacked a point of reference. I did, however, know it was exactly 1:27 p.m. when I awoke. Twenty-seven minutes past the beginning of my history class or maybe anthropology. I am not sure which, because I could not have told you what day of the week it was, or even month. I understood only winter and lateness.

I felt bad for the poor rat. It was hard not to. Wet rats are not cute, of course, even lab rats. Pink sickly eyes, bony paws, thick fleshy tail—she was not exactly a sympathetic figure. But I pitied her all the same.

That afternoon, I stood among twenty or so other students encircling the edge of what amounted to an oversized kiddie pool, a hard blue plastic cylinder brimming with still water. This was my psychology class, I am sure, because it was my last class of the day, beginning at 3:30 p.m. As I was generally awake by that hour, I regularly attended. Beyond it's convenience, I made special effort to show up to class while we studied the unit on memory. Memory was a mystery to me, puzzle pieces that no longer fit together. I was anxious to learn all I could. Knowledge would bring me back. (As though back was a place. As though I could return.)

Sipping from a thermos of my characteristically weak coffee, I peered into the wide tub. The professor was gently placing a lab rat down onto a small clear platform situated above the waterline in the center of the pool. The rat sat for a brief moment unmoving, then sniffed, then paced, walking her circular perimeter, stopped, tested the water, and dutifully began the process again. We watched. She seemed to be conscious of our observation. Perched on her hind legs, she checked the air, her nose bobbing, and scanned our intent faces.

Without warning, the professor grabbed the rat by the tail and flung her unceremoniously into the water. The dull thunk of impact was followed by the splatter of splashed water returning to water. The rat broke to the surface, stunned, confused, but after only two panicky turns, she swan directly to the platform, slipping easily onto the plastic refuge, as though a penguin emerging from an arctic ocean onto ice.

The professor repeated the test again and again. Each time the rat responded in much the same way, now even more rapidly returning to the center platform, shocked perhaps, fur matted from successive dunks, but largely unfazed. We watched, and the rat knew we watched.

The professor spoke. "The rat experienced the platform. She remembered it as dry and safe. Thus she returned to it repeatedly once in danger." As he spoke, he unsheathed a syringe. "That memory is built by proteins in the hippocampus. Anisomycin is a protein inhibitor. We can target the specific cluster of proteins that is the rat's memory of the platform by injecting Anisomycin while she is thinking about it, or, in effect, committing it to memory. We can make the rat forget."

Leaning over the tub, the professor held the rat firmly in one hand and injected her with the contents of the syringe with the other. Then he again lifted the rat by the tail and dropped her into the pool. This time there was no beeline to the platform. She spun in the water, seeking dry land. She paddled to the edge of the vat and tried fruitlessly to scamper up the side.

"She has lost the memory of the platform," the professor said, as we all watched the lab rat swim this way and that, each turn more frantic than the last. "The platform is clear Plexiglas and is difficult for her to see against the blue background of the tub. She may yet still discover it, but it would be a revelation, not navigation. She currently believes she is in open waters."

The rat splashed, swimming in desperate circles. Her nose twitched and whiskers quivered just above the water's surface; she began to squeak intermittently, soft and sad. It occurred to me as I watched that I was witnessing the forgetting. I wanted suddenly then to know the rat's name, so I could call to her, that she might remember herself. I did not even know if the rat had a name, maybe a number had been assigned to her. But what was the name she understood as her own? Her true name, perhaps a precisely pitched sequence of squeaks, might ground her, remind her of who she was and what she knew. Then perhaps she might remember the platform. Yet was that even possible now? Maybe there are no reminders in the forgetting.

The audience became anxious as the rat's squeaking increased in frequency and volume, her head below water occasionally now. The professor plucked her out of the pool and placed her mercifully on the platform. She sat there, sucking quick sharp breaths, soaked and spent. I felt inexplicably exhausted myself at that moment. The smell of rubber filled my nose and I was unsure why.

"I'll need a detailed analysis of this experiment by Friday. The data you'll need can be found..." the professor began, but I was not listening. I was instead captivated by the poor drenched rat. She was studying me, I felt certain, with her little pink eyes. I wondered if her mind had become a blank slate, or whether she, like me, now experienced memories in a foggy haze, out of order and upside down—not a bright clean washing away of past, not memories erased, but instead made murky, dark and confused.

The events of the last few weeks were jumbled and heavy in my head. I could not comprehend how my life had altered so quickly, and moreover, I could not decide how I felt about any of it. Was this the life I had wanted? Was this who I was supposed to be? Or merely the kind of person I had become?

I found Dave outside. He sat as though he were modeling. I wondered whether he was aware of this, whether it was conscious effort or distracted pose. He was on the front cement steps of his dorm, leaning elbows to knees, one leg bent to the first step, the other leg relaxed on the second. A cigarette hung from his mouth, it straightening occasionally as his lips tightened to inhale, then the casual removal for exhale. He stared off into the distance, his head turned slightly away from my approach so that my arrival was almost a surprise, but it was just me, and I was a fixture at his doorstep.

"Hey," I said, still walking across the small patch of front yard.

"Hey," he returned, not yet broken from his trance.

"How was class," I said, now standing before him.

"Fine. Bullshit. Whatever. Hey, you know that old store over there?" He nodded toward the empty 50's deco style building at the end of the block.

"Yeah."

"You know it's for sale?" He said, still staring intently at the corner.

"Yeah, I saw the sign, I guess."

"It's a great location, right on the main drag and all. Why doesn't somebody buy the thing up?"

"Don't know."

"I mean, Jesus. A pub." He was not really talking to me, he was just saying it to the yard and the street. "If you could get a liquor license, of course. Or a coffee shop. You know, 24 hours would make a killing around here."

"You're right," I said, as though it mattered what I thought.

"I mean, I don't want to move boxes forever."

Dave had recently started working the graveyard shift for UPS. It was grueling work, unloading semi-trailers of packages onto a conveyer belt from midnight until four in the morning. It fit his school schedule and paid benefits. He said he had learned two things at his job. The first was, whoever invented the heating pad was a genius. The second was that a 70 lb big box weighs less than a 70 lb small box. "It's true. You're ready for it when it's big," he had explained.

I had thought there was something profound in that, about the distance between perception and reality. For him it was just a practical matter of fact.

Dave flicked his cigarette out into the street and looked at me finally.

"But to buy a place I'd have to have some kind of money. For a down payment. And I'd have to care," he said and stood up. "Want a beer?"

"Sure," I said, feeling as though I had been left out of some key piece of his internal discussion. Perhaps it was that big dreams weigh less than small ones. Or something about how boxes were not the only load he carried.

I woke often in those days next to the warm, naked body of a woman. And lying in bed in the mornings, smoking, I would watch her dress and put on makeup, watch the curves of her breasts as they were cupped into a flower patterned bra, watch her reflection in the mirror as she pursed freshly painted lips and felt at ease and a little in love.

"You going to class this morning?" Lindsay asked as she scrambled around the room looking for her books, tossing clothes and moving ashtrays. She was late as usual. I was still in bed, half propped up, groggy, watching her.

"I should." I leaned over and grabbed my jeans off the floor, rifled through my front pockets, successfully retrieving my pack of cigarettes and lighter.

Lindsay handed me an ashtray which she was in the process of moving. She waited patiently until I grabbed it, all the while scanning the room for a missing book. It was nonchalant and familiar.

"Thanks, babe." I settled the ashtray in my lap and lit my cigarette. "I missed the last one, but I don't know if I'm going or not."

"You seen my psych book?" she asked as though it were a response.

"Abnormal or Developmental?"

"Abnormal."

"Yeah." I lifted my shirt off the floor and snatched up her hefty textbook. I held it out to her with one hand, my wrist bending with the weight.

"Thanks." Her book stack now complete she edged toward the door. "Well, you know you're welcome to stay all day. I'll be back around four. Lock the door if you leave."

"Sure," I said.

She looked in the mirror by the door. I could see her face in the reflection. It was expressionless yet calm and content. She was soothing this morning. Us was soothing on this day.

She placed the books on the edge of her dresser still facing the mirror and then in one motion tossed, caught and pulled her long brown hair into a ponytail, securing it with an elastic band. She grabbed her books and swung around to face me, smiling with a satisfied air of accomplishment.

"I love you," she said and opened the door.

"Have a good day," I sneaked in before she vanished into the hallway and the door swung shut.

What I hoped, what I dreamed, what I wanted desperately to believe was *this*. This moment. Lindsay made my heart light. Being with her somehow confirmed that school was not all important. She had a tacit understanding that there were things worth more, things of beauty, things that deserved more attention. She made me feel as if I was not a failure. We could stress out about school, be upset if we were not doing well. We could argue and even yell at each other, as long as we stayed healthy. The darkness dwarfed all else. In the end being happy mattered most. Claiming joy was not only our right but our duty.

The voices were common now. Loud and steady. But Lindsay knew them. They were her voices too, but I did not understand that yet. Did not understand that she knew the field of battle firsthand. I did not yet know I was sick. I only knew that she made everything easier, better.

She spoke to me of teddy bears and model trains.

We danced often in my room to no music—me holding her, my nose lost in her auburn hair. She always smelled of an old woman perfume—lavender or something—she said it reminded her of playing dress-up when she was a little girl. But she was no longer a girl. She was powerful and confident and stood tall, all legs and torso. I could not read enough of her body to fill me up. She wore tight T-shirts that revealed her soft midriff and bellybutton ring. She and I would dance, sway to the rhythm not of sound but of our own bodies, slowly, gently melting into one another, the linoleum tile of my dorm room our ballroom parquet.

She spoke of horses, all sinew and speed.

And slowly, nightly, listening and talking, we began to know each other. Her desire to know me made me strong, made me feel alive. Being considered, being discovered, those are the first timid inklings of love. And I needed above all else to be loved. So I gave myself to her, and she to me. Each night we shared the heat and touch of our bodies, our inner-selves erratically illuminated orange-grey by the quivering candle light, I slipping fast into her like a symphony all at once.

She whispered lightning and rain.

(There is a picture I still have of Lindsay and me sitting in a restaurant. The waitress had taken it. Lindsay sits tall and graceful, her long hair dyed chestnut by shadow and light. I sit next to her with my arm around her. I look a bit ragged, honestly, like I have had a bad nights rest. In reality, it had been more than one rough night, it had been a year's worth. But I am smiling wide, pure and genuine, a smile almost like laughter. She, too, is smiling, confident and content. "We look so incredibly happy," Lindsay had said, touching the photo lightly with her index finger. And it was true. We do look happy. We were. This moment, now trammeled in glass and frame, is proof. It is a picture of health. A picture of love. I peer occasionally at that photo and marvel at the strength of young hearts. She and I were individually crumbling, nightly combating demons of the dark. But together, there at some restaurant, a photograph captured the whites of our teeth and joy in our eyes. In that moment, we shared a sacred and inarticulable understanding, a dream of something more.)

"Dreams?" Nathan stood up and began to pace the distance of our room. Mara and I watched him as he pondered my question.

"I have all sorts a dreams," he said. "For example, last night I had a dream I was wiping my ass with a toothbrush."

"Okaaaayyy. Not quite what I meant," I said, trying to stop him before he got rolling. "I mean stuff that affects you, you know, shapes the way you plan your life."

"You think that dream didn't affect me? I had to go out this morning and buy a new toothbrush." He grinned.

"I mean, dreams, like hopes and aspirations," I said needlessly, knowing he knew what I meant.

Nathan jumped on my bed and put his hand on his chest. "I have a dream that someday all the world will gather 'round to witness human equality created through the perfection of the military-industrial-corporate-technocracy. And we (those not killed or imprisoned or exiled) will all join hands and sing Kumbaya." He hopped down with a bang. "You mean that kind of dream?"

"Yeah," I said. "Something like that."

"Well then, not really."

Mara and I laughed.

"What about you, Mara?"

"For as long as I can remember I've wanted to be a rock star. You know, touring, playing packed arenas. Drugs, sex, money, the whole thing. I was going to be famous."

"It can still happen," I said.

Air shot from her nose in a skeptical laugh. "Not so sure about that."

"Seriously, your music is incredible," I said.

"Thank you, but once you've done it for a while...played enough coffeehouses and shit bars, you start to realize it's all a crap-shoot. I know some really great bands, people way more talented than I am, that never caught on."

"Well, if it's a crapshoot, then there's always a chance," Nathan said.

"I suppose, but I think I'll just end up going to law school...be a lawyer like my dad."

None of us spoke for a few moments, so that the silence seemed to get heavy, and Mara took the initiative to make it seem less sad. "It's not a bad thing, ya know. I'll be a great lawyer. And dreams are just that, dreams. They're not real. They're wonderful, great to have, and then you wake up to real life."

I was reminded of T.S. Eliot then and said, "Human voices wake us and we drown."

"What?"

"Nothing." I said.

Nathan walked over to our sink and pulled open the mirrored cabinet. "Here," he said and tossed Mara and me toothbrushes. "No hidden hygiene message here. I just went a little overboard this morning." As he slid a toothbrush out of its packaging and began the work of brushing his teeth, I could see that his cabinet shelves were stocked full with boxes of new toothbrushes.

"I never know when to believe him," Mara said to me.

"Unfortunately, the answer is *always*," I said back, and we laughed.

After a minute or so Nathan turned off the running tap water and wandered back to us. "Well, Waylan, what about you? What are your dreams?"

"I want to own a professional basketball team," I said, telling them the breezy big dreams and keeping the small significant ones for myself.

In high school, after I had been accepted to Macalester, my dreams at night were of snowball fights and northern lights, each embedded with the hope of my coming collegiate career. But in Minnesota the dreams came only of the southern sun. I wondered if Lindsay knew that when I held her close after sex I dreamed of Anna.

"You're a dumb-ass." Nathan said, smirking.

"Why?" I shot back, tiring of his abuse.

"Because you refuse to get over Anna."

"What? I'm thinking about telling Lindsay I love her!"

Nathan's smile widened. He was enjoying himself. "Listen to yourself, Waylan. You said you might tell her you love her. Why didn't you just tell *me* you love her. Can you do that?"

"Of course. Yes, I love her." I said, but immediately began to falter. "I mean, she's great. We're great. I think I really feel like I love her."

He laughed and pumped his fists in the air triumphantly. "You see? What, man, is your problem with loving her? Is this about Anna? About Dave? Or just about you?"

Nathan looked at me in a way that made me uneasy. Something changed in the energy of the room. Something in Nathan's glare perhaps. And then I realized he was not moving. No flashing grin, no tapping feet, no dancing red eyebrows. Nothing. And I looked away, not understanding my embarrassment.

Nathan spoke coldly, "Why are you ashamed to be in love with Lindsay?" And then he began to move again. He tossed his head back and threw his arms out flamboyantly. An actor on his stage.

"I mean, you sit here and talk to me about Lindsay all the

damn time. But it's like you're blowing her off. You say, 'We get along' and 'It's cool.'"

In saying this he changed his voice to do his highly regarded impression of me, which I disagreeably thought sounded much more like Al Gore than me.

"You talk about her passion, her strength, her capacity for joy, but then you always imply that those are the very traits that annoy you. 'I don't know…she's over the top. Stubborn. Immature.'" Maybe it was more Eeyore, than Al Gore.

Nathan meandered over to one of the walls of our room and began hitting his fists lightly and rapidly against the cinderblocks, ducking and weaving his rock-hard opponent. "You tell me the sex is good, as though she's some whore."

He stopped boxing the wall and looked out the window. He searched the snow-covered streets and perhaps the play of shadow and light on the church across the intersection.

"You love her."

The way he said it, I felt like he had more to say, but he was done. Something in the shadow and light had silenced him. Or maybe he had said all he could say. And in the silence that followed, I realized I did not know whether he was talking about Lindsay or Anna.

Darkness came sudden and deep. After a heavy snow fall in Minnesota I was always taken by the silence. St. Paul had incredible winter weather maintenance. The roads were always plowed quickly, people cleared their walks promptly. They were accustomed to the snow. They knew how to deal with it. But they also knew better than to brave it unnecessarily. On work days everyone went about their business. On weekends, children, bundled and wrapped, mittened and muffed, went sledding and had snow ball fights. But in the evenings after a particularly heavy snow the world became eerily silent. I stood outside on a night such as this after talking to Nathan and listened to the nothingness. For a while, at first, there was the distant sound of someone who had arrived home late still shoveling his sidewalk. And there was the occasional loud rumble of an unhappy car on the road, the sound of wheels easing over packed snow, the crunch and give. Beyond that, nothing stirred. No traffic. No horns. The chirps of insects and birds were hushed by the bitter cold and muting snow. The night was clear and quiet, and the silence blossomed cruelly inside my skull. Some nights are filled with the things we are not. With the things we will not become.

"We made a rat forget today," I said, lying in bed with Lindsay.

Maybe I spoke the phrase at a whisper, and she did not hear me. Maybe I did not speak. Either way she did not respond; instead she stroked my hair and hummed a lullaby. Perhaps I could not get over Anna, but I felt whole with Lindsay in a new and mysterious way. She completed me on a basic level that I could not pinpoint. Our darknesses communed when we held each other close. I remember how my cheek rested half on the softness of her left breast (it was smaller than her right) and half on the firmness of her sternum. I remember thinking that I was not really thinking, thinking that I was feeling. That I was aware of the heat of her body against mine. That I was consumed by the rhythm of her breathing, and I matched it with my own. My unthinking mind was clear. All made sense. We did not speak. The only things we knew, we felt. Can I stay here? A brief moment beyond the haze, like a plane gaining altitude to avoid a storm. Breaking free of the dark, ominous clouds, the air was clear and my breathing matched hers. It was impossible to sustain such control, such lucidity, such bliss. It always is. It was not her fault. Or mine really. When I would wake, I would wake late, the day already slipping, the responsibilities untended, the heft of hours accumulating until my lower back muscles cried out in earnest and knees would give out. My agonizing self-doubt and hyper-sensitivity to pressure would tomorrow make me inept and likely wholly immobile. So let me stay here a while with her. Engulfed in her breath and heartbeat. In her soft and bone.

XIII

Alone in my room, I lay in bed fully clothed. *They all hate me. Something is wrong and they know it. Quit being such a downer. Just get over it.* The smell of a bed long slept in and never washed consumed me. The stench of my sweat clung to the fabric—it smelled of failure. Every time I laid my head down to rest, the embedded scent spurred a recollection only of defeat. I do not know how long I lay there, do not recall if I slept. My sleeping and waking hours were so much the same then. So I am not sure when I heard the gentle trickling of water.

As if asleep, perhaps dreaming, I peered over the edge of my bed. Water covered my floor, a slow-rising black lagoon girded me on all sides. Had a pipe burst? Had a toilet overflowed? As I watched, there from within the inky depths, three solitary lights flickered beneath the waters, grew bright, then faded. Orion's belt! Then a cotton nightgown. Things emerged from the dark still pool, floating alternately shallow and deep. A beer cap chess piece. Curve of stone. A lab rat struggling and splashing and then under. All flashes—blood and white—porch lit snippets, coalescing briefly, quivering as if by candle light. Images and half-moments (her fingers stroking guitar strings) arose from moonless waters, then sank again and down. These images I recognized, memories perhaps, but I forgot each one immediately as they were consumed and disappeared. In the dark mirror-like surface, I saw a vast forest of trees, all upside down and backwards, and as though viewed from a great height. With a touch, the reflected trees trembled and moved out from themselves, repeating as echoes.

It is only a bad dream. Sleep, I heard the voices say. *Sleep*. The voices were familiar, I theirs and they mine, so I did not fear them. *You are exhausted. So tired. Just sleep. I just need sleep.*

I believed I could sleep enough to catch up, sleep and find rest. I closed my eyes to shut out the world, trying to block the ghostly images, ignoring the amassing waters. I lay there in bed, my face pressed to the pillow—the sweat of a hundred endless, agonizing, tossing, unbearable nights saturated the fibers of my pillow case; it reeked of shame. Suddenly something flicked the back of my head. I flipped over and was hit in the face by a fat drop of water. My ceiling was leaking. Perhaps this was the source of my swamping. Perhaps the dorm room above had flooded.

Stay here. It is safe here. Someone will come and take care of this mess. You are not capable. Stay. Sleep.

The heavy drips quickly became a stream pouring onto my upturned face. I pulled the sheets over my head and tried to sleep. My eyes shut, my head hidden, I could hear the water in the darkness. The sound of rain slapping open waters was like an argument in my mind.

I must get up and deal with this. No, you are too tired. You need rest. But I am all alone and the seas are rising. Hush now. Sleep.

The steady rhythm of hard rain on puddles crescendoed to loud splatter of torrential downpour on expanding lakes. The roaring of the water filled my ears, deafened me, seemed even to become my thoughts, so the things I knew and remembered washed away. Suddenly, yet as if drawn out, my mind held only rushing noise and, too, some snippet of song that I might have known, something familiar, but lost. *You'll have things you'll want to talk about...* Confused, terrified, I peeked out from beneath my covers, squinting in the darkness and could see the grey outline of my bookshelf. I held my vision steady to ground myself amidst the surrounding upheaval. I needed the words from those books, stories that might remind me of something, words that might speak to me of myself. I lay there in my bed, staring at my bookcase through sheets of rain, trying to stare into the books, that I might know all that knowledge, hear a thousand stories all at once, as if that might save me.

Perhaps words might save you. Perhaps. Words are not death, but they still suffer the same fate as the dead. Either praised or judged, eventually forgotten. Coffined, rubbery with formaldehyde, death waits for us the mourners. The lights pink and soft, music quiet and conspicuously soothing. The dead are groomed, made presentable, laid in quilt-topped beds, or sprinkled across the surface of certain seas. The dead are honored, but enjoy such praise with silent lips. The dead are judged, but remain defenseless in their permanent state. But the dead care not. Death is darkness and lack of guilt.

The ceiling crumbled and fell, collapsing under the weight of the flood above. A waterfall cascaded down, crashing in and crushing my room. My bookshelf disintegrated beneath such force. My bed rocked and lurched, a dinghy on violent storm-lashed oceans. I clung to my soaked bedsheets, desperate to stay afloat. How long can I hold on? How strong is the instinct to survive?

Perhaps in a few days or months I could release a bird, like Gilgamesh's raven or Noah's dove, and they might return to me, grasped in their beaks some hope. But the raven is salvation and the dove is peace, and I had neither in my heart. Darkness alone informed my disposition. (The darkness came and stayed.) Nights at some point become so deep that they are dreamless. "What do you want?" is the wrong question for someone who cannot project anything hopeful into the future. I only cared for chaos, only ached to be destroyed. So the waters came up over the sides of my mattress-ark and I was submerged.

XIV

Ring.

"You've reached Waylan's room. I'm not in. Please leave a message."

Whatcha sayin', Waylan? Just calling to see how you're doing. Haven't heard from you in a while. So when you get this just give me a call, okay. Love you.

Ring.

"You've reached Waylan's room. I'm not in. Please leave a message."

Waylan. It's Mara. Thought you'd said you'd be home. We've got that History test on Friday. It'd be great if we could get a head start on it. Maybe tomorrow. Coffee's on me this time. Talk to you soon.

Ring.

"You've reached Waylan's room. I'm not in. Please leave a message."

What's up, buddy. It's Dave. You weren't at dinner. Just making sure you're all right. You forced me to eat with some random hot chicks. Bastard. I'm assuming you'll stop by sometime tonight, so, later.

Ring.

"You've reached Waylan's room. I'm not in. Please leave a message."

Hi, honey. It's Mom. We usually talk on Sunday evenings, and we hadn't heard from you yet. But that's all right. Maybe you have a big paper or something due tomorrow. Well, good luck with whatever you're doing and give us a call as soon as you can. Love you. Bye.

Ring.

"You've reached Waylan's room. I'm not in. Please leave a message."

Hey. Haven't talked to you in a few days. I know you were upset with me the other night, but it's not like you to hold a grudge. Maybe you're just busy, but call me, just so I don't worry. I'm kind of going crazy not knowing why you're not talking to me. If it's nothing then forget about this message. Oh, God, that sounded stupid, didn't it. I'm awful on these machines. Just call me okay? And know that I love you.

Ring.

"You've reached Waylan's room. I'm not in. Please leave a message."

'Sup. Dave again. You musta done one of those emergency isolation trips to Perkins. You must have a shit load of work or something. Call me, I'll be up.

Ring.

"You've reached Waylan's room. I'm not in. Please leave a message."

Waylan, this is Professor Unseld. I'm calling in regards to your recent attendance. I have not been notified about an illness or a family emergency. I hope everything is okay. But know that I am concerned about your continued absence affecting your final grade irrevocably. Please contact me as soon as possible so we can set up a time to meet. Thank you.

Ring.

"You've reached Waylan's room. I'm not in. Please leave a message."

Jesus, Waylan. Did you drop out of school? It's been three days since anybody's seen you. You missed the exam today. I really hope everything's all right. I have no idea how you're going to talk your way out of this one. Anyway, call me as soon as you get this.

Ring.

"You've reached Waylan's room. I'm not in. Please leave a message."

It's Lindsay. At least I know you're not just avoiding me. Nobody's seen you. I came by earlier today, but no answer. Dave says you might have left with Nathan, but it's not like you not to tell anybody. I'm starting to worry. So, at least, just call and let me know you're all right.

Ring.

"You've reached Waylan's room. I'm not in. Please leave a message."

Dave here. I know Nathan's playing hooky this week and went to Florida. I guess you went with him. But I'm going through withdrawal, so call me when you get this.

Ring.

"You've reached Waylan's room. I'm not in. Please leave a message."

Honey, it's Mom. Where are you? Dad and I are starting to

worry. We know you're busy, but give us a quick call. Shoot us an e-mail, maybe. Dad says to keep up the good work. Just call, okay. We love you. Bye.

"Mom. Mom. Are you there?"

The other end clicked and became the melancholy hum of dial tone.

"Mommy?"

XV

I cannot express to you the effort it took to walk across campus. My legs were heavy, my gut shook uncontrollably, my mind rushed. *What can I say? What am I going to say? Fool, there is nothing to say. Will he be angry? He will be disappointed. They are all so disappointed. Whata terrible waste. I cannot DO THIS. Ofcourse you can't. HewillBEsoANGRY.*

I had become stunned by the beauty of the raging unbridled world. I was amazed by the strength of humanity. That each morning they found the resolve to get up in the morning, to dress and shower, maybe to make breakfast. To get the kids off to school, to brave rush hour traffic, or to wait patiently in the predawn snow for the bus or to change three subway lines to get to work. To work long hours on assembly lines, in cubicles, behind counters. The world got up every morning, for different reasons certainly, but with reason. This great mass of individuals functions and so the world functions. And it was beyond my capacity to fathom how any of it got done. I was baffled by the astonishing collective will, and, yes, it amazed me that anyone could organize and motivate themselves enough to succeed in college.

My anxiety and despair in general forced me to avoid any form of confrontation. But I understood my academic career was at a breaking point, and the anxiety of that slowly but surely began to outweigh my anxiety over a conversation with my professor. And so, one afternoon, after sleeping through Professor Unseld's 2:15 class again, I decided to head to his office to apologize.

I stood outside of Old Main smoking, trying to talk myself into going inside, seriously considering returning to my dorm room. My bed seemed to beckon me, promising safety and warmth. I shivered in the cold and lit another cigarette. I paced and smoked until I ran out of cigarettes. Finally too cold to remain in the wind, I pulled hard on the massive oak front doors and reluctantly slipped inside.

Once inside I lost my nerve again. I eased up the stairs, up a few steps and then back down. Occasionally a door would open on some level and someone would enter the stairwell. When this occurred I avoided eye contact and pretended to be heading either up or down the stairs until they were gone. This routine of alternating hesitant dance and determined step went on for maybe twenty minutes before finally arriving me on the third floor. *I can still go. I can always run. It is easier to run.*

I eased open the door to the hallway. It was quiet—classes had already ended for the day. I stopped in the middle of that silent, carpeted hallway, paralyzed by my anxiety. Taking long deep breaths, I stared intently at a bulletin-board along the near wall in an attempt to look as though I belonged, as though there might be some viable reason for standing there directionless and alone. Suddenly a door down the hall opened, "Ah, Waylan. What a pleasant surprise." Professor Unseld stood before me with a welcoming arm gesturing me into his office. And for a moment I did not feel afraid.

I went in and sat down, searching for the right way to apologize.

"We missed you in class today," Unseld said, positioning himself behind his desk. His leather chair rolled slightly with the force of his sitting.

My ease left me. I had spent so much energy to just show up, I had not thought yet of what I might say. *Lie. It is easier to lie.* But the effort to lie seemed then more than the effort to share some semblance of the truth. "I've not been feeling well lately."

"Sick?"

"Yeah, for a while now," I answered, staring at the corner of his desk.

"I should say. Weeks. That is very concerning. Have you been to see a doctor?"

"Not like that." I stopped, cleared my throat, hesitant to go on. "More...more like everything's harder than it should be."

Professor Unseld looked at me for a while and did not speak. Finally he stood, and rolled his chair out into the middle of the room so the desk no longer separated us.

"Listen Waylan, don't worry about class. We can figure that out later. I'm just really glad to see you. Can you stay for a cup of coffee?"

I nodded.

"Great," he said with such genuine feeling that I caught myself smiling. I caught myself wanting to be somewhere other than my bed.

We talked for over an hour. I told him about my struggles with attendance, about my difficulties with self-discipline, about my feelings of anxiety and guilt. I told him what I cared about and how I was frustrated by my inability to grab hold of the opportunities being offered me. I spoke of Anna. I spoke of Lindsay.

Unseld listened. He was patient and kind. He told me about his own college experience, "all those many years ago." And then he said a funny thing. He said that I should go and talk to the Macalester counseling staff. To this day I still find it amusing because that is exactly what you say to a kid who comes in to talk about absences and ends up telling his life story. I do not know if he knew exactly what he was suggesting, the kind of impact he would have on my life, but he did know something I was unable to arrive at on my own; I needed help.

As I was leaving, he reiterated his belief that I should make a therapy appointment, because, as he said, "I find it's useful to talk to those who are trained to listen." I gave him a kind of nervous look as I nodded in response. At that moment it must have dawned on him the courage and enormous effort it had taken me to show up at his office because he smiled, said, "Hold on just one minute," and picked up the phone. That beautiful man scheduled the appointment for me.

"Well…" Lindsay said as she pulled herself into the booth. She looked at me across the table as though trying to ascertain my mental state unsure how to approach me. Autumn sunlight streamed pale through the plate-glass window and caressed the side of her face, her brown hair glowed blond. She smiled at me in the hanging silence. I looked at her shimmering hair and then out the window at the football field across the street. The grunt and crush of football practice toughened the brisk early evening atmosphere. I had forgotten fall. It is so brief in Minnesota. By the time department stores erect Halloween displays, there is inevitably snow on the ground. But the bridge from summer to winter is heart-rending in its artistry. Shadow and light dance closer, heavier, more deliberately, as the music of the equinox slackens its pace. Nature's color pallet alters—green to yellow, yellow to orange, orange to red. Autumn is the dying of the land. It is the season of dying, but it is not yet death.

"So how did it go?" she probed.

I took a deep breath. My recent struggles appeared clearer to me now, yet the answers laid out before me engendered confusion. I did not know how to articulate my feelings.

Earlier that day Lindsay had said, "I'll meet you after, at the Broiler. Say, five o'clock?"

"But baby, the session will be over by three," I had answered.

"You'll want some time," she said and gave me a sympathetic half-smile. "Five o'clock then."

I did not know why she thought I would need time, but now I understood. Maybe I needed more than a couple of hours. After my first therapy session, I was emotionally spent. But I needed to be there with Lindsay. I needed to try to put voice to all that I suddenly felt. In sharing it might become understandable. The voices were screaming, oceans in my ears. I had to speak, to force my own voice through the den of noise. But I could not find my own voice; my actual voice. It had atrophied from disuse. I did not know where to start or how to begin. Her hair glistened sun.

"Waylan, we can do this later." She paused then, perhaps thinking what it was that I needed to hear. "Or not at all. What you talked about there is for you. I just want…"

"He said I am clinically depressed."

She nodded in silence.

"He was nice. He listened. He had so little doubt about his diagnosis."

Still she said nothing. Even sitting there I felt I was falling. "Surely this deserves response," I thought. But there was only her quiet and her nod. So I continued, trying to find words amidst the debilitating torrent in my head.

"The sleeping, the anxiety, the apathy…it all adds up, he said. He said certain people are more susceptible. And how he figures it, the pressures of college triggered some preexisting condition. As though it was always in me…as though I was born with a see-saw for a brain that has now been tipped to unstable."

The anger began to roil in me. I was starting to put language to my pain. I spoke loudly to hear my own words.

"I mean, what the fuck, right? This guy doesn't even know me. It's not like I haven't been happy over the last year. I'm coping, just like everybody does, ya know? And, Christ, come on, the clinical definition of depression makes everyone I know depressed. Right?"

I looked at Lindsay. The sun was setting, and the light faded from our window so that she was now more muted grey than radiant. She reached her hand out across the table.

"I don't even know what any of this means," I said, letting her take my hand. "It's all just so stupid. This guy doesn't know shit."

"I don't think he's wrong, Waylan."

A couple of days later Dave and I stood on the bank of the Mississippi. It had been a twenty minute walk in a bitter coming-winter wind, but I had needed him to make this journey with me. Even though he did not understand the importance of the quest, he accompanied me all the same. We were like that, Dave and I. There was an unquestioning devotion between us that made our connection unheeding to the brink of dangerous.

"Depressed? Come on, you know I don't believe in that shit," Dave said.

We stood there in the silt and mud, tossing stones, alternately large and small, into the river.

"You know, this is because you've got a fucking psych major for a girlfriend. Always diagnosing everybody with something. It's a good thing you saved me from that woman."

That made me smile, how I had "saved" him from Lindsay. It was how Dave had settled on speaking about my indiscretion, my betrayal transformed into a selfless act of love through a turn of phrase.

Dave spit and smiled. "If you hadn't stepped in, that bitch would have me in a straightjacket by now."

"So you think I'm depressed?" I asked Lindsay.

"Waylan…"

The waitress approached our table hesitantly. She stood with a pot of coffee a foot or two from the table, and an uneasy silence arose among the three of us. Lindsay and I released hands so she could top off my cup.

"Can I get you anything, dear?" she said to Lindsay.

"Yes, ma'am. A coffee." Lindsay looked at the full dish of creamers on the table and said without missing a beat, "and I'll need some extra cream."

"Anything to eat?"

"Just a club. Oh, and a side of cheese grits."

"All right. Anything for you, dear?" The waitress looked at me.

I managed a smile. "Thanks. I'm not hungry."

She smiled, stuffed her pen into the back of her hair and headed to the kitchen.

"Waylan," Lindsay said. "You know my dad died when I was in high school."

I nodded.

"That was just four years ago," she said to herself. She paused before speaking again to me. "But what you don't know is how it affected me. It hit me pretty hard, of course. It's only natural. You know I dropped out of school for a while. I couldn't concentrate on anything…not school, not work. I started sleeping all the time. And at first everyone understood."

"It's understandable."

"Yeah, but it wasn't entirely. I was devastated. I spent whole days crying. Whole days! And I started to feel alienated because no one really got it. Even my family, who had loved him as much as I did, they weren't broken like I was. So I got angry. I felt all alone."

"But, baby, it sounds like you're splitting hairs. It sounds like you're saying there is a proper way to grieve."

"It's not that simple. Yes, I was reacting to a terrible loss..."

The waitress returned with Lindsay's coffee and a handful of creamers.

"Thanks," Lindsay said.

She tore open the first of what I knew would be four creamers. She did so without losing her train of thought. "But I didn't get better with time. I got worse. I thought about killing myself all the time. Something short circuited. I was depressed, Waylan. And I couldn't reason my way out of it. It was not normal grief. I needed help."

She took a sip of her coffee to create room for more creamer. "And I can say to you in all truth that therapy and medication are the only reasons I am here today."

"Baby, I had no idea."

"I recognized the signs in you. I recognized my own experience in you."

"Why didn't you say anything?" I suddenly felt a sharp stabbing pain behind my eyes. Between Professor Unseld, the therapist and Lindsay, I began to feel like the only one in the room that had not noticed the elephant.

"You needed to figure it out on your own."

"On my own! Christ...I've been...figure it out on my own...Jesus, Lindsay."

"Just imagine if I'd come to you a month ago, or yesterday for that matter and said that I thought you were clinically depressed. You would have blown it off and maybe never ever gone to a therapist out of some bullshit sense of pride."

"Do you really believe that?"

"Am I wrong?" She said stirring her coffee with a spoon.

"I don't know, babe. I just...I just feel..."

"You've got to stop feeling sorry for yourself," Dave shouted from his perch atop a fallen tree. "Do you know how many people are out there right now working their asses off—waking up every morning, doing some job they hate just to make ends meet, just begging for a break?"

He stopped and steadied himself, regaining his balance on the damp bark. "Or in some god-awful passionless marriage with a bunch of bratty kids? Do you know how many people are out there living their lives fucking depressed?"

"No, I don't," I said, while scavenging the river bank for a particularly aerodynamic rock. "How many?"

"All of them."

"No Dave, they're not. Just because we're depressed doesn't mean the whole world is."

"Hey, don't drag me into this clinical bullshit." He jumped down from the prone tree trunk with force. "If you want to claim depression, then fine. But that's you. That's on you."

"Okay," I said, intentionally passive to break the ascent of his anger.

It was quiet for a while between us. We paced the riverside and tossed stones in silence. But it was not really silence. There was instead the infernal rushing in my mind that passes for silence.

"I don't really get any of this, you know. I mean, my mind is my only reality," I said eventually. "But what if he's right? What if I *am* depressed?"

"Of course he's right," Dave said. "Are you really that surprised?"

While going through a book from my Elizabethan England History class, I discovered these two portraits of King Philip II of Spain. In the first he sits strong and proud, with dark hair and intelligent eyes. Painted in the early 1580's, he would have been in his fifties and the ruler of the greatest nation in the known world. The second portrait was painted just ten years later, and it is of a seemingly different man. His hair white, his facial expression grim, his eyes sad and tired. It is an amazing and profound change. During those ten years Philip had seen the execution of his Catholic ally Mary Queen of Scots and the defeat of the great Spanish Armada by the English. A man known for his patience and thought had begun to make rash decisions. He reportedly spent less and less time with his family and had stopped frequenting his garden. I wondered what those ten years had done to the King. Whether it had anything to do with the Catholic cause or the defeat of his seemingly invincible Armada. Perhaps he knew himself in the first painting and had lost touch with himself ten years later. Or maybe he had instead learned finally who he was by the time of the second painting.

I began to wish there could be two such portraits of me. I wondered what they would reveal about my heart. How might I look before depression and during? How would my eyes look? How did my eyes see differently? I wondered whether I knew myself before depression and had lost some sense of myself, or whether I now understood myself better, deeper, more fully than before. I wondered whether Jack or Anna or my parents even recognized me now in my second portrait. There had been profound change in me, but it had not come on suddenly, it had been a natural evolution. I decided that Phillip's transformation had nothing to do with the circumstances of his reign and instead had everything to do with the weight of years, and though tired, he had grown wise in his second portrait. I cannot remember why I decided that. Maybe because I needed to believe it. Maybe I was afraid—because trees grow for hundreds of years just to fall brittle and silent. There are changes that are not about growth.

"If he's right…if I'm depressed and too, if school in fact triggered some chemical imbalance…" I said. "If he's right, then, God, no one in college knows me not depressed. You don't even know me," I said to Lindsay there in the diner. I said the same later to Dave on the riverbank.

"I have always known your heart," Lindsay said.

"Well," Dave said, "you're my boy, so unless you were a total dickhead before college, I have a feeling it doesn't make a difference."

(But there was something about the cold cement of Anna's front steps, a floral scent on the wind, and softly sharp words regarding the change she saw in me.)

The clouds hung grey and low over the Mississippi. The Great River moved swiftly and seemed to soothe the wounds of my confession to Dave, but I changed the subject all the same.

"I wonder how fast the water moves, you know?" I said.

"Yeah, I guess."

"I mean, like how long it takes the water right here to get to the ocean."

Dave picked up a small ragged stone in silence, reared back and released it in a high arc out into the river as though in response.

"If I were to get on a raft, like some crazy-ass Huck Finn shit, how long would it take to get to New Orleans? A week? A month?"

"You planning on rafting down to see Anna?" Dave grinned.

"No, not like that. We're united by this, me and Anna." I chucked a stick out as far as I could. "All the stuff I want her to know, I can give to this water, just toss it out there like that stick and it'll eventually get to her. I guess I just kinda wanted to know when."

I had this vision of Anna relaxing, laying out on a grassy levy with her friends. She is enjoying the sun, drinking some cheap beer and talking about something, when all of a sudden she gets quiet, maybe mid-sentence, because she hears something—not exactly hears it, but senses it. Her friends give her strange looks as she gazes out onto the broad swath of river, searching intently among the cargo ships and tankers. And perhaps she is quiet for some time as she takes in all that I have sent her on the water. Then finally she returns to the group discussion, but there is something different in her, something strong, emboldened now by the knowledge of our connectedness.

"You're kind of pathetic, you know that, Waylan?"

"You're kind of an asshole," I said, slightly hurt, but more pleased, because I knew Dave well enough to know he understood all that I felt.

I checked my door. Locked. Nathan was not back yet, or would not be. I had to hand my books to Mara. My hand was still a mitt of bandages from the stitches two nights before. I had to do everything with my off hand, take notes, smoke, and unlock doors.

"*Viola*," I said, opening the door. "*Apres vois, mon cherie*," presenting the entryway with a flourish.

"So you've actually decided to attend French class on occasion." Mara laughed.

"Sort of. I'm pretty sure I butchered that."

"Well, you are checking with the wrong *Senorita*."

"Spanish is the smarter move on your part. Half of America will be speaking it before we're dead," I mused.

"Oh, is that an official stat?"

"It might be an approximation."

Mara sat on my bed as I retrieved two Icehouse bottles from the mini-fridge.

"If you're such a proponent of Spanish, why French?"

I began to respond when Mara cut me off. "Oh right. Another Anna hang-over."

"A what?"

"Anna hang-over. It's like a holdover or a hang-up from an old relationship. One night I was drinking and talking about Peter, and instead of holdover or hang-up, I said hang-over. Drinking like I was, it seemed appropriate."

"Not bad." I took a swig off my beer. "I still can't believe his name is Peter Little."

"Come on. Peter? It's Biblical."

"It's too funny."

Mara returned her hair behind her left ear. "Tell me how you got into college when you have the mind of a twelve-year-old boy."

"If I knew him, it might be different. But, Jesus, he dumped you for some bimbo. I'm allowed to make fun of him."

"Hey. We don't know for sure that she's a bimbo."

"God damn! You are too nice! She's not you," I said. "How good could she be?"

I sat next to Mara on the bed, and I tilted my beer bottle neck out for her in cheers. She clinked it.

"You're a fucking goddess," I said before drinking my toast.

"And you, my friend, are a sweet talker." She paused, took another sip of beer and smiled. "With absolutely no room to talk."

I feigned indignation.

"Two women." She spread two fingers out from her hold on her bottle. "Two."

"Come on, Mara. You know it's complicated."

"What I know is that you are too good of a guy not to get this figured out quick." Her tone got more serious. "You're not being honest with anybody, including yourself."

I got still and whispered. "That's fair."

She looked at me with big eyes. "Oh, Waylan."

"No," I said, "that is definitely fair."

"You got a cigarette?" she said loud and off-topic.

We both moved to the window sill. She opened the window and the air poured in clean and cold. We sat on the sill edge. We called it the smoking section, and we had hung, cleverly we thought, a No Smoking sign on the wall next to the window.

"So, how you doing with this whole Peter situation?" I asked.

"Pretty good, I guess. I mean the truth is, I'm having trouble getting over it."

"You know what you need to do. Go out and get yourself a piece of ass."

"What is that with men? Get a piece of ass? What about taking time to process the lessons of the connection? What about trying to forgive? Or gaining strength from independence?"

I smiled at her, but she was rolling now and not about to stop.

"For all the millions upon billions of men that have had their hearts broken throughout the entire history of humanity, you would think one of them would have come up with some sage advice about how to cope. But still, to this day, the best any of you can come up with is, 'Go out and get yourself a piece of ass.'"

She looked at me, and I said, "Well, hey. It worked for me."

Mara began laughing. "No, it didn't"

"Oh yeah." I laughed too.

I held out my cigarette pack with my good hand and pawed at the cigarettes with my bandaged hand. I worked intently for a moment before producing two cigarettes.

"So what happened, Waylan, Wednesday night?" she said, while grabbing my lighter and lighting both cigarettes.

How could I explain to Mara what I did not understand?

I do not remember why I threw my fist through the thin elementary school window pane. I can still feel the cold glass give against my knuckles. And the warm blood release on my numb hand. Blood on snow.

It is strange how memory works. I can hear the sound of the window breaking as I struck, but I do not actually remember it. I have reconstructed the sound from a thousand beer bottles broken against pavement, from the dropped plates at restaurants, from movie sound-effects. No, I do not think I remember the sound of the window breaking. The sound I remember is the thud of my hand before the break. It is a sound I felt—against my flesh, up my arm. I feel that sound in my body. I do not remember pain, though my hand was sliced open deep enough to require stitches. Cannot recall that. I am not even sure it hurt.

I do remember the school. It was late night. March in Minnesota. The school was dark yet alive. Schools, especially elementary schools, are organic. They have a way of being full even when empty, alight even in the dead of night. It is the spirits of children. The energy they possess and exude lingers. Schools breathe at night—breathe with the collective eager breath of youth. I remember as the window broke feeling as though a thousand eyes were watching me, looking toward the direction of the noise. The eyes of the school. And I remember having a momentary vision of curious children bending over the bright morning-lit snow soaked in my blood. I felt their wonder, their fear. And from the evidence they would create stories to scare one another. As I stood there staring at the snow, those stories began to form already. The school building seemed to get loud with the rumors, its thousand voices clamoring. And the voices closed in and surrounded me. Thousands of eyes searched for me as my feet fell alternately shallow and deep in the frozen snow. My shoes heavy, my hand hot and red. The eyes followed me until I rounded a corner out of the school's sight.

Dave got me on the first bus to leave for the hospital that morning, 5:29 a.m. Still dark. Stepped onto the bus, my hand wrapped in a white towel soaked through with blood. The florescent bus lights were eerie and unreal. I was lightheaded. We sat silent, Dave and I half drunk. But I was concentrating too. Riding the bus is often a determined action: I had learned to will buses forward. Constantly alert, scanning the streets, calculating the distance to my stop, hurtling the bus forward in my mind, passed the liquor store, the seasonal Dairy Queen and the Super America where I walked for cigarettes. Soon now I can pull the cord. Soon now. One more stop. Open the door for the elderly woman with the grocery bags. She steps down slowly. And down. Soon now. Close the door. The familiar abrupt unfolding door, the hiss and scrape, heavy closing of the door. The grumbling push of the bus accelerating. Soon. The bullying into the lane. Soon now. This is how I willed the bus forward.

On this morning I moved it with my energy, bleeding urgency, but my focus was on the towel. The florescent unreality of the bus in that coming dawn made my towel appear bluish. The blood was ever consuming the towel with maroon. And the fibers pulled and probed my open wound. I began to believe the towel was blue.

"We get it to stop bleeding yet?" Dave's voice shattered my blue towel bus-willing concentration.

"Man, I don't know if we got all the glass out."

"Oh yeah, they were big pieces. It'll be all right."

I shot him a nervous look.

"Alcohol thins the blood," was all he said.

My hand continued to bleed, but I remembered now that the towel was white. Soon now, the cord, though the bus driver needed no cue. Half drunk college boys with blood covered towels at 5:29 a.m. are not headed very many places. The door folded loudly and the Minnesota morning burst in cold and harsh.

By the weekend everyone knew the story and took turns teasing me about it. I think, because they could not comprehend my actions, perhaps because laughing seemed a better option than crying.

Like when Mara and Lindsay entered my room Saturday night. Dave and I were on the floor playing chess. Nathan sat at his desk, surfing the Internet.

"Hey guys," Mara said.

"What's up?"

"Well, my cousin's having a big birthday bash tonight at her place. Lindsay and I are going and just wondered if you guys wanted to tag along."

Nathan turned around in his chair, "Is she hot?"

"Who?"

"Your cousin."

"Oh." Mara paused. "She's got a fiancée."

"Hey, fiancée is just a French word meaning Nathan didn't get there first," he grinned.

Air shot out of Mara's nose, half laughing, half exasperated. "If you're going, you better behave."

"Who are you talking to?" Nathan put hand to chest and drew his face into its most innocent look. "I always behave."

"Right," Mara shot back. "Like the time my little brother came to stay with me, and you totally had him convinced that Puerto Ricans hate Canada."

"Look, *you* go into a bar in San Juan and order a Labatts. See what happens."

"So you guys coming?" Lindsay asked Dave and me.

"I don't think so," I answered, while Dave shook his head no.

"All right. Then get some rest." She bent over and gave me a goodbye kiss.

Nathan stood and began to put on his coat. "Hey, Waylan, if Mara's cousin happens to be a school teacher, I'll tell her I've got a buddy with a great idea for school reform."

All my friends were smiling as Nathan did a little celebratory tap dance. I threw my bandaged hand up in his direction. "This is me flipping you off."

"You know, Nathan," Mara said, "on our way out we should make some sort of announcement. I'm sure all the windows will be relieved to know that Waylan is staying in tonight."

"No Mara. No window is safe until this man..." Nathan pointed to me, "...this bandit, is brought to justice."

"You guys are fucking hilarious," I said. "Get out of here. Go drink somebody else's beer for once."

Mara opened the door for Nathan and Lindsay, then blew us a kiss before following them out. "Goodnight, boys."

Dave had not asked me what happened. Not when I stumbled into his room sometime before dawn. He had been asleep. I moved furtively toward his bedside.

"Dave," I said in a half voice.

"Hmm." Some involuntary reflex made him moan a response from his REM state.

"Dave," I said louder, "I'm hurt."

"What?" He said, stirring. "Okay." He turned on his reading lamp. How I must have looked to him then, one hand clutching the other, blood smeared on my face and clothes, my hands drenched in red.

"Fuck!"

And he leapt out of bed and led me to his sink basin. Flipping on the florescent mirror light, he looked at me hard, examining me.

"It's my hand."

He looked down and took my hand, hunched to his task. "Glass, eh?"

I nodded.

He turned on the water and ran his hand under the stream until it warmed. He wore nothing except his boxer-shorts, and his bare toes wiggled on the tile floor, one hand gently under mine, the other checking the water temperature.

"This might hurt a little," he said as he began washing my hand, my blood diluted by the running tap water, blending and swirling, disappearing down the sink drain. While he carefully pulled out splinters of glass from my wound, there were no questions, just action. Even on the bus Dave did not push me. But there in the Emergency Room, after he had filled out the forms for me and we were told to wait, he asked.

"So what the fuck'd you do?"

"I don't know," I said.

We sat then in the Emergency Room waiting area surrounded by the sick and wounded and waiting. Hospital visits for me have always had a dreamlike quality. The existence of hospitals are a necessity, their conception an absurdity, their structure sterile and bureaucratic. There is always a sense of disassociation, a kind of morphine induced trip that dictates the whole experience be comical or excruciating, but always unreal. The disassociation is surely due to the human coping mechanisms for pain, grief and anxiety because hospitals are situations so unconnected to the outside world. Think of the wife whose husband is dying slowly. How unnatural it must seem to have the man she loves for his humor and strength atrophy before her eyes. She sleeps in a too small chair, and every time she wakes he seems smaller and further away. She must daily make decisions regarding his treatment about which she knows nothing. Or think of the father who must feed his college-age daughter and change her bedpan, after doing those same things twenty years prior when she was an infant. The memory of her first tooth and her prom and high school graduation becomes muted as though merely a vision or dream, now that the only difference in his parenting some twenty years later is her matured body and the whisper of a life lived.

Hospitals have always seemed to me similar to airports—as though the same architects designed them, the same corporate oligarchies manage them. There is an other-worldly feel, the fading of one's own constitution. The airport, with its thousands of souls in limbo, exhausted, standing in lines, handing over their possessions, milling about, killing time, sensing vaguely the final moment when they or their loved one will depart on a tin-can hurtled through space at five hundred miles per hour, and that building, that environment, will not allow the power of the moment to coalesce.

Like the day Anna left me. Vague, clouded sense. The apple sweet vanilla scent of her hair, the smell of a song—thick harmony. We stood there awkwardly in the airport terminal, alone in a crowd. She said my name.

"Yes, baby? Please just touch me—that for a moment we may remember, we may for a moment know each other again, that I may feel your softness again," I ached, but did not say. "Remember? You used to cry with laughter. You used to wear my sweatshirts, and they used to smell of your skin. Remember?" I thought, but could not share.

"Waylan, don't do this," she said.

"Do what?" I said, dying on the inside. I was never enough. But she loved me once. "Anna, forget our today. Forget and remember that we were in love. Touch me, and be here and feel nothing else," I wanted to say but found no voice.

"Don't be so quiet. Don't be sad."

I coughed nervously, and we then talked of nothing, everything impossible behind my eyes. But I had no energy for small talk and no capacity for truth, so I fell silent. It was better that way, me wanting, hurting, needing to scream. "I could make you forget and remember all at once, if only you would touch me."

When I got quiet, she looked beyond me casually. I smiled and tried not to look hurt.

I think hospitals and airports are both about a giving up of control—in the trust granted to a surgeon or pilot, the way our body is no longer ours. Independence to dependence, coherence to semi-coherence.

"You've got to remember what happened, Waylan," Dave implored. The waiting room was filling up now, as those who went to bed healthy woke to illness. The sun was up full now, heating our backs through the window.

"Were you in a fight? Did you break into a house? Jesus, man, what happened?"

"I wasn't angry," I started slowly. "Or sad. I wasn't anything, really."

"And..." Dave prodded, unsettled now.

"It was just all the dark. And the kids."

"There were kids there?" he said too loud, and the old woman across from us looked up.

"No," I whispered, "but the kids, you know, they're just so young and clean."

"Waylan, you're not making any sense."

"I don't remember. I guess I just wanted to feel something."

At both the airport and the hospital there are always people around twenty-four hours a day. Some arriving, some departing, but so many people waiting. The mind numbing waiting.

Regulars have routines, ways to make the waiting bearable: reading novels, doing crossword puzzles, browsing the gift shop, their humanity drained just a little more with every stay. First-timers often possess a discernible awe tempered by an uncertain composure; the anxiety revealed in them persists in all of those waiting, suppressed or not. Waiting for test results or planes, waiting for a new baby or the arrival of a long-exiled love are nearly identical in their anticipation. There is understanding, however dim, that life is about to change. Waiting is a preparation of the heart.

Yet exactly when you are least ready, when you have decided the change is too much, the surgeon steps into the lobby to speak to you. It is always too late when the stewardess calls her boarding row.

"It's time," Anna said.

"I suppose it is."

"So…" She stopped and looked at me sympathetically.

"I'll miss you."

"I know."

"I love you."

"Me too."

"Call me when you get there," I said.

"Sure. And you have my number?" She grabbed at her bag as though to indicate she could produce the number upon request, that somehow the number could alleviate the pain of her departure. She wanted to fix what she could not. I loved her for that.

"Yeah, I got it."

"So you can call me too."

"All the time."

"Okay. Got to go."

"Yeah, I..."

"What?"

"It's just..."

"Baby, don't."

"Yeah, okay. Be safe, all right?"

"I love you. I'll call you."

With that Anna moved toward the gate. She looked back over her shoulder and smiled, but that was it. She handed over her ticket and disappeared down the corridor. We lose people that easily sometimes.

XVI

"Waylan," Mara's voice came muffled through the door. "Come on, open up."

I pulled the sheets up over my head.

"We're gonna be late," Mara said and opened the door. "All right, up and at 'em." I could hear her cross the room toward me.

"I'm sleeping," I moaned.

"I can tell." She sat down on my bed. "Come on. I brought you coffee."

Mara pulled the covers from my face. "Good morning, sleepy head. Or as a cynic might say, 'Good afternoon.'"

I rolled away from her. "Do you mind?"

"Well, yes, I do. You asked me to come by and get you. And if you keep dickin' around, we're gonna be late."

"Go ahead then. I'll catch up."

"Nice try." She took an audible sip of coffee.

"I thought the coffee was for me," I said, looking back over my shoulder.

"What? You can't share."

"Fine. Just go, okay." I grabbed the sheet back over my head.

"Jesus, Waylan. Get up."

Mara paused then, perhaps waiting for my response. I said nothing.

"All right," the bed creaked and returned as she stood. "At least let me drop off your paper."

"Mara, just go."

"Look, you asked me to come by. If you aren't going to class, let me turn in your paper."

"Mara," I said, my voice getting louder.

"You didn't write it? Waylan…"

"Goddamn it, Mara."

"Fine. Go back to sleep. But I'm taking the coffee," she said, followed by the sound of the door closing hard.

She spoke of ocean waves.

Lindsay made a miniature boat with bark, twig for mast, leaf as sail, and captained it along the currents of my faded blue jeans.

Her childlike joy usually struck me as immature, or at least worthy of ridicule, but she never wavered. She never apologized for being herself. I do not know whether she ever tried to put language to any of this, but if she had, it probably would have been something about choosing to experience rather than possess, or something about making a conscious decision to live rather than intend. But she would instead just say to me, "You act too old for your age. You are too sad for such days."

She spoke of lilies and sparrows and larks.

It was a springtime afternoon. The world was thawing—the sun held high and beckoned us to life. We lay in the shade, Lindsay on her side and me on my back, my head propped against a root. We lay as lovers do and spoke quietly all the things that comprised who we were: school and friends, thoughts and observations.

She spoke of fireflies.

Eventually we discussed my most recent therapy session.

"I believe his exact words were 'spiraling out of control.' And I was wondering whether that is like an official psychiatric term. I mean, have they taught you that one yet?"

"I'm glad you think this is funny," Lindsay said, her voice sarcastic, shooting me a look of disapproval.

"Look, I'm having a good day. Can we not do this?"

"Okay, that's fair. But this is serious stuff, Waylan."

I ran my finger up her bare arm and back down.

"He thinks I should go on Prozac."

"Well, then you should," Lindsay said matter-of-factly.

I guess I should not have been shocked by her clarity on the issue, because of her own positive experience with medication, but I was hesitant. Taking Prozac, it seemed to me at the time, meant sacrificing control.

"I'm not so sure. I feel like mind-altering drugs is a little extreme."

"Mind-altering? Listen to you. It's not LSD. Prozac is a serotonin reuptake inhibitor. It basically allows the brain to produce and intake the correct amount of serotonin, stuff your body should be doing naturally anyway."

That made absolutely no sense to me. She could have been speaking German for all I knew. Reuptake inhibitors sounded like something out of Star Trek. There had to be a better way to make sense of it.

"Well, maybe I could try some of yours—just to see, you know, if it works for me."

"That's not how it works, Waylan. You can't just *try* a couple. It builds up in your system slowly."

The truth was, I did not know how it worked. What little I had heard about Prozac came from hearsay and anecdotes.

One such story came from Nathan's renowned tale, affectionately referred to as *Crazy Bitch*. The first time I heard the story was over dinner at Kagin Hall with Dave and Mara and a half a dozen other kids.

"I was dating this hot-ass girl once." Nathan sat eating from a plate consisting of various starches: rice, mashed potatoes, and a healthy dose of macaroni and cheese.

"It was like our fifth date. We'd seen a movie. Something awful. Can't remember what it was. Doesn't matter really. But it was a nice date, ya know. And a nice night. She's a cool-ass girl. So we went and got some ice cream and walked to this nearby park, or whatever. Just date shit, ya know. So we end up on this park bench, making out and all, when she gets up and motions me into the bushes."

Nathan grinned and looked at his loyal fans grinning in response. "Yeah, so I'm like, all right, sounds good. Then when we're all hidden in the brush she starts strippin'. And I'm thinking this is the best thing in the whole wide world, ya know. Girl's spontaneous."

I remember he got numerous nods of approval from the boys at the table.

"So we're going at it and all of the sudden, like out of no where, she slugs me. Now I don't mean slapped or jabbed or anything that could be construed as anything close to accidental or maybe playful. The crazy bitch hit me, closed fist, straight in the face."

Nathan grabbed his jaw as though he was still sore from the hit years ago.

"But, ya know, at first I'm just shocked. Been kind of out of it, if you understand what I'm saying. And I hadn't gotten freaky with the girl before, so part of me is like, maybe that sort of thing gets her off. But then she does it again and starts screaming."

Nathan noticed the dubious looked that passed between Mara and me.

"You gotta believe me, I did nothing to her. She was the aggressor the whole time. She dragged me into the bushes. She took off both of our clothes. She was on top of me. And then she's beating on me and screaming. So I'm like, 'what the fuck? Calm down!' Well, then she jumps up, grabs her clothes and runs off all naked."

"Holy shit, dude," Dave said.

"Yeah, no shit, holy shit. So I jump up to go after her. That's when I realize she took my pants."

"What?"

"Yeah. When she took her clothes she took my pants."

"What about your underwear?"

Nathan shot us all a repulsed look. "Haven't owned a pair since I was ten."

Knowing Nathan, I believed him.

"So you're stark naked?" I said.

"As the day you were born?" Mara added for emphasis. Nathan, I think, loved this about telling stories above all else. There was a way in which his stories were organic, how others helped him tell them—heckling or questions or prompting pushed his stories in new directions and to new heights.

"No. I was not, as my grandfather used to say 'Naked as a jaybird in June.' I still had my shoes and my shirt."

We all laughed, some with food in our mouths.

"So there I was in some bushes with a shirt and no pants in the middle of this park."

He gave me the pained look that I knew would turn into a smile. And it did.

"So I tie the shirt around me loin-cloth style. I mean, my scrawny-ass white butt is out there, but not Captain Dick and his crew of two, ya know."

"Wait..." Mara started. "No, don't. Never mind. Keep going."

"My first thought is this can't be happening, ya know. Like she got startled by a possum or something. Or maybe she's just screwing with me. Like I said, this was a pretty cool girl. Maybe she's being funny. So I head back to her car, 'cause she drove and all, but the car ain't there. She is gone, my friends, and so are my pants.

"Well, its pretty late, I guess, maybe midnight, so there aren't a lot of people out, but the park is a good hour walk from my house and I have to huff it in the shirt diaper. It was a nice night, though, so it wasn't so bad. Kind of freeing really."

As he spoke I was reminded of our first Halloween together at Macalester. I thought I had been decidedly risqué with my costume choice of a Freudian Slip. Mara had let me borrow a slip, and to it I had safety-pinned an index card that read "Freudian?" I was proudly modeling in the mirror when Nathan walked into our room. He had constructed a hula-hoop hat, and from it hung a clear shower curtain liner. He was completely nude beneath the see-through curtain.

"Freudian slip. Awesome," Nathan said striding into the room.

"Yeah, thanks."

"Ya know, that reminds me of this joke." He spoke through the plastic of his costume, like some perverse boy-in-a-bubble.

"Yeah," I said, consciously keeping my eyes trained on his face.

"Two guys, right. And they're trying to figure out what a Freudian slip means. One of the guys is like, 'I think it's when you say something, but you really meant to say something else.' And his buddy or whatever is like, 'Hey, yeah, that shit happens to me all the time. Like last night at dinner I meant to ask my wife to pass the butter, but what I said was, "Bitch, you ruined my life."'

Nathan smiled wide. "Huh? Pretty good, huh?"

"Yeah," I said. "Great." I was smiling broadly at him, amused by the unbelievably bizarre context of standing in the middle of my room in a woman's slip while an essentially naked Nathan told me jokes.

He did a little tap dance and the hula-hoop hat bounced and the curtain liner swayed and shook. "So…How 'bout my costume?"

"Reminds *me* of a joke," I said. "Guy walks into the psychiatrist's office wearing nothing but plastic wrap and the psychiatrist says, 'Well, I can clearly see your nuts.'"

"Good one," Nathan grinned and pointed at me approvingly. "So you got a guess at what I am?"

I purposely looked up to examine his homemade headgear.

"I'm a shower, dude! What do ya think?"

I darted my eyes to his bare feet. "I think there's a foot of snow outside."

"And…" Nathan said, on the verge of being crestfallen.

"You need flip-flops."

"Fuck yeah! Good call."

I smiled to myself as I pictured Nathan, tall wiry redhead, completely comfortable walking down a city sidewalk at midnight in a loin-cloth.

"Well I get home sometime after one in the morning. And all is well, except one thing—I don't have my pants."

Dave laughed. "While still funny, you already established that part."

"Right, but no pants means I don't have my keys." Nathan stabbed his fork into a pile of mashed potatoes and released it as though thrusting a sword into the ground. "And I'd be damned if I was going to knock on the door and wake up my parents wearing nothing but a shirt."

He leaned forward and spoke in a hushed tone, like telling a secret. "So I start going around the house trying to find an open window, but they're all shut. After a while I realize the only open window is the one to my room."

All of us had leaned in to hear his whispers, and so we all exploded back as he unexpectedly yelled, "...which is on the second story!

"Lucky for me, there is this old tree right next to my room. I used to sneak out that way all the time. So I shimmy up the tree and get to my window. Well, the screen is on, so I kick it out. But the window is only open a crack. And this isn't one of them slick-ass plastic energy-saving windows, this is an old school wood-frame, paint chips flake off every time you open the goddamn thing window—not the kinda thing you just slide open from the outside. So there I am, one arm hugging this tree, the other trying to push up on the window, half-hanging really, wearing nothing but my tennis shoes and my shirt shorts in the middle of the night."

He waited. He always waited in moments like this.

"That's when the floodlight shines on me."

"What?"

"What I didn't know is that my nosy-ass neighbor saw me creeping around the house and called the cops."

"Son of a bitch," Dave said.

"Pig's got his car floodlight lighting up my bare white ass for the whole friggin' neighborhood to see." Nathan had a distant look in his eyes, as though, despite it making a great story, the humiliation was still palpable. The table got quiet.

I would feel later that I had lost him. It is funny, sort of, because he is not the type of man that you lose—because he was the type of friend you never have. He was theatrical and intoxicating, hilarious and thought-provoking, but he was ephemeral. He was an almost daily presence in my life. His stories and advice helped balance my all but collapsing mind. But he was too big to hold, too outlandish to trust. Perhaps all his frivolity was his true nature, or perhaps it was a protection mechanism. I will never know.

Because as close as we were, I never knew him. Later after college as our communication diminished over time, phone tag for weeks that stretched into years, I began to feel again the distance, created by the width of a bed or the span of a tiled bathroom floor. And the distance was too broad for my mind to draw together. His humor had steadied me, his wisdom had buoyed me, but I began to believe him a dream. So he slipped from me as if I had once held him. He faded as though he had once been real.

"So what'd you tell the cops," I asked, to bring Nathan back.

"I told them I'd lost my keys." He laughed. We all laughed.

"How about your parents? What did they say?"

"What could they say really? They just never asked. Ha!"

"And what about the girl?"

"Ah, yes, crazy bitch." Nathan leaned back, easing into his epilogue. "What I found out was that she was really into me. She felt things were going so well, she was so happy, that she decided to stop taking her Prozac sometime between date four and five. Apparently crazy bitch needed to stay medicated."

The way Nathan told it, Prozac was some sort of antipsychotic drug. To Nathan Prozac was on par with Lithium. He reminded me of this when I brought up my dilemma over whether or not to go on medication.

"You really believe in this model mental health shit? Like there is some perfect mind that we must stack up to or we need to be medicated? Brave New World? 1984? Ring any bells? Christ, this is some creepy shit."

I had been mulling over the issue for a couple of days when I finally brought it up to Nathan. We were hanging out in our room one day after classes. He lay flat on his bed, staring at the ceiling.

"Some of the world's greatest minds...no, not some, I'm pretty sure *all* of them fought the darkness of their own psyches," he said and then rolled onto his side to look at me, his arm bent to prop his head. "I mean, Waylan, our greatest art, culture's greatest advances, our most profound goddamn thoughts, have come from facing the void. You're telling me you think that needs fixing." Nathan threw himself onto his back, once again facing the ceiling. "That's just giving in, ya know," Nathan said, as though he were not speaking to me, but instead speaking to the ceiling, about me. "Taking pills to numb you to the truth of your existence. Fuck that."

"Look, Nathan, I can't sleep at night. I can't wake up in the mornings. I can't get to class or even answer the goddamn phone. I'm tired all the time. If this tortured soul bullshit is supposed to make me an artist or a philosopher, then you can keep it. You can fucking keep it! I just want to feel better."

"Good for you, man!"

"What?" I said and immediately felt manipulated.

"There is still some fight in you."

"Fuck off."

"No. Seriously, dude. Do the whole goddamn thing. Prozac and whatever. It doesn't matter what I think. Because you believe in it. That's all that matters, right?"

"But Nathan, I'm not sure what I believe."

Despite the pleas of Lindsay, my parents, and my then current therapist, it took me months to decide to go on Prozac. Beyond Nathan and Dave's aversion to the idea, I lived in a collegiate culture that did not take to the medical world kindly. In my classes I was reading texts with titles like, *Toxic Psychiatry*. And when Macalester offered free immunizations for meningitis, I had to cross a picket line of "conscientious objectors" holding homemade poster board signs like WE HAVE ENGINEERED OURSELVES OUTSIDE OF NATURE and NATURE WILL HAPPILY BE THE DEATH OF ME!

It did seem to me a bit too typical—our societal answer to everything is to medicate. There is a pill for everything—pills for ailments we did not know existed until there was a cure for them, while the pharmaceutical companies laugh all the way to the bank. But perhaps in the end it took me so long to agree to go on medication because I could not really comprehend my mind as chemicals and synapses. I did not entirely understand the dynamics of serotonin levels, the exact function of a neurotransmitter, or what any of it had to do with how I felt. Too, I was uncomfortable with the psychiatric tendency to characterize my struggles in terms of mental disorder. My darkness was my own. By naming it depression and assuming it could be remedied (*REMEDIED!*) by popping pills, I lost something sacred in myself. The idea that I could be labeled and cured stole the mysteries of my depths and cheapened them.

Not surprisingly, I suppose, it was Lindsay who finally convinced me to start taking Prozac. It was partly that I trusted her advice on the matter, but it was mainly her relentlessness. As I sat at my desk pretending to study but actually staring out the window, there came a knock at the door.

"Come in."

The door opened, and Lindsay stepped into the room. "Hey," she said.

"Hey, babe."

"I brought you something." She held a hefty textbook closed around her index finger to keep the page. She sat down on my bed. "Take a look."

I sat down on the bed next to her. The springs gave and returned and I eased into her body, touching as much of her as I could—my leg against hers, my hand on the small of her back, my face half lost in her hair. She opened the textbook in her lap to the page her finger had been marking. The two-page spread before me was largely text. Along the border of the right-hand page was a orange box of bullet-points. In the top left corner of the left-hand page was a picture of two multicolored blobs.

"Okay now, I wanted to show you this picture." Lindsay pointed to the two blobs. "These are two CAT scans of two different brains. This one," she pointed to the left blob, "is a healthy brain. And this one," she slid her finger over to the other, "is the brain of someone suffering from depression. So what do you think?"

I studied the two photos. The "normal" brain was made up of an intermingling blue and green color base, with a yellow blob spreading out across a good 75% of its area. The "depressed" brain had a similar blue/green base, but that was the predominant color scheme—yellow covered maybe only 20%. I focused on the CAT scans for a long time in silence. I did not exactly know what I was looking at or what Lindsay expected me to say.

"Huh," I said finally. "The healthy brain has too much yellow."

"Quit being a smart-ass."

"Okay, so what? I don't have enough yellow."

"Baby, the yellow is chemical brain activity."

"And..."

"Waylan, you say to me all the time that you like therapy, that you find it useful, that it has helped. The things they suggest, the way they listen—it's good, right?"

"Yeah, sure. Definitely."

"Well, it's been like, what, ten months? Almost a year? And you still don't have a good hold on this thing."

She was right, I knew. Learning that I was depressed was a good thing; identifying the problem is essential to recovery. But my mind now existed only on the playing field of depression. In certain ways learning about depression was damaging, in the sense that I allowed it to paralyze me. I let depression become an excuse for my wasting away. I was Hamlet: too busy exploring my own darkness to live, take action, or take control. I made myself weak with self-analysis.

"I'm trying," I said, because I was. I was exhausted and spent, but I was trying.

"I know, but in some cases therapy isn't enough to repair damage of this extent. I mean, your sessions have hauled you from the bottom, anyone can see that, but what are we shooting for here? Christ, Waylan, you still can't sleep at night, you still sleep too late into the day, you still get freaked out over stupid shit. And you always talk about how you have trouble making connections, or can't remember like you should, like you aren't smart enough for college…You can't use your brain or your body like you should, because it's not working properly."

Lindsay had leaned away from me so that she could look me in the eyes as she spoke. I leaned further into her, hiding my face in her hair.

"Just imagine, baby. To have your mind back. You forget what it's like. I know you do, because I did too. Prozac won't steal anything important or make you something you're not."

"Okay," I said, pulled back her hair and kissed her neck. "I get it."

"The darkness never goes away, Waylan," she said, softening. "I know part of you is afraid of losing it, but it never goes away."

I stared for a long while at the two photos, one brain yellow and radiant, the other dark and cool. I was reminded then of the two portraits of King Phillip II of Spain and was overwhelmed by grief. I thought of how tragic it was that over the years he stopped spending time with his family. I thought of his second picture, grey and vacant, and then I thought of his famed royal garden untended and empty. I felt suddenly and inexorably bound to Phillip II, across oceans and centuries. I spoke a silent prayer for him—my brother, my King.

"Thanks for bringing by these pictures, babe," I said, "but I've seen them before."

XVII

Time for me became simultaneously meaningless and suffocating. In one sense days and hours passed in a muted blur, uncountable, uncontrollable. Time was the background noise of my incessant mind. But in almost the same way time was all consuming for my lack of it. Time slipped away, and with it the burden of responsibility grew ever heavier. And as I let yet another minute disappear, something else was missed, another moment lost. Human life, or at least American life, is organized almost solely by time—appointments, deadlines, due dates, show times, alarm settings—it is our collective addiction. "What time is it?" "Do you have the time?" "Where does the time go?" In the mornings I put on my watch without thinking. It is pattern and habit, the leather band and clock face have become one with my wrist, so that I will not be without time. So that I will know that I am already late. The ticking of the clock enslaves us all.

One night Lindsay took my watch, pulled the shades, and covered all of the clocks so that I could finish a paper. Panic had seized me. I was unable to write in the face of diminishing time. It was maybe nine at night, and I had a ten page paper due at eight the next morning.

"All right. An hour a page, then an hour to edit and revise," I said heavily, staring at the computer.

"Just write," Lindsay said.

"It's not enough time. This one has to be good. I'm failing this class."

"Based on attendance, not your work. It'll be fine. Just write."

"Jesus Christ, it's almost nine-thirty," I said. That is when she covered the clocks. Thoroughly, she even placed masking tape over the clock on my computer screen.

She sat up and read while I wrote. About six pages into my paper I stopped and leaned back in my chair to stretch. "It's late, isn't it?"

"I don't know," she said.

"It feels late."

"I'm still up. If your tired, make another pot of coffee."

"I'm running out of time."

"How do you know?" Lindsay smiled, then turned back to her book. She stayed up reading next to me all night.

She understood. She understood my anxiety, but she also understood the meaninglessness of time. That time is in fact a cosmic joke. It is a figment of our collective imagination. In the end it is like any addiction. The beer or the cigarette is never about the beer or cigarette. It is always about comfort or rage or freedom or emptiness. We have, all of us, bought into arbitrary numbers and dates, and we daily worship the false idol of time.

But surely, you might say, there is science behind it all. The space-time continuum, the rate of decay of atoms—it is math, it is science. But can you blame me? For time in my growing confusion escaped me. How could I see it as sequential when it was all a roaring fog? And can you blame me for resenting time after being continually punished for existing outside of it? I could not meet the world's time demands, and so I was forced again and again into hiding. For my own sanity I had to come to the conclusion that we were all bound by the atomic clock of folly.

But surely, you might say, we see the passage of time in everything; in the growth of hair, in the changing of seasons we see time. We see time as we age daily in the mirror. I no longer believe that we grow old. Or more precisely, I do not believe we age through the passage of years. The beating of my heart is the only clock I trust. Only the wax and wane of effort and despair in the heart marks time.

The heart grows at a rate based on experience, not time. Phrases like, "wise beyond his years," "old soul" and "emotionally immature" are ways in which we try to articulate the distance between what we perceive and what we expect. There is a chasm in our acceptance of what is real because we cling so tightly to the "truth" of time. But the heart holds its own truths if we listen. Lindsay taught me that. I am not sure, however, that she understood the consequences of my learning it.

"It's just not fair," she screamed, one night. "How can you ask me to do this?"

"Baby, ask you to do what?"

"You can't ask me to be with you, and you still not leave her."

It was a conversation held a thousand times and yet never held. It was in the silences, in the long glances, in eye contact broken. It was held while we slept and while we made love. My ambiguity over my relationship with Anna was continually under discussion, but it was never spoken.

"But I'm here. I'm here with you."

Lindsay scoffed, her face tightening with anger. "You are some piece of work." She got up, grabbed her coat, and thrust her arms into both sleeves in one forceful motion. "And I fucking knew better."

I did not know what to say. What could I say?

"Sure. You're here now. While she's not here, you're here." She flipped her long hair from under the collar of her hastily pulled on coat. "I'm just some substitute." And then she said, as though to herself, even as her voice rose in volume, "And I'm letting him do it."

"Lindsay, don't go. I'm sorry."

"You're always sorry, but you never make a choice." She began to walk out.

"Wait. Lindsay, wait." I stood up.

And then she spoke without prompting, as though continuing a conversation I could not hear. "Do you know what it's like? Do you even care? I can't play this game anymore. I won't come second anymore."

"Baby, you don't believe that, do you? God, I hope you don't. You're not second. You never have been."

"You're right, I guess." She paused with the door half open. "Maybe I'm not second. I'm one of two." Lindsay looked at me, and I thought how her eyes seemed hollow, infinitely empty and sad. Then she stepped out into the hall, and before the door slammed shut I heard her say, "Asshole."

I followed Lindsay into the hall, she was walking fast and already at the far end.

"Lindsay!"

She did not stop.

"Okay!"

At the top of the dorm stairwell she stopped and spun around. "Okay, what?" she fumed.

I walked quickly to meet her.

There was something about the lines of her face, or something about the way she stood with her arms crossed against her body, then shuffled and readjusted, and the way she was constantly rocking, her weight shifting from her heels to her toes and back again. No, it was the way she looked at me, her gaze steady and deliberate, in utter contrast to her body. Her being spoke of the ethereal. It begged to be held, but would not be compromised. She was indecision and confidence. She was awkward and elegant. I had been mistaken, misled even, into believing I could ever be enough for her.

"Okay, what do I need to do?"

Breath shot from her nose in disgust, and shaking her head she said, "You know, Waylan, it's not always about you."

"I don't understand."

"Of course you don't," she answered.

Later I told Dave about this moment, about my failure at the top of the stairs.

"Dave, man, I've spent my entire life trying to be a good man, thinking I was being good to women. I always try to treat women with respect without demeaning them. To walk the line between gentleman and chauvinist. I try to be aware of their oppression, their second-class status. I try to be sympathetic to how men objectify women and work on seeing their beauty not as object but as cohesively part of their being."

Dave smiled and looked as though he wanted to speak and so I stopped. "What?"

He took a sip of his Jim Beam and Coke and waved at me to continue.

"But then, then I apparently don't understand at all. I'm just like every other asshole guy. I mean, I know I continually fail. I lust and ogle. Sometimes I really do care too much about basketball and not about how her day went. And sometimes I just want to go to sleep after sex instead of cuddling. I think maybe I'm fighting something bigger than myself. I don't know—genetics, DNA, evolution, something, ya know?"

Whatever it was, at my very core, I felt dirty. It clung to me, and I could not scrub it away with brush or soap.

"Jesus, dude, you are all tied up," Dave said.

"And I know that I have betrayed both of them by loving them both, and I see the injustice of that...but no matter what I do, I can't fix it. I can't win. I do love them, I do. And isn't that a gift? I just wish women could understand that I'm really trying here."

"Yeah maybe. But I'm not sure you do feel the injustice. What if you were one of two guys? You're assuming that women are different than men. You see them as all mythical and magical, and to some extent they are. But women are not a different species. In your head women are some alien creatures unfathomable to the male psyche. That's some straight Freudian shit. Women are human, man. By making them mysterious and special you deny them your own capacity. They see that."

Dave was right. My inability to understand women was closely related to my inability to see them as I saw myself. I could not comprehend that women were the same mass of chaos, the same mess of insecurity, the same desperate vagabonds, that I was. And I looked at Dave, knowing he was right, and felt like crying.

"You don't know shit," I said.

"Granted. But the difference between you and me is that I don't care. I will never know shit. I'll never have it figured out. And I'm okay. But it terrifies you. It drives you crazy. In the end you have to accept that you will never get it right and be okay with that. Otherwise you'll go insane."

"You're on a roll tonight, aren't you," I said, flashing a smartass grin.

"Piss off," Dave said, "I'm just trying to help."

"Help would be explaining to me why even though I love Lindsay, I know now I have to leave her. That I have to be with Anna."

"Jesus, I can't believe she chose you over me." His voice was partly flippant; the other part was pained.

Lindsay had started down the stairs, and I had followed, stopping her on the landing.

"What will it take for you to trust me?"

"Listen to your heart," she said.

My first reaction to this response was annoyance. I was bothered by the corny sentiment at what I had felt was an important moment. I had heard that before, of course, in a thousand pop songs, and it was the lesson of every *Chicken Soup for the Soul* story. It was seemingly good advice, but impractical. The problem is that the heart fails you. There are times, crucial moments, critical situations, in which the heart aches and hides, moments when the heart falls silent. And courage falters.

"Come on. Don't feed me bullshit," I retorted.

She flinched almost imperceptibly at my response, but instead of lashing back, her tone softened. "I'm serious, Waylan. You're thinking too hard, too *much*."

"My professors don't ever accuse me of that," I smiled, trying to meet her calm. She grimaced.

"You know at night, when your mind is racing, and the voices are shouting, and you stare at the ceiling praying for sleep?"

It always surprised me, every time, when she understood so well. I knew that Lindsay had fought these same demons. I knew that she knew the darkness, but it was a jolt again and again that she could see into my soul. I felt naked and vulnerable at times like these, but it was her uncanny understanding—our shared secret— that drew me to her.

"When your head won't shut up, do you ever try to concentrate on something else? What is it that your heart is saying then?"

"I don't...I don't know," I stammered.

"It's not so much about a choice as it is about being honest. With yourself. And with me."

"I love you," I said. It spilled out of me, unchecked. She had said it to me many times before. I had thought it, of course. Felt it, surely. Had even discussed it with Nathan. But I had never spoken the words to Lindsay. Simple, stupid word—love. I was stupid to fear it and put so much weight on the use of it. I loved her. She knew that as much as I did. But I had successfully protected myself somehow by not saying, "I love you." And in the sharing, in the confession, it was made real.

She looked at me as though I were a well meaning child with his shoes on the wrong feet, or perhaps a lost dog. Then she kissed me gently and walked away. Feeling strange and false, I turned slowly and headed back to my room, and she not looking back over her shoulder and me not looking back over mine.

And so in one cruel evening, Lindsay had asked me to search my heart and in it I had discovered the strength to be vulnerable with her, but just long enough to understand that loving her meant I had to leave.

In such ways the heart ages. In such ways we note the passage of time.

If ideas can save, then Lordy, Lordy, I was reborn. I began to fantasize about my new life with Anna. The seasonless Big Easy. An apartment. Just the two of us. And the little things living together entails. Studying together across the kitchen table with Joni Mitchell playing lightly in the background. Grocery shopping. I imagined us there after a long day of classes. Bluish in the florescent light, young looking, playing grown-ups. Me pushing the metal cart with the rickety right front wheel down the symmetrical isles. Anna walking in front, her hand resting occasionally on the wire framed cart, her eyes scanning the shelves of food; tuna (spring water or oil), endless pasta options, and the ecstatic wall of cereal. She glances now and then at the grocery list, pausing at a particularly difficult decision. "I know it's a bit more, but we've got to get name brand peanut butter." I smile disapprovingly as she pulls the Extra Chunky Jiff off the shelf. She stiffens at my mock sternness. "You get your expensive toilet paper. I get my peanut butter," she says with finality, then grins and continues to lead the cart.

I thought of us cooking together. And doing dishes. Her hands moving methodically over the dishes in the hot soapy water. Her shirt wet from splashed water. And me on dry duty, the plate warm in my hand as I pull the damp towel from my shoulder. When dried I slip the ceramic plate onto the others in the cabinet, it making the familiar hollow clank that is neither quite like glass nor like metal. I turn back to find yet another steaming glass waiting for me. Until finally Anna is to the heavy work of pots and pans, and I have no more dishes to dry. I stand behind her, place my wet hands on her hips, pull myself close and kiss the top of her head. Pulling her hair aside, I kiss lightly her neck. She softens, and the music seeping in from the living room seems to grow louder as we sway quietly to the beat.

Our space. Our home. I thought of us sharing stories and aspirations late into the night. And folding laundry, our clothes mixed up and stacked together. In the evenings, she might pour herself a glass of red wine, Bordeaux maybe, and curl up to read a familiar book, something she has read before, something by Dickens or George Sand. And later, her falling asleep, her head in my lap, while I watch the final minutes of Monday Night Football. And us making love. Often and in every room, drenched by the bayou humidity, her hair slightly damp and falling in my face. Our moist bodies sticking and sliding, steadily, then quicker, grabbing and holding on. Wet from love making, we hold each other, her head on my shoulder, naked, covered by an extraneous sheet. We fall asleep there and dream of what we might do in this world, of who we might become in this life, having each other like we do.

Alleluia! I was born again. My sweet savior—Hope. Alleluia! Amen.

XVIII

Eventually the therapy sessions, drug regime and psychobabble just became a part of my life. I had therapists point to particular ailments in the Psychology Dictionary. "Classic case," they would say. I began to believe that they had merely heard some key word or series of words that triggered some memory. I would speculate about their thought processes. "That sounds familiar. Oh, what was that again? I remember reading that. It was at the coffee shop on Grand at 2 A.M.. No, no, I was on the can. That's it. Depression."

> depression - A clinical syndrome consisting of a lowering of mood tone (feelings of painful dejection or an irritable mood), loss of interest or pleasure in comparison with the subject's pre-morbid state, psychomotor retardation or agitation and difficulty in thinking or concentration. Complaints of fatigue or loss of energy and of feelings of worthlessness or guilt are common. The patient often has recurrent thoughts of death, and many attempt suicide or make plans to do so. [Biological Symptoms] sleep disturbance (insomnia or hypersomnia), diurnal variation of mood, loss of appetite, loss of weight, constipation, loss of libido. —used by the layman, depression refers only to the lowering of mood tone (dejection, sadness, gloominess, etc.)

It seemed so clear to me that this was just some mental exercise for them, like some college quiz in diagnosing mental illness. I had so many professionals in those first years, searching for someone I liked and could afford. They often disagreed on the details. Clinical Depression? Generalized Anxiety Disorder? Usually some combination of both. "GAD often co-occurs with Major Mood Disorders." No matter the diagnosis, the answer was most often the same—Prozac (dosage varied) and, of course, regular visits to see them (from $60 to $220 an hour.)

By my third therapist I had learned the game. I was whoring myself for meds. And that first session was set up for me to convince the doctor that I was, in fact, ill. I worked hard not to make it too obvious, and I made sure not to tell them my diagnosis by other professionals. That information usually just annoyed them; they liked to figure it out themselves. So I dropped hints. "So you are experiencing dysfunctional sleeping patterns. Hmm, I see. Uncontrollable rage? Interesting. I'd like you to talk more about this sense of alienation."

I learned to revel in their "ah-ha" moments. I eagerly anticipated the end of that first session when they were finally ready to speak after listening to my ceaseless droning. They usually spoke cautiously in that soft yet professional tone, "From what I've been hearing so far, I am inclined to believe that you may be suffering from some form of clinical depression. I'll have to see you again, of course, but I'd like to start you on Prozac." Whatever they said about dosage did not matter, because after a short while I knew myself what I needed. Normally 400 milligrams a day was fine, 600 milligrams when it was real bad and 200 milligrams when I ran out of money.

I do not want it to sound too cynical. I speak from the position of a weary veteran, not of a skeptic. I have enormous respect for most of the professionals who cared for me. I learned a great deal about myself and my disease. I was taught valuable mechanisms in my fight. I cried and laughed and came to important realizations under watchful guidance. In therapy I was listened to and cared about. And in my darkest, even when I could do nothing else, I usually found my way to my session. That in itself may be a testament to its value.

Of course, the process of recovery was slow and arduous. I experienced continual setbacks. But there were moments of triumph as well, increasingly frequent, mostly modest—at least until the morning I remember vividly as my first major breakthrough. I remember it because it was the beginning of my memory returning.

That morning I awoke late as usual and staggered to the shower in a sleepy haze. I remember the water against my skin hot. Water dripped into my eyes, and I closed and rubbed them to free them of sting. Blinking my eyes clear, I remember being stunned by the appearance of yellow tile. I had daily showered among that same tile and had always experienced the space as drab and melancholy, dirty white bordered by eggshell white. But here, this day, for the first time the distinction between the white tiles and the yellow accent tiles around the window was sharp and bright. Yellow was vibrant and alive. It struck me that I was seeing differently this morning, my vision clear in a way that was new and strange to me. I opened my eyes wide and felt a surge of emotion—it was grief strangled by joy. Regret and relief interlocked. Depression had robbed me of my senses, as film over my eyes. I had for two and a half years lived as a blind man and not realized it. Suddenly, on this morning, my sight returned to me. The fog lifted, and I was inundated by the contrast of white against yellow— lemon, sunshine, daffodil yellow! The water was hot against my skin, and I began to weep, sobbing uncontrollably in the shower. Yellow was yellow again.

With help I had begun to emerge from my cavern of discontent, and I began to realize that there were things worth living for, things in which to believe.

"I've been thinking a lot about Anna lately," I said, my words tumbling into the silence. I always felt though, that my words, even harsh words, never disturbed the peace there. My words seemed cushioned and caught. I sat comfortably in my customary chair, attending my weekly therapy session.

My psychologist's office was stereotypically designed not to offend. I wondered often if interior design is required reading for a psychology degree, perhaps a chapter on office décor between conflict resolution and Freud's dream analysis. There were two lamps, one on a small end-table next to her and one on the end-table next to me, both with low-watt bulbs. Next to my lamp was a box of tissues. Next to her lamp was a small clock. The clock always faced away from me, and I did not know whether that was true for all patients or just for the ones like me who were neurotic about time. Her desk, which she never sat at during a session, was uncluttered, it suggested order. A few small framed pictures sat next to her computer. They were of her family, and when I had asked her about them she had answered politely and then quickly steered the conversation back to me. An African art tapestry covered the entirety of the wall behind her desk; bookcases consumed an adjacent wall. And then a wall of windows. This is the wall I remember well. I stared out the windows every time the answers became difficult and watched the movement of leaves in the wind, or the pattern of rain against glass.

"I've decided to move to New Orleans."

"Okay. Good. Why?"

"I don't know," I said. "I just was always supposed to...to spend my life with Anna."

"I want you to push further, Waylan. Why is moving to New Orleans appealing to you?"

"I guess I feel like Anna is good for me."

"Okay. What does that say about how you feel here, in Minnesota?"

"The opposite, I guess," I said, grasping at the obvious answer. "I don't know though. I love these people. They care about me.

But...I do feel less pure."

"Does that have anything to do with them?"

"I don't know..."

She waited.

"Probably not, right?" I stopped, looking for approval. She continued to wait.

"It's not about my friends here; it's about me. It's my perception."

"Okay."

"But perception is reality," I said, the ideas beginning to flow. "So the reality for me is that Anna is better for me than anyone here."

"Can you change your reality then, by changing your perceptions?"

"Isn't that what I'm supposed to be doing with you?"

"You tell me."

"Do you believe that Anna is better for me than Lindsay and Dave?"

"It's not important what I believe."

"It is to me," I said.

I thought she would smile at that, but she did not. Instead she put her writing pad and pen down. "Why?"

"Because I trust you," I said, feeling vulnerable toward her in a way I had not experienced before.

She seemed to brush the sentiment off and continued to push me. "I appreciate that, Waylan, but I don't know any of these people. I only know you."

"And what do you know about me?"

"I know only what you tell me."

I grimaced. I felt as though I had talked us into a typical doctor/patient scenario, something she had navigated a thousand times. It seemed trite and no longer useful. She sensed this perhaps and continued.

"I know that you are a million miles from where you were when I met you."

"And…" I lead, still unsatisfied.

"Just that, Waylan. You've made great strides."

"Why am I still so unhappy?"

"Are you?"

"Yes, damn it." I felt a flood within me, waves crashing against the inside of my chest. I was suffocating, drowning. Sobs choked me, but there were no tears. "God, yes."

"Are you unhappy, or are you just used to being unhappy? Have you convinced yourself that you must be unhappy here?"

"I don't know. I…" I looked out the window. She waited, but I did not continue.

"You need to start trusting yourself."

"But all of the voices you told me not to trust…"

"You must begin to take control. You are an intelligent person and stronger than you think. You have the tools now to separate out the voices. I will not be here forever. It is up to you."

"Maybe…maybe I'm not ready." I said, weak and ashamed.

"Ready for what?"

"Ready to make decisions on my own. I still don't know which voices to trust."

"You trust the voice that says you are unhappy. Why?"

"I don't know. Maybe because it's the most familiar."

"Okay. What about the voice that says being with Anna is the answer?"

"It's the same voice, I think. I'm just tired of being sad. I'm just tired."

"I know, Waylan. But hang in there with me. You're doing good work."

She smiled at me, her light exploding through my darkness.

"What is the voice that makes you unsure about moving to New Orleans?"

"It's…it's reason. It's rational. Moving is an outrageous risk. To drop out of school. To leave my life—for something that I can't guarantee will work."

"So a voice of reason keeps you here?"

"Yes, but there are other voices too. Guilt. I can't leave these people. I can't fail the expectations of my parents and professors. I can't abandon Dave. He needs me. And Lindsay, too."

"Do you trust guilt as a voice?"

"It protects others," I said.

"What about the rational voice?"

"It keeps order. It maintains."

"So guilt and reason maintain others' happiness?" She asked.

"Yes."

"What about your happiness?"

"That is secondary," I said.

"But you just told me how tired you were of being unhappy."

"Are you saying that I should actually move to New Orleans?"

"I have not said that, Waylan. You have said that."

Whether I was, in fact, ready to move across the country is debatable. But in the move was hope. So by the time I finally told my friends in Minnesota, I had no regrets. No thoughts even for their feelings. No remorse. I loved them. But Dave, Mara, Lindsay, and Nathan were part of a world I hated. To turn away from that felt more like relief than loss.

"Hey, Dave." I caught him after his last class of the day. "Want to have a smoke?"

He nodded. We shielded each other's lighters from the wind, hands warmed by the flame. Then the first few rapid puffs to get our cigarettes started. Lit, we walked back toward my apartment.

"Ya know that thing I was talking about the other night?"

Dave tensed.

"You know, about how I've got to be with Anna?"

"Yeah," he said, the affirmation half choked by exhaled smoke.

"Well, I'm going."

He looked at me nervously, but not quite yet comprehending.

"I'm gone. A month from tomorrow. Moving to New Orleans."

"You were serious about that shit. I thought...you know, we were drunk..."

"Yeah well, it's what I'm doing," I said callously. Then catching myself, "I mean it's not you. You're the one reason to stay." This too I said coldly, unconvincingly.

"Jesus," he said, "I thought it was drunk talk." He got quiet then. Perhaps the reality of me not living in Minnesota began to dawn on him. But probably not. Neither of us could fathom being apart. It would not be real until I was gone.

But I did not care, about his grief or my ambivalence. This was about me. About saving myself. If I could cleave a part of me, slice through muscle or chop through soul and then rise, why should I not? And why mourn the waste when its amputation was my salvation? If my friendship with Dave would be lost with my move, so be it. Dave was a part of me, but I hated myself. Something at my very base ached to be free.

Maybe Dave understood. Maybe. That I wanted to love him, but could not. That hope was all I had left. That my faith in my past, though foolish, sustained my pulse. Maybe he too for a moment could envision my plan succeeding, see me there in the hot Louisiana sun, happy and stable. Maybe part of him believed and in that moment could forgive me. But all he could say was, "Jesus, Waylan. Jesus."

"I don't understand," Mara had said, just above a whisper. "I mean, I guess I do, but Lindsay sure as hell won't." She looked at me blankly. "I don't know how you can just pick up and leave."

"I've done this all wrong, I know," I said. We sat at a large round table in the library. We had been studying for finals when I told her about my plans to move. "But everything feels wrong here. I don't know how to do it any better."

"What's so wrong with here? Why do you have to leave...us?"

"It's not you," I whispered, "it's this place. It's crushing me. It's killing me. I *have* to go."

Mara's jaw was clinched, and even though we spoke in muted tones her voice was forceful. "You can't run from yourself."

"It's not running...It's starting over." I said quietly. Even as I spoke the words, I did not believe them, and I could sense Mara did not either. But then I found the courage to share the truth. "I need this."

"Then do it," she said. She began closing her open books and gathering together her notes. She was no longer looking at me. "Don't let anything stop you." Her words were hushed and detached. "Not me. Not anything."

With her arms full of books Mara rose hastily and began to walk away. But before she left she stopped behind my chair and stood there in silence for a few moments. Finally, she kissed the top of my head and whispered, "Make this work."

I left in the middle of the night. I had packed up a small moving van. I did not own much: a big green armchair, a toaster oven which largely handled my cooking needs, a mattress and box spring, some clothes, college papers and old love letters. The last thing I packed took the most space, and it took me hours of packing and repacking before it all fit. In the end I crammed it in, slam-

ming the door quickly before it fell out—my hope. I carried my
depression with me as well, but it, like everything else I traveled
with, was crushed under the load of my hope. I could barely see
out my rearview mirror; hope ballooned and obstructed the view.
It was so weighty, it killed my gas mileage. Somewhere amongst
all of those things, maybe thrown into a box of trinkets with other
odds and ends, I also carried with me the guilt of leaving. I did not
know I had packed it; I would find it only later—because at that
moment I was driving fast on a highway headed south. And free.

I drove, chasing the darkness with my headlights. The hills
of Wisconsin surrounded me but grew weary during the night and
eventually lay down. There was something about heading somewhere; there was purpose in my movement, and it was refreshing
in a new way, a traveling way. The road-stop coffee shops populated by strangers were even comforting, because they were a part
of my journey toward relevance. I traveled down from the world I
knew, that world at the top of the river, tearing through darkness,
following Highway 61—the Great River Road. It follows the grand
Miss down, ever down. I was tracing its contours, riding its rapids
into the unknown.

Somewhere in Iowa the day dawned, sky slate-grey, leaking
light. I washed down my Prozac at a rest stop water fountain like
some junky. And then onward, heading south through Missouri.
61 led me through Hannibal, Mark Twain's river town. Hugging
the curves of the Mississippi, the river always near me, sometimes
visible, sometimes hidden by trees, occasionally miles to the east,
but always near, the highway swept me headlong with its current.
St. Louis and the Arch. Memphis. I pulled off to see the Lorraine
Motel where Martin Luther King, Jr. was shot. It is a museum
now, but the balcony is still the same, the same balcony in the photo
where King lies, obscured by railing, men in suits standing around
him, all pointing in the direction of an unseen assassin.

I was following the Big Muddy, barreling down Highway 61, Dylan's highway, the Blues Highway. Outside of Clarksdale where Bessie Smith died in a car wreck, past the crossroads where Robert Johnson sold his soul to the Devil. History and river wove, meandered and fell away. Days and nights blurred together with each mile made.

There is an all-consuming cold to a Minnesota winter—eventually shivering gives way to numbness, until you cannot feel your skin except as ice against your clothes, and you feel you have no body. But the earth changes as you drop south. The world warms. I rolled down my window. The air smelled different—full, lush, heavy. There is an itchy saturation to a Louisiana night. Sticking to your clothes and to yourself, you grow utterly aware of the smells and movements of your body. My body, slowly, measurably with each hour south, knew itself again. The chill thawed, the freeze left my limbs, and I began again to feel myself.

I was close now. Exhausted and dirty from sleeping short nights parked at rest stops, I was close. As the sun disappeared, once more slipping beyond the western horizon and ushering in the third night of my journey, I pulled off onto the shoulder to stretch my legs. As I did, I was suddenly overwhelmed with emotion. That which chased me and that which I raced toward seemed to collide. I do not remember exactly what I felt, but it had something to do with the sensation of having escaped and that I was not only beginning anew, I was journeying back into time. As the weather changed and feeling returned to my body, I began to believe I was being recalled to life. I stepped out of the rental van and leaned against the open passenger door. Out there on the road, away from major cities, all was dark except for occasional headlights and the sky of stars.

There along the southwest horizon, Orion bestrode the Mississippi which lay beyond my vision to the west. My new life beckoned me. I jumped back into the van and sped away, tearing through the night—pushing hard through the last stage of my move. I was yearning for rebirth, and so when I finally entered New Orleans, it was as though I was mounting the shore at the mouth of the Mighty Miss like some freshly baptized believer. I had arrived.

Taking the off-ramp I moved my attention from my atlas to the directions I had shorthanded on a scrap piece of paper and began navigating the city. Glancing around as I drove, I was struck by the people. People were everywhere—on street corners and balconies, sitting outside of cafes and walking leisurely down the broad, grassy medians. New Orleans was bustling with life. Not frenetic, it was casual almost, yet an energy seemed to exude from the people and, too, from the yucca plants and begonias and flowering dogwoods that lined and hedged the streets. The whole city seemed to generate a unique quality—part vivacity, part lethargy. The very air hung with distinction, bearing the aroma of stale beer and rotting wood, decaying flowers and diapers left in the sun. The stench was subtle but pervasive and it seemed to mingle with the percussive rattle of the street car and the music that seeped from shaded bars. New Orleans had rhythm—all heat, life, green.

I followed the street car tracks along St. Charles until I found Napoleon Avenue and turned south toward the River. Anna had taken care of everything. She had staked out a place for us to rent, had signed the lease and by now had probably moved in all of her belongings. I pulled up to the address she had given me. It was an old Victorian style two story house brandishing a white columned front porch and skirted by a decorative wrought iron fence. It was like something out of a movie, a mansion standing proud and close to the street, its upper windows peering out at me like eyes.

I suddenly felt dirty. I had not showered in three days, and I smelled appropriately. My face was scruffy for lack of shaving, but more than that I felt dirty inside. Parked in front of the grandeur that was to stage my new life, I, in contrast, was obtuse. My depression felt almost petty here, too dark and vile for my Anna, for this new house, for this city in the sun. I suddenly, desperately did not want to leave the van.

Make this work.

Remembering Mara's words, I took a deep breath and stepped out onto the street.

I opened the iron gate and staggered up the front walk toward the house carrying a backpack of overnight gear. Mounting the porch I read the listings on the massive glass double-door. *A*, *B* and *C*. I stepped back confused and suddenly felt very much in a strange city 1,500 miles from the world I knew. But there on the front left edge of the house was a black iron *D*. I followed the concrete path around the side of the house. There the door stood. My door. Our door. And the old anxiety crept back up. I had not the nerve to knock. I turned back to look at the van parked on the street.

I could run. This is too much. Too hard. I can still run.

Perhaps I was dirty and broken, but I had come too far to give in to my fears now. With a surge of strength I rapped on the door. I fidgeted with my Pacers ball cap, nervously pulling it off and then back tight on my head and waited.

The door swung open and a tall college-age brunette towered before me. Probably already a few inches taller than I was, our height difference was exaggerated by the fact that I stood on the second step of the stoop, so that I had to look up at her. She wore a tight black leotard top and jeans. I had no idea who she was.

"Oh, hey," she said as though she had expected someone else.

I was devastated. It occurred to me in a flash that all of my long years of depression, all of my therapy and medication, all of

my courage and the many miles trekking the length of the Mississippi River had led me finally to the wrong apartment. I stammered
to find the words for my predicament.

"Hi. I...I'm looking..."

Ignoring me, she leaned her head back inside the house,
extending her long neck and shouted, "Anna! Your boy is here!"

With that the brunette wandered off leaving the door wide
open. I stood there still on the second step of the stoop like a fool,
uncertain about what to do. Then, in a moment, Anna appeared,
leaning into the doorway from the left door jam, smiling at me.
There she was—my Anna, looking just as I remembered her, and
different. She had been transformed by the southern sun. She was
not exactly tan, but her skin had color, and her previously dishwater
blond hair was bleached nearly platinum. She had gained a bit of
weight and it suited her. She glistened sweat and seemed to me to
glow, the embodiment of health and contentment.

"Hey," she said.

"Hey," I said back.

There was silence then, neither of us knowing how to proceed. She held the door frame and I stood below her. Her hair was
longer than I remembered. I wanted to step up and hold her. I
wanted still to run.

"Well, come in," she said finally.

I stepped inside and found hardwood floors and blank walls.
Boxes populated the small front room, some open, some stacked
in a corner. A desk-lamp sat on the floor plugged into an outlet
but it had no bulb. To my right was a closed glass door. I could see
that it led to another small room, strewn with clothes. An inflat-
able mattress lay beneath a low slanted ceiling, its pitch dictated
by the position of the house's main staircase.

"How was your trip?" Anna asked. She stood to my left, several feet away. She put her hands in the back pockets of her jeans.
She always did that when she was nervous.

"Good," I answered. "Long." My voice sounded strange to me after three days in silence. It was raspy and quiet. I cleared my throat.

"So you met Courtney?"

Courtney, who had wandered into the galley-style kitchen beyond Anna, waved at the mention of her name. She opened the fridge, pulled out a beer and disappeared into a far room.

"She's my roommate. Or used to be." Anna smiled at me. "We were just having some beers in the new place." With her hands still in her back pockets she began to sway ever so slightly back and forth. She always did that too when she was nervous. "So, what do you think?"

I continued to scan my surroundings—the blank walls and empty rooms were canvases of possibility. One can begin anew like this, I thought. I looked back at Anna, but could find no words to speak.

"Welcome home, Waylan."

XIX

"Are you ready for this?" Anna said.

"I think so," I said, but I had never been more ready for anything. Moving in together was natural. Living with her was something that always was a given, and yet it had been so far away. Now, finally, it was time. "Yes, I am ready. I have been waiting my whole life. I have been waiting to begin my life with you. Of course I am ready." I did not say this, however. Instead I just continued to unpack.

"Do you want this picture on this wall or this one?" I said, moving across the room with a heavy framed poster.

"I don't know," she said, standing from her hunched work of distributing cases into the CD rack. "Do it again."

I grimaced playfully, "Yes, ma'am," and dutifully repeated placement of the frame to its potential wall positions.

"I like it there."

"Yeah?"

"Yeah."

"Okay."

"But higher."

"There," I said, sliding the picture up the wall. Anna squinted as I did so, like a surveyor evaluating land.

"Perfect," she said, breaking her squint and holding her hands out in front of her to indicate "stop."

"I do like perfection."

I made a mark with a pencil and set the frame on the floor leaning against the wall. I walked across the room to retrieve my hammer and a nail. Anna, who was still standing, stepped in front of me.

"You're pretty handy," she said coyly.

"My gift is in knowing that women are always right," I said.

"I knew there was a reason I liked you." Grabbing my hand, she pulled it to her lips.

"I missed you," I said. I should have said more then. I should have told her about how I believed she could save me from myself. If only I had been more desperate. If only I had conveyed even a little of the magnitude of my emotion. I was broken. I had escaped death and traveled by a secret road in the night to get to her. If only I had been able to express the depth of my gratitude, my hope. I wanted life, believed in life with her. I was dirty from my years in the darkness. I was fragile from my years of torture. Now I just wanted a chance. I just needed the sun and a reassuring touch. I was, for some reason that is beyond me even to this day, unable to reveal to her my true self. I was unable to share my crumbling heart. I needed to ask for forgiveness. Instead I came to her there in New Orleans stilted and confused.

She kissed me. It was long and suggestive. She tasted acid sweet familiar. She tasted like home. And I thought immediately, and for the first time since my move to New Orleans, how different her kiss was from Lindsay's. Lindsay always tasted of Marlboro Reds and Corona. She always tasted of desire. Suddenly Anna's breath and mouth felt foreign to me. I was uncomfortable and awkward, and Anna felt it in my body, in my lips.

"How 'bout a drink?" she said, smiling, defiant, her hands on my hips.

"I thought you'd never ask."

Anna and I walked down the street to Ms. Mae's. It was a dark and smoky one-room bar consisting of a half-dozen or so tables. Electronic poker machines stood on one wall below covered windows. A pool table and foosball table were in the back. Anna explained to me that in France foosball was called *baby-foot*. We thought that was funny. The only light in Ms. Mae's was created by neon beer signs, poker screens and the jukebox, which was currently (and almost perpetually) playing Patsy Cline. Over the next year, when we said we were going to the bar, we meant here. It was two blocks from our house, so it became our first stop or last stop, or sometimes both, on nights out.

"So me working at a video store. What do you think?" I asked, starting promptly on my first beer.

We sat perched on stools at the bar. Anna was taking a swig of Dixie beer when I asked her opinion on my new vocation. Her glass glinted cinnamon and sapphire.

"It'll be great, babe." She wiped her mouth with an open hand. "Free movies…you can't beat that."

"I mean a couple days a week. It won't be much money, but with splitting the rent it should be enough."

Anna smiled and nodded. I lit a cigarette.

"Nice thing is, it should be low stress," I said, breathing smoke. She and I were quiet for a while. Patsy Cline seemed to effortlessly permeate the respite.

"Something I'm worried about…the stress…with school and work. I mean, I really crumbled under the weight up there." I said.

"Yeah, but it'll be different here. You're better now. And you're with me." She put a hand on my knee. Silhouetted against a video screen, she was dark and yellow. "We'll make sure you take a light class schedule. There's no hurry to finish."

I nodded and turned to watch the bartender moving up and down the bar. I felt suddenly safe. Patsy and Dixie and colors in the dark, I felt then that I had righted the ship. Anna was saying that life was now what we made it, as opposed to what depression dictated.

"Thank you," I said, but she did not hear me, or if she did she probably did not understand.

She leaned over and kissed me briefly. "We're finally together again, and we can do this however we want."

I believed her. Finally we were together. Finally I was home. I smiled and simultaneously pushed my empty glass forward to indicate I was ready for another drink.

"Jesus. Another already?" Anna said, holding up her half-full glass as proof of her amazement.

"One thing college has taught me is how to drink," I grinned. The bartender grabbed my glass casually, slowly, in the way all things are done in New Orleans.

"Well I've been in the Big Easy for three years...I will not be put to shame. How 'bout shots?"

"Whiskey?"

"I can tell you've been holed up in the snow," she said, her eyes widening in mock disapproval. "I'm having a Red Headed Slut."

"The mouth on you, my word," I said. She stuck out her tongue in response.

As the bartender returned my glass, now brimming with Dixie, Anna said, "I'll take another round, too. And two shots. Red Headed Slut and a whiskey."

"Make it two Red Headed Sluts," I said.

I remember this night because it held within it all that was possible. Anna and I were building a life together, one surprisingly unafraid of my recent past. The changes she had discerned in me a few years back were forgotten, or lost to the joy of our reunion. Two years, that was the plan. Time enough for me to finish school. She would graduate from Tulane after a year, but she could work, or get her Master's—the details did not matter to me. I was now with her. Two years and then we would be married, and so now all the pieces that had for the last three years seemed misshapen were falling into place. From now on and forever my mornings would begin with her, with our daily ritual of coffee and conversation over the newspaper. Us together. Errands and dinners, disagreements and cross words, furniture arrangements and crossword puzzles. Careers and kids and pension plans. Years upon years of us. Finally my life was unfolding as it should.

"Wacha' doin'?" Anna said through the screen door.

"Just smoking. I'll be in, in a minute."

She opened the screen and sat down next to me on the stoop.

"Can I have one?"

"Okay," I said, pulling my pack of cigarettes out of my pocket and handing them to her, "but don't get hooked."

"Deal," she said in a childlike voice as though we were kids making a spit pact.

I smiled at that as I lit her cigarette.

"Nice day," she said.

"Fuckin' hot." I returned.

"Welcome to the Big Easy." She smiled and with one hand pulled and spun her long hair into a bunch and held it atop her head.

"It's the most wonderful place I've ever been," I said.

Anna was quiet for a while, smoking. "Stinks, though," she said finally.

"Well, that," I said, laughing. We both laughed. "The smell is part of it's charm."

"Charm," she said. "I like that."

I kissed her damp forehead.

Anna took a drag and exhaled immediately. She smoked like that, rapid shallow intakes, nervous almost, like a hummingbird might if a hummingbird were to smoke, I thought.

Lindsay always smoked like an actress on stage, exaggerated and dramatic, so that even those in the back row could interpret her movements. Forceful, with flare to sell the act, she would pull the cigarette hard and then extract it, her arm falling all the way to her knee. Then she would toss her chin into the air to exhale, the plume of smoke pouring up.

"I'm beginning to see New Orleans differently now that you're here," Anna said, releasing her hair and leaning forward.

"Good or bad?"

"Good, if anything, but neither really," she said.

"Okay."

"I've always loved it here, but now I feel like I don't just live here…" Anna trailed off and looked out at the street. "This might sound strange," she started again, "but I feel now like New Orleans is something I wear, like it's part of me."

There was the sound of the trolley in the near distance, the rumble and familiar cry and whine coasting forever back to us and away again. She waited, perhaps for the expected bell—clang, clang—before going on. *Clang clang*.

"I don't know what I mean exactly, but it's caught up with you being here, too." She fidgeted with the ring I had given her in high school. "It's nice," she said with a shy smile.

Fat drops of water began to slap our front walk. We rose quickly and ducked inside, the rain having surprised us once again. Despite it being a nearly daily occurrence, it often surprises because when it rains in New Orleans it comes in sheets, it comes in waves—torrential all at once.

I remember Anna and I getting caught along Magazine Street

one afternoon, dashing and splashing through puddles before finding shelter under some antique store awning. Laughing, soaked, and breathless, she and I kissed, her hair wet, warm water dripping into my eyes and slipping down my nose. Then, my hand on the small of her back, we peered out at the world through a curtain of rain. And I was struck by the sky. Though not quite overcast, it was discolored a greenish-orange hue, so that the world seemed to glow electric and the air felt potent, all rinsed clean and made new. The change in color was like the morning in the shower a few months before when my vision began to return, when off-white had transformed into yellow. I thought of that moment because of how it rains in New Orleans, hot rain, the way it rains like a shower.

After five minutes, maybe twenty, the deluge is nearly always over. And almost immediately there is no record of it, no proof. The cement dries instantly. The droplets beaded upon ginkgo leaves are discreetly absorbed or evaporate back into the thick air. The earth drinks away all memory in moments as though the rain had never poured. But the mid-afternoon is cooled briefly, providing relief, granting strength to endure the heat just a little while longer.

Perhaps those afternoon showers were like my arrival in New Orleans—my depression soothed, my strength renewed—so that Anna and I could be united on fresh grounds. Yet my move was, like the rain, only a short reprieve. Even though the length of a river was no longer between us, the years of separation distanced us now in ways we could not have foreseen, in ways we did not understand. While I hoped Anna's new feeling of envelopment was connected to feeling safe and secure—that wearing New Orleans related to being consumed by our passion and potential—part of me began to fear that the weight of all of my hope had descended upon her with my move. The burden of my disease and the baggage of my recovery were now partly hers to bear.

Thick air blasted in though the up pulled windows of the trolley as it trundled down the grassy median of St. Charles Avenue. I watched the conductor as she swung her arms back and forth, clacking the clutch up a gear and then down. The car slid and scraped on its metal tracks, alternately braking and jolting forward, slowing occasionally, always reluctantly it seemed, to stop in response to a buzz from the pull cord. The wooden doors smacked open to release or admit passengers, people moving in or out slowly, as they do in New Orleans. And then off again, the acceleration accompanied by percussive clatter and a clang of the bell. The jerk and scrape of wheels hammered my body through the worn planked seat. I peered out at the splendor of the Garden District, magnolia and honeysuckle in bloom, wind hot on my face.

Then the bell rang sharply, repeating in quick succession. The trolley car screamed and lurched, metal on metal whistling an urgent whine, jarring me forward in a sudden, yet excruciatingly sluggish, halt. I darted my eyes forward, and through the front glass I could see a car sitting in the median along the trolley's path, waiting to merge into a line of leisurely traffic. It was a common occurrence in the city, trolley and car vying for the same position. I had even a few times seen the two collide, never violently, always at low speeds, property damage and delays the most tragic outcomes. But this time the hiss and scrape, the slow motion nature of the situation, the metal cries of wheel on track, thrust me once again to the train wreck. Those three brothers among the elementary aged victims as the train barreled into the school bus. "It is done," they all must have sensed then in those last seconds. Perhaps at the point of impact there was comfort in such finality. All fear stripped away, the warm darkness wrapping them in peace. Surely the engineer could not have stopped, but that moment would continue long after the wreckage had been hauled away. Those deaths would live with him forever, so that it became more than a tragic instant, but rather an infinity of frozen disaster. There are moments time cannot hold, days and months so burdened by grief that time itself breaks under such weight.

We there on that trolley, stopping well before a collision, then lunging again forward, rattling on west, heading toward the Universities and Audubon Park, we did not carry with us such burdens. We traveled, in comparison, so lightly it was as though we might in fact lift off, take flight, the trolley and all of us in it, lumbering into thick New Orleans sky. The conductor clutched up again with one wide motion of her arm and the trolley soared on, breezing through the mid-afternoon humidity until it came time for me to pull the cord. Buzz-buzzzzz! And we all jerked and thudded back to earth. The map-clutching, camera-clicking tourists and the ancient-faced denizen in a full suit and tie watched me as I followed the rubber-ribbed mat out, grabbing the back of every other wooden bench on my way and then down, slowly, as all things are done in New Orleans.

"You're late," my manager said as I walked into the video store.

"I took the trolley," I said.

"All right then," he responded, accepting my excuse without misgivings. My issues with time management had improved significantly with Anna's prodding, but I also now found myself in a city far more relaxed about timeliness. It was as though I had discovered the only place on earth calibrated to my internal clock.

"Rachel's backed up with checkouts. Help her before you reshelve."

I hurried behind the counter. The hours flew by in a blur, a steady line of customers and a constantly amassing pile of videos to return to their categorized, alphabetized positions along the wall-sized shelves.

"You ever seen this one," the next lady in line asked, handing me a video. I enjoyed recommending movies but was always anxious about this type of question. They had already made a semi-commitment by bringing the video to the checkout counter. If I had seen the film but had no strong opinion, the customer inevitably still connected me to their choice, often blaming me for their bad pick. Even a hint of disappointment from a customer stressed me out to no end. On particularly hard days, I returned home distraught, racked with guilt. Anna would say, "It's just a stupid job. Relax." And I would smile and nod and turn on the TV.

I took the video from the woman and read the spine of the generic white box: *Searching for Bobby Fischer*.

"They're not patzers!" I heard Dave yell, as if he were with me. I could see him there in his room, scanning the chess board, plotting his attack. Everything back then seemed achievable, hope of a set board not yet put into motion. I missed chess with my friend, our lives interacting in hypothetical futures, math and jazz, shapes in space, expectation of the possible.

"It's an excellent movie," I answered the customer. "One of my favorites."

I remembered sweeping the pieces clear of the board, how I had lost the king. The king went missing and we replaced it with a beer lid.

"Really?" she said. "I mean, it's about chess."

At the beginning of college I believed I would preside over the vast expanse of my destiny like a king. That seemed to me long ago. I thought of King Philip II and wondered again if Anna even recognized me now.

"It's about way more than chess. Even chess is about more than chess," I said.

The customer frowned. "I guess I'll take it then."

"Good choice. You won't regret it."

The image of Lindsay asleep, curled up on a bathmat, flickered before my eyes. And then I remembered Dave sitting cross-legged on my bed. Staring at the ceiling as though he might be counting stars, he spoke to me, quoting the kid from *Bobby Fischer*. "You've lost. You just don't know it yet."

The next day I was late to work again. The day after that I forgot to go in at all.

XX

See Anna there in our house. She is surrounded by plants, by greenness and life. She is tending to her plants—watering, trimming, repotting—the chores of patience and care. She is humming soft almost distinguishable hymns, yet she jumps and skips among many, and they fade and blend with her own internal song. Her humming is only broken by the occasional pep talk to a plant. (Her Norfolk Pine needs particular encouragement on this day.) She continues on, shuffling from orchid to fern, the green reaching and growing about her as she moves, as she sings. Having a green thumb is something I do not understand. It is a gift I do not possess. But *green thumb* does not do Anna's ability justice. Her very essence speaks to her house plants. There, amongst all that life, her life unifies, and in turn encompasses the life around her. She is never self-conscious here, never sad. It is the work and reward, the focus of their need being her task, that spurs a calm in her. She thinks of things as she tends—like the underside of leaves. How often the bottom of a leaf is pale, not quite sickly, but fragile looking compared to the bold vibrant green of the sunny side. The bottom of a leaf is a ghostly reflection of its other side. She wonders how a leaf chooses such a thing, one side weak so the other can be strong, wonders if there is ever a power struggle. She decides in passing, as she ties a drooping branch to a stake, that the underside of a leaf is noble. It is beautiful for its sacrifice. Her fingers are damp and earthy from the work. She likes this. She feels counter-intuitively cleansed by the dirt. She bemoans how separate her life is from the earth, how her life is so much pavement and steel. She smells her tulip—the pink one—and smiles. She returns her watering can to its place on the hook above the sink. She does so reluctantly as she always does. She thinks then, right before she will think of all the many things that constitute the immediacy of her existence, that life endures in a great many forms, but growth is all too rare.

Mara's voice sang out from the CD player like milk, all chilled-cream smooth, pouring from one note into another, the guitar strumming bass and her words soaring high.

> *My dreams of flying*
> *Always end in a fall*
> *I wake before dying*
> *But live for nothing at all*

"You've got to hear this. I mean really listen to it."

Anna had appeared in the doorway of our living room, perhaps stretching her legs. She had been in the other room. Writing a paper, I think.

"I have, Waylan. You play it all the time," she said. It was not cruel, the way she said it. She was rarely cruel in such ways, but it was clear that she was exasperated.

"Sorry," I said. "She's just really good. And I know her, ya know? It's…important to me."

"I know." She shuffled into the room. Her jeans were faded an almost grey from wear. She wore a cotton blouse with long flared sleeves. It was too big for her, the sleeves nearly engulfed her hands, and the neckline slid according to her movement from revealing the blades of her back to collar bone to almost falling off her shoulder. She always looked best this way—comfortable, casual, unselfconscious. She threw herself into our big paisley chair. She had broken the springs long ago this way, so it returned no bounce; she landed with a thud. Mara's voice seemed to get loud then, and I closed my eyes, surrendering.

We all wait for morning
Beneath this cold broken sky
With everything crumbling
His lips do not lie

One night Mara and I had come back from our weekly dinner together. We stopped and stood in the courtyard.

"It was great, ya know. Nice." Mara said.

"As usual," I retorted, but she meant something more than that.

We became strangely quiet then. Snow fell lightly, and it seemed to fill the silence with a contrived profundity. I studied the arched buttresses of the dormitory behind her, strong simple curves of stone.

"Well, thanks," she said and hugged me. But neither of us would let go. It was wild and desperate and easy as Mara held me there in the snow, in the darkness. Something about her hold, or the curve of stone or the soft pad of falling snow pulled me from my haze. It was like a boat aiming for shore finally coming out of the fog, gaining bearings and seeing land.

"I'm a fool." The words spilled out in unchecked confession.

She shushed me, and it made me smile.

"No," I said, releasing my hold and facing her, "for not seeing your beauty."

Her nose was red and ran slightly from the cold.

And I kissed her. She had felt it coming, but our lips still met in surprise. It was a kiss of uncertainty, but it was what I had felt at that moment. It was then. I had no thought nor any sense of her thoughts. My mind willed itself not to think; I only wanted to feel her lips. Beyond consequence, beyond Lindsay and Anna, beyond even Mara. Beyond anger and fear, beyond depression and its insidious name and gel-capped antidote. Beyond even fight and strength—just to be held there and kissed. To be beyond myself.

Her lips were chapped and dry, but soft, like sitting in an old comfy chair after a long day, and all my tension seemed to drain from me. I had been a fool for not seeing her in this way before, for not being here my entire life. I had often lamented that I needed to trust my instincts, my emotions. Now I had, and it had led me here.

We stopped kissing, but she held my bottom lip with her lips. She moaned slightly, ever so quietly. I hugged her abruptly, before either of us could open our eyes, before we could rejoin the world, before I felt cold again. Maybe before it became real.

But I wanted to say things to her. I wanted to apologize for my blindness, for not loving her in the right way, in the way she deserved. I wanted to tell her about the boat and the fog. But before I could find the words, she spoke. Looking at the ground, while snow fell lightly in her hair, she said, "You make me tired, Waylan."

My mind rushed, but again no words came. I looked at her, waiting for the eye contact that would not come. What the hell is that? I'm tiring? We had kissed. I had taken a risk and been slapped in the face. What did she mean? What did she want from me? Not a kiss clearly. Apparently I had been racing along a track, one that led us from this beginning to one that needed to be played out over days and months. It had come on me in a flash, but it was real. It was truth, being here, together. Was not this the exciting beginning, not the mired middle? She knew this surely. She had been a part of that kiss, a part of the slow years that had led us here. Surely she understood. But how to ask, how to convince her and make her see? How to explain that I was present tonight, beyond the depression? Maybe if I asked her to envision a sunrise, the soft timid light, the smell of hope and damp earth. But how to say it so that it might reverse time to the point before she felt whatever it was that made her say that?.

"Wow, thanks. Tiring. Usually after a kiss I get a negative response." Sarcasm was all I had.

"I want this to be…to start…"

"I want that, too. I'm sorry it took so long." I began to regain my footing.

"But, it's not real." She stopped then and scanned the night, her eyes moved steadily, as though following the walk of a person on the far end of campus, but I did not look with her, only watched her face intently as she struggled for the words to explain what in her heart she knew.

"I can't depend on this," she said finally. "Don't forget that I know you."

"Of course you do," I thought. "And that is the beauty of it. You know my soul. The soul I have tried to keep secret and safe from so many here. More than anyone here, you know me." But I could not respond in that way. It was not entirely true. And she was saying something else. I knew that.

This was a rejection based on more than the superficial, which is the most dire blow to the psyche at these moments. This was not about me being ugly or dumb or dull. She had even met my darkness and held her ground. These things did not keep her from loving me. Beyond what I hoped, she meant something else, something sinister. What I understood but could not think or articulate at the time was that what she meant was something more than any of my fears. It was that I could not love. And whatever had brought us to this moment was not about love, because my love had all been spent. My love was reserved for Jack and Anna, and I did not have enough left for anyone here. Not for Dave or Lindsay, not even for Mara. She was protecting herself, and for a moment I believed she was right.

"I'm sorry," was all I could manage.

There was silence. She shivered in the cold, and I grabbed her arms and rubbed them to warm her. It was instinctual and odd.

"Waylan…"

"Love me. Despite all of me." But I could not say it. I was afraid of saying too much, of being too real. I really believed that night I could start over, that loving her was the answer and that I could convince her, here, now. But she was right. In doing so I would be taking even more of a risk than I already had. For all its madness, Lindsay and Anna, drinking and school, my life was mine. I could not give it away. I should have—should have at that moment given myself away. For Mara.

"We've both had a lot of wine. Go home, sleep it off. We'll talk tomorrow."

But I knew we would not. That was not the way we were. And somewhere outside of myself I realized I had missed my only chance. That I had taken a risk, but could not see it through. The kiss was soft and comforting, and perhaps a beginning, but I had said nothing to convince her of it. It was a beginning that I, in fact, was not willing to see through. Mara saw this somehow. Maybe it was something she always knew.

> *Words are for giving*
> *But taken all wrong.*
> *Time's unforgiving*
> *Why have we waited so long*

"You miss them, huh?" Anna asked.

"Yeah, I guess," I said, bringing myself back from song and memory. "I mean, of course. Of course I do."

"And her?"

"Who, Mara?"

"No, not Mara."

"Yeah, sure," I said before I had thought about how it would make Anna feel. I tried to recover. "But not the way you think."

"She would have understood this, right?"

"Ah, come on, babe. What are you talking about? I'm here. With you. Because this is what I want."

Anna had been looking at the floor, but she looked up now and smiled. "I know."

I do not know how many times we had fixed it, Anna and I. We had a knack for tackling obvious issues and smoothing them temporarily. My relationship with Lindsay was a lapse in our relationship Anna seemed to accept and dismiss immediately. But I think what hurt her was the piece of me she could not see. I had secrets now, where there had never been any before.

"This is just different than I thought, ya know," she said, and her smile faded.

She came to me then (oh, I wish she had) and grabbed me by the shoulders, gazing into my face until I bowed my head in shame. "Look at me," she shook me slightly, her voice was powerful then; it held within it great certitude. "You cannot do this," she warned as though I knew of what she spoke. But I did know somehow and began to tremble with both fear and relief. "She knows," I thought. She finally understands, but she did not really. We did not know anything, but were compelled someway to be stuck there entangled, pretending to be profound, forcing ourselves to love that it might come about, that we might find ourselves in the place we believed we were supposed to be. We were both actors hoping our costumes and masks would sell the part, or pianists playing lightly snippets of old songs hoping within the combination of keys we might fumble upon inspiration.

"I cannot lose you," she said. "This is too good." (Ah, if only she had said, "This holds too much potential," then I might have believed her, but I knew we were far from good—she knew too.)

"Dear," I said. "I must let this fall away. It must fade. I cannot be happy. I cannot be loved." (I did not say any of this. It is what I felt.)

Her finger curled and lifted my chin. "Look at me," she said again. The refrain of it made it true, and I looked into her eyes—green ever fading to blue—and saw the hope beneath the lies, the small part of her spirit yet uncrushed, there was a piece still unafraid.

"It is too late," I said and wept. (In truth I could no longer weep, which makes me incredibly sad, but not sad enough to cry.) "The hour draws near. I will make you hate me. I must. In the end you will strain to be free. It is our lot, you and me."

With force she embraced me. (I wish any of this were true.) She held me with a fervor I did not know she possessed. There was a violence in her almost. I had drained the gentleness from her, I suppose, with my daily despondency. "I cannot hate you," she cried.

"You begin to already," I returned. The day had drifted to night, and our lampless room grew dark. The dark drew up around us until I could not distinguish her from me, me from her, us from the room.

"The day is coming when you will be made sick by my presence."

"No. Stop it. I won't."

"And you will say to yourself in disgust, 'What a waste. What a waste.'"

"Please stop. It cannot be. We, you and I, are indestructible."

I smiled at this in the dark. "You have no idea the depth of this pit. It will consume us both and hunger for more."

"Perhaps if we stay here, like this, believing…" (Pretending to believe, sitting here adopting the posture of belief.)

"Perhaps. But we will not. You have not the patience, and I have not the heart."

"So it is done then," she said.

"Not yet. No, not yet. It must hurt more first. We must bleed a little more."

None of this is true. It did not happen like that. Instead I sat on the floor next to the speakers listening to Mara sing. Anna sat in her broken-spring chair looking at me.

"Hang in there, kid," I said and winked at her.

XXI

Anna's hair was soft and thin, blond that caught the sun and made her appear angelic. She and I would sit up on the balcony and talk over a beer. I never fully appreciated that peace. By then she was always somewhere else—on a different plane. So to have her there, to have her present for the length of a slowly sipped beer bottle on a hot afternoon was a secret joy, because she instilled calm, if not confidence. There was an ease and grace about her wispy frame, as though she were part of a different era. The age of movie stars—she was Hepburn and Kelly. Some of it had to do with her classic look: lithe body, slender fingers, delicate features and fierce eyes. But her elegance resided in her economy of motion, in her concise eye blinks, in the subtle way she touched her neck. Her stillness stirred in me the sensation of vast fields, like beholding an endless expansion of level space, only a stark sky stemming its infinite progress at the horizon. To sit with her was to be with the land, to feel small and insignificant in the face of such expanse. She always had little to say to me, like quiet on the prairie, as though saving her words for something or someone more worthy, yet she granted these brief balcony moments. Her measured speech, our drawn out stretches of silence, became for me like prayer. Thus this became my weekly mass. This was my experience of the Holy.

I do not mean this as blasphemy. I believe in God. I have in fact met God. In my darkness I have confronted God, wrestled with God like Jacob before me, and finally killed God. In the deepest illness of my mind, in the loudest darkness of my disease, I amputated myself from the world. I rejected love and abandoned hope. And it was then that I understood the existence of God by feeling God's absence.

"Do you believe in God, Dave?"

The night before I left for New Orleans, Dave and I sat up late into the night drinking and talking.

"No," he said swallowing his Beam and Coke with a sour face. "I mean, I was raised in the church. I guess I kind of believe in the whole idea of religion. I understand its purpose. I just don't believe there's anybody out there."

"Why not?"

"I guess I feel like this world should make a little more sense. I feel like it would be a little better, I mean, if there was an omnipotent being out there."

"Yeah, I guess."

"You believe?"

"I have to, Dave." I looked at him, then at the floor and back at him. "I have to believe in redemption."

He began to speak and then stopped. He lit a cigarette instead and waited.

"The whole Lindsay thing. I mean, Christ, how could I do that to her?"

"She's a big girl. She's gonna be all right," he said condescendingly. I could not tell if he meant it that way or not.

"But what if she's not? What have I done?"

"Hey, how did Lindsay's life become about you? You're not her keeper. You don't have to save her. And..." he said, getting animated, "you don't have the power to destroy her."

"I love her. I want to take away her pain."

"If that was ever your job, it is definitely not now."

"Okay, okay. Not Lindsay. Not just Lindsay, but everybody. The way I've been. The way I've hurt...you. I have to believe that there can be redemption. For me and for this whole goddamn fucked up world. That it can be saved." I could no longer look at him, but I realized I was on the edge of my chair and that I was probably shouting.

"So why? So you can pray and not act. So that you can hurt and not regret."

"No," I said. "So that things can get better...that I can be better. I just have to believe there will be another opportunity. If there is a God, then there is forgiveness, and there is such a thing as a second chance."

"You think New Orleans is that chance?"

"Maybe," I said sheepishly.

"Well, maybe it is." He smiled, and for some reason I was shocked by his gift of approval. Perhaps because it smacked of placation. I felt my face flush in anger. "And then what?" he asked.

"I'm not a fool, you know?"

Dave began to respond and then stopped. He was thrown off guard, as though he had planned for a different conversation, as though he had listened to his own response in his head and began its answer, then only belatedly heard my own.

"But...but of course you are. You are naive to believe in anything in this world. Stop hoping. Stop believing in a change in this world. This world is too old and broken down. It's too uninspired."

He stopped and took a breath. There was a glassy pain in his eyes as though he had just confessed his greatest sin. "You...you don't fit, Waylan. And it seems to me..." He sighed, his confession had exhausted him. He looked ancient. "You need to get your shit together or just give up, because nothing in between is worth the effort."

"You know me better than that," I thought, but did not say, though I smiled at him to remind him of who I was. This did not put him at ease. He looked at me hard, and I realized that he was crying. There were no tears, no sobs. He was not actually crying, but he was somehow; I could feel it. And I did not know why. I tried to think. What had he said that had been so painful? Why did I not understand the gravity of this interaction? Maybe he had shared with me a secret. My God, he has been holding it in for so long—believing that he was protecting me from the cruel reality of a world I could not handle. There was something about life, about love and knowledge that I did not understand. And that he believed I could never understand. I felt weak then, and small—crushed by the world and his imperceptible crying. Either I *am* a fool or my closest friend believes that I am. Somehow that felt just the same.

The silence had been too long. He looked as though he might collapse. He had stumbled down a dark tunnel from which he could find no escape. I grabbed him forcibly, gently, my hand on the side of his face. It was intimate, yet masculine—the line he and I always walked. I pulled us together and spoke in his ear.

"I'll be all right." I did not understand what was happening. I was not strong enough or smart enough. This needed more perhaps, but all I could find to give him was my reassurance.

Dave pulled away from me and looked at my face. He was almost angry. "Of course, man. I know. I know." He got up then, almost embarrassed, but not. We were too close for embarrassment of that kind. He was more distracted than anything. We were done, I guessed. He walked away to mix another drink. I sat where I was and did not think of anything. He had let me off the hook. We would probably talk about basketball or sex, and I could relax, could back off the edge of this uncertainty. But when he returned, he sat down and stared at me hard.

"What I'm saying…what I'm trying to say…it's not just that there is no God out there to save the world, Waylan. It's that in the end it's not worth saving." He lit a cigarette. "So what is left, ya know? You've got to let it go."

And then I understood.

"Well, boy, I may be a fool, but you are sure one jaded son of a bitch."

We laughed, but not hard, because it was more true than funny. Because my hope gave him hope. He did not really believe in anything—except me. And in telling me to give up hope, he was admitting his own nihilism. He was the realist in the relationship. He shouldered our reality, carried all our dirt and anger and potential, all that we were and had been and would yet become; he held it all, for us both. It had been too much weight. It was killing him, and he needed me to help carry the load. Perhaps in that moment I failed him. In a way that could not be recovered. Because I refused the load. But it was because it was a false burden; nothing real ever holds any weight.

Some two weeks after my decision to leave, I got up the courage to tell Lindsay. When I went to see her that day, I had long since said goodbye. I had been saying goodbye for two weeks. So it was dreamlike. I believed somehow that she would understand. That I had somehow communicated it to her without words. Surely she knew. I was so convinced, so already gone—she would sense that, even accept it. She knew me better than anyone in the world, and so she knew that this was coming, she understood this was the right thing. At least, that is what I believed. I think. I am not sure I really thought anything coherent. I was callous, oblivious to the fact that even though I had thought this through, had mourned and was here for closure, for her it was new. Over the last few weeks I had been, if anything, only a bit detached. I had given her no sign. "I'm leaving. Going to New Orleans," came as an utter surprise. It must have been so unreal for her. She broke slowly as it came over her.

I had talked her into it, into loving me. That still gets me. She did not choose me. I was not in her mind until I put myself there. I spoke of my dreams. I spoke of times that were not yet. I made her believe in the me I could be, so that she no longer saw the shell that I was. I spoke of my passion as though it were something actual. I spoke to her of her eyes, the way her hair fell. I kissed her, my lips, soft and gentle, belied the realities of my rage. I made her see the me I wanted to be. "I love you," she would say. And I would think how she loved the idea of me. She loved the same me I loved, that illusive me of my longwinded, circular reasoning. There was a scrim always between us, between the truth and the false. I had created it. She was not a fool to not see it. She believed, because I believed. I had lied to myself for so long, that I was no longer lying. I know it hurt her when the real me came inevitably crashing in. Surely she felt betrayed by my constant cajoling followed by utter disregard. It surely made no sense.

"I thought, I mean you said, you convinced me...that you loved me," she said, her voice growing loud, then descending to whisper, as though to me and yet also to herself in disbelief. "But now, it is just so easy for you to let it end. For it to end. You didn't...you never loved me." I could not explain it away.

I could not explain the lies with which I had beguiled her, because they were the same lies that I believed. Like the night I decided to move (the night I told Anna), Lindsay and I had gone out to dinner. A nice Italian place. Candles. Red wine. We talked about marriage, possible names for our kids. She would hate me for that later.

"You knew. You fucking knew already!"

But what she did not understand, what I could not explain was that there was a division for me between mind and soul. Between possibility and reality. I had meant it: the marriage, the kids. I could envision it all, our lives together. I wanted that life, even though I would betray her, even as I was betraying her already.

I sat there on the edge of a vast field. I looked out and scanned the crab grass and butterflies, the distant shelters, the land meeting cloud sky.

Lindsay spoke from somewhere behind me. "You're so selfish. You're killing me, you know that? And you don't even care."

"Of course I care. I love you." The words slipped slowly around in my mind, but I could not speak them. I knew she needed them and did not need them, and I turned my head to look at her. The silence rising to crescendo.

She wore a sundress. The skin of her neck and collarbone beckoned my lips. Her auburn hair, wavy and tucked behind her ears, dropped past her shoulders. She sat cross legged; the dress was taut between her knees and loose about her breasts. I ached to hold her as I once had, to comfort her, make her understand, make her whole. But I looked instead back to the field. Her desperate eyes, deep crevasses and dark bruises of suffering beneath them, stayed steady, penetrating the back of my head.

She swallowed audibly. "Waylan Gray," her voice hit the field and fell to silence abruptly. "I want you to feel the pain of being responsible for my death."

I turned quickly to look at her again. She was no longer crying. Her eyes looked through me, past me to the darkness and found comfort there. Life was much more complicated and painful than following her father.

They say time heals all wounds, but I only half believe it. There was an acute sense of loss that never left me. It was not a missing piece. It was not a hole. The loss was somehow something added. Like a small lead weight in my chest that was always there. It was a feeling of regret and shame. A concentrated agony. Small and heavy. I believed that it would fade as the shaking had done, pass as the crying had. But it did not.

Over time I began to imagine myself as a Civil War veteran. I believed I understood how it felt for him to be shot. Thought I could feel the hot lead ball tearing into his body, the sting of it, the heat, the surprise and then exquisite pain. And how many years after the War the old vet would still feel the lead shot under his skin, in the muscle. How he would recall lying in that open field, with the boom of canon and the cries of dying men all around, soldiers running, stepping, tripping over him, the smoke and spectacle, and beyond, the pale white sky. I knew how that day on the field, that moment being shot, must have finally become a part of every day.

I believed I knew how the Civil War must have changed a man—not a growing up experience, but a growing *in* experience.. The vet must have seemed quieter when he returned home; he must have seemed more reserved, more deliberate. It was because of the way the lead ball resided in his flesh. Like a grain of sand in an oyster, always present, irritating the soft tissue. But instead of wrapping it in pearl, instead of the body containing it, smoothing it and healing, it was wrapped instead by silence. And with each new layer came a change in the man until the ball was not merely in him, not a part of him, but was him. And all growth, all change thereafter, came from this new essence—the hidden metal orb, the added loss—until finally the vet might look in the mirror some morning while shaving and not recognize himself, would only see the pale sky and feel the lead weight at his core.

I loved Lindsay, but she will always remember me as the man who did not love her enough to sacrifice for her. He who would not sacrifice. And she will sit some nights when it is quiet, smoking a cigarette, and wonder if it was truly love, if I could not sacrifice. She will be right to question. To question everything we had been. I wish she would not, but I do not blame her. I have little to say. For I was the one who left.

Later I would hear that she apparently cut her hair short and took a bunch of pills. They put her in a hospital where they made her wear a paper gown. I only heard this. I did not phone her. I cannot remember why. Perhaps it was because she was with me all of the time, in my thoughts, in my heart, but I did not call.

XXII

As Jack and I descended the mountain, that hurried, halting hop-trot down steep declining trails and concerted effort to beat the growing darkness, there was a near indefinite silence. It was after our climb to the peak, after a precarious butt slide down a shale and slate slope from our peak back to the trail. We were perhaps listening to our own thoughts, but finally Jack spoke—loud and jerky with the movement of his body, half running, half stopping. But it seemed to me a whisper, a mere breath released.

"You know, up there, I thought I was going to die."

I let a moment pass, because a statement like that deserves a moment. I wanted him to know that I was hearing him fully, that I was taking him seriously. But I did not need a moment; I had felt his fear already. I had known his heart on the cliff.

"Yeah," I said finally, still moving down, Jack a little in front, so I could not wholly see his face, me a little behind.

"That rock. It just fell from under my foot," Jack said, slowing his pace.

I matched his gait until I could stop my momentum and labored toward a stump alongside our path. While turned away from Jack, staring at the stump, I said, "I was more afraid for you than for me." I sat on the old rough wood and looked again at my friend. He seemed exhausted by the downhill run and perhaps aged by the events of the day. His glassy eyes searched my face.

"Yeah," he said.

The forest was loud with the pulsating hum of cicadas—that constant rhythmic backdrop that passes for silence—unnoticeable until you stop and listen.

"Like the river," Jack said. His gaze was so strong that I could only hold it briefly. My eyes darted around him, to trees and rocks, to his shoes and the sky. "You were right there, you know. And then you weren't."

Jack and I had been white water rafting the week before on the Colorado river with my parents, uncle and cousins. He and I had been in front. The guide was in the back. He prepared us as we approached the rapids. It was a difficult stretch we were told— a level five. If we fell in, we were not to swim to the shore or to any of the rocks. They were all undercut and would sweep us under and trap us below the surface of the water. That was the reason this particular rapid was responsible for several deaths.

I was tossed into the rapids almost immediately. I do not remember it. There is no recollection of trying to hold on or of being thrown. There was only the paddling, and then the water.

"I wanted to jump in after you, but you were already gone." Jack walked over, took off his backpack and leaned against a thin pine tree next to me.

"I looked back and couldn't see you, and we still had to get through the rapids."

I had been under water then. By the time I surfaced for a moment the raft was a distant orange dot down river. And then under again. I could not think of anything except the rushing of water and the desperation for breath. Then the current forced me onto a rock. I had been spared. Pushed upward instead of under, the width of maybe five feet being the calculable difference between saved and trapped.

I lay like a rag doll, my body's position dictated by the curve of the rock. Spitting, gagging, hanging on. The jagged surface of my island oasis cut the skin of my cramped fingers. Blood mixed with water washed away. The waves were violent, cold, relentless—until inevitably I was swept back into the river.

"I couldn't do anything. I felt...helpless, but more than that," Jack said, as he kicked distractedly at a fallen pinecone, "it was emptiness."

The frigid depths pulled and forced me down. Crushing greys, undulating lights and darks, I was thrashed about by the sheer power of nature. Desperate breaths filled my lungs with water. Flailing, choking, my screams beneath the roaring rush made no sound except in my head. My thoughts were only of breath and an emerging acquiescence to death. There too was a moment near the end when I thought of Jack and Anna and my parents somehow all at once. They were with me, and their love filled me and made me infinitely sad.

The struggling stopped, and the water tore me utterly at will. I was with the river. I was the river. Wholly engulfed, wholly resigned. The icy waves enwrapped me, and I began to fall unconscious. So this is how life must end—in darkness, alone in the swollen void. Perhaps. But I cannot be certain, because a hand ripped me back from the edge.

The next raft on the tour had seen my orange life jacket bobbing alternately shallow and deep. I was pulled from the river by old men, they lifting the weight of death and oceans, pulling me onto the rubbery smell of resurrection. My face pressed against the raft, coughing, gasping, I was still submerged somehow, as though the air too had become water. The darkness still clung to me; I was saturated by it. I lay there on the raft, weeping, drenched with death yet too heavy with life to move, tasting vulcanized salvation.

"Good thing for those old farts, huh?"

"Yeah," I said, the memory of river still roaring in my ears, "good thing."

And slowly I realized Jack had made a connection between the peak and the river which was beyond the mortal danger, but I could not quite grasp it. It was something about emptiness. It was something about the nature of our relationship, but the cacophony of the river made it hard to think.

XXIII

New Orleans is a great place to go and die. It is a grand city all its own. It is a vibrant place of carnival and debauchery. The opulence of old Southern money displays itself along St. Charles, in the Garden district and Uptown. That wealth accrued from the slave trade and black marketeering sits amidst the descendants of slaves and pirates. The utterly poor and the obliviously prosperous live side by side. Yes, like all cities, New Orleans has ghettos and suburbs, but in the old city the rich and poor are tied to one another, one mingled mass of life and heat. And it is hot. It is sweltering, oppressive heat: swamp heat, the air so thick you must wade through it. But the bars never close, and so they drink away those long, humid nights.

A dirty and defiant city, New Orleans drinks its cares away. Already below sea level, it sinks slowly day by day, hour by hour. Even the streets are sinking, so littered with potholes that they are nearly impassable. But no one drives fast in New Orleans anyway; New Orleans does not do anything fast. It is too hot. And the city is too old and wise to be in a hurry. Leave that to the fools in New York and Boston and Los Angeles. Here everyone waits. They wait in long check-out lines for groceries and sit for long drawn out meals in seafood shacks. They wait, and the city sinks, and no one minds. There is an easy amble, a pace into which everyone slips. The city and the great people of the city have chosen a kind of steady strength.

Sinking into the ocean and mutilated by termites and mold, the city dies but does not care. New Orleans is unafraid of death. They celebrate death in the streets—long parades of trumpeters and dancers, umbrellas and horse drawn caskets—because they know death. The city is dying, crumbling, and sinking. It is drinking, gambling and losing, yet it does it slowly. Everything in New Orleans happens with a kind of underwhelmed flare. That is why the world is in love with New Orleans. It is a place to go and experience filth and pageantry simultaneously. It is a city that will take on your sin and smile broadly, unimpressed. Because it is a grand, beautiful city, a city in which the poor are not shunned or hidden, it is the great American city of the poor. "We are poor," says New Orleans, incredulous. "We are sinking into the ocean; we are dying, America, but we are doing it with style. And we are in no hurry, for it is too hot, and we have seen too much to be concerned about something so certain."

I held her close every night, my mistress New Orleans. With each breath I was filled with her—hot and seductive. She engulfed me with her heaviness. She wooed me with her music. New Orleans whispered to me, "Hush now. Hush. You are here now, here in the majestic city of despair and death. Come. Sit. Rest and listen. You have found your warm safe place to lie down."

I would sit across from Anna many nights at the dinner table and say nothing, all the while lying to her. "What is two years?" I would say to myself while slowly fork-stabbing the last of the canned green beans from my plate. What is two years to wait?

Nathan would answer, "A whole lifetime to a two-year-old." I had laughed when he said that on the phone. But later that night I would cry over that same phrase. Two years was a damn long time to lie.

I could, of course, still look at Anna on good days and love her—us there in our small apartment off St. Charles Avenue. She was still in many ways the girl I had known my whole life. She was, in certain ways, the woman I was destined to love. Not so long before I had called her and said, "I am coming to New Orleans to live with you. To finish school. Just two years. And then I will marry you." When I had said it, I had meant it. She was beautiful and brilliant, and she loved me. On most days I could recall all the trauma of my life in Minnesota and realize my relative peace. My relative happiness. And yet when I stepped back, even in my most fulfilled, serene moments, I had to admit that I was not happy. There was something in me that was suffocating, something in me that ached to be free. I kept thinking, "This is not what I meant, when I used to mean something. This is not what I meant, not what I meant at all."

Of course I thought about Anna's pain sometimes. Like when she came home with her heavy backpack, sweaty from the Louisiana heat, the mail held tightly in her hand. I was lying on the couch in the middle of my James Bond marathon I had planned for the day.

"Hey, baby."

"Hey," she said, dropping her bag and surveying the scene.

"How was your day?"

"Fine. Long. Hey, I thought we decided you were going to stop smoking in the house."

"Oh yeah, I know, but I'm doing a marathon thing here."

She looked at the screen. "Bond, eh?"

"Yeah. Sorry about the smoke."

"It's all right," she said flipping through the mail, dropping the keepers on the dining room table and discarding the rest.

"I'm starving," she said, leaning on the living room doorframe for balance as she slipped off her shoes.

"Oh yeah?" I answered, trying to be interested, trying not to watch the television, trying to appreciate Roger Moore for what he was and not condemn him for being a second-rate Bond.

"I'm going to make dinner. Want any?"

"Sure, babe. That'd be great."

"Any requests?"

"No. Whatever, you know."

As she turned toward the kitchen I said, "Are you sure, kid? I mean, if you're tired, I'll make something."

"No," she smiled. "It's fine, really. I'm fine. Watch your movie."

"Thanks."

"Sure."

She entered the kitchen, and I followed her path with each familiar sound she made. The creak of cabinet doors as she scoured the cupboard for ideas. The clatter of pans, the running of water. But later I thought I heard her crying. Not loud, but softly, among the hiss of the stove and whir of the microwave, I thought I heard the reflexive intake of air from stifled sobs. I thought, but could not be sure.

I was not an easy person to live with. I was not an easy man to love. I wish I had had the strength to get up and go to her. But depression was like a boulder on my chest that kept me pressed to the couch. My failure separated me from her. My failure surrounded me like a bubble and held me at a distance from everyone. I could not find the reserve to apologize for all of my transgressions. Nor could I ignore the failure and break the bubble and begin anew because I knew I would fail her again. How could I ask for trust which I knew I would betray? So my failure, both actual and anticipated, forced me alone. To break that cycle, that amassing silence, took courage I no longer possessed.

Eventually, inspired by curiosity or concern, perhaps fueled by frustration, Anna took the initiative that I could not. We sat reading one night, as we often did, after dinner. We had been silent for a long time when she looked up from her book and said, "So are we talking about suicide?"

I was somehow not surprised by the question. We had been living together for several months, and we had never talked about my depression. It was a question that had surely built from the very first letter she received from me about seeing a therapist. But I was slow to answer. I knew she did not really want the answer I had to give.

"Yeah, I guess, partly."

She closed her book. "Partly?" Her eyes narrowed. She bit her lip.

"Well, that's not all it is. It's more than that. But, yes, suicide sometimes."

She tried to hold my gaze, but could not. She looked at the television screen, dark and quiet.

"Don't worry, babe," I said, trying to bring her back from her emerging dread. I needed to be concrete so that her imagination would not distort what I meant. "Kid, I don't have the guts to kill myself. I mean, the way to go really is carbon monoxide. Car in the garage. That's the way to go. Just fall asleep. But that's too easy. If I'm going to kill myself, I need to know that I'm doing it. Need to feel it. Like razor blades. But I don't have the guts."

She sat silently looking down at the coffee table, hands folded in her lap. She was shaking, eyes glassy. I realized I had said too much. She had asked, but she did not really understand what she was asking. I had made it too clear.

"Too easy?" she whispered finally. A single tear escaped and slipped down her cheek.

"Ah, baby. No, come on. It's okay. I told you. It's fine. I'm not going to."

"Just fall asleep?"

The voices were like a constant rushing in my mind. If you have been to Niagara Falls or an obnoxiously loud bar, you know the constant noise can make communication difficult. And once you have said "huh?" or "what?" enough times you give up trying to listen. It takes too much energy, too much effort for too little gain, so you begin to nod politely. Or in more honest moments, you point to your ears to indicate that you cannot hear the other person and put up your hands in a kind of merry apology of resignation. And then you kind of fade out, glance around the room, try to look comfortable and coherent as the cacophony overwhelms you.

The voices of Minnesota haunted me, woke me in the dark. The land was chasing me. That land which had been stretching before me since my decision to move to New Orleans was now tumbling backwards. Wide open fields were narrowing, closing, receding on me, and I longed to spread them wide again, to run again, to flatten out the tumultuous earth and grass that seemed to crave me, calmly, surely, preparing a grave for me.

To run was the only answer which made sense to me, because I am a runner; my life is a marathon. Everything slightly challenging, frightening, or difficult, I avoid. I run. The phone rings, and I pretend not to be home. I have a paper to write, and I watch TV. Dishes to wash, I go out for a beer. It is more than procrastination; it is an endless race. Can I outrun responsibility? Can I outrun myself? Can I run fast enough and long enough before I am caught? And it does not ever end. Sometimes it gets easier. I get out in front—a comfortable lead—and I can jog for a while, but most of the time I am running as hard as I can. I am in the thick of it, and I cannot see the finish line.

I came to believe I could create my own finish line, or at the very least forfeit the race. Razorblades seemed just as good as tickertape parades. Because some journeys do not end fast enough, some roads too difficult to pass, sometimes the burn in your chest too painful to outlast, and your knees give out. At that point razorblades and tickertape parades are just the same.

Perhaps I should start with the fireworks—how I laid out on that little league baseball field and stared up at the night sky. Anna was next to me, her face gently lit with bursts of color then back to dark. She was so beautiful, the way she smiled at me. We had "oohed" and "aahed" at each increasingly impressive pyrotechnic display. And laughed. That was back in Indiana, back in time, a time before pain, a night before I really knew darkness. Sitting in my dark place, I remember thinking that fireworks would be nice.

And do you remember, Anna, when sometimes the nights were like liquid—warm and thick so that we felt like we were wading, slow and easy through the humid air? We would walk around the block holding hands, pulling the landscape with us, it seeping back into our wake as we passed. And then we would come back and sit on the porch, the night like water. Remember how much you loved me? And how I could barely breathe?

The tiled room was warm and thick. I could barely breathe. It was not quiet. The water poured upon itself in a rumble, and steam bellowed up from the hot cascading liquid. There, too, was loud rushing in my head. The voices screaming now, coming on quickly. Quick, like they do. How they sound in the darkness. I was exhausted. My resignation was complete. I had no legs enough to run more.

I could see them all there; they were with me just as before, suffocating beneath the waters of the Colorado river; my loved ones seemed to wash through me all at once. My parents, Jack and Dave, Mara and Nathan, Lindsay and Anna. But they were not themselves. They were ghostly reflections of my failure. Instead of comfort, the images of my loved ones brought only agony. They had become part of the voices. They were within the darkness— the very darkness coming, penetrating every crevice of my mind.

See how you fail them. They love you and you only hurt them. So selfish. You've lost them all. Fool. I have lost them all.

"I wanted to jump in after you," I heard Jack say, "but you were already gone."

Waking up in the middle of the night and finding Lindsay's bed empty, that was with me. How I had opened my sleep-crusted eyes and glanced at the half open bedroom door. Light seeped into the hallway from under the bathroom door. I remember how her side of the bed was cold, how I had laid there for a moment, paralyzed by fear before I tore off the covers and rushed into the hall.

"Hey, baby. You all right in there."

There had been no answer.

"Baby." I said, cracking the door slightly.

Lindsay sat on the floor in her nightgown, kneeling near the toilet. It was clear that she had been throwing up and crying, but now all of her fluids were spent. Tears no longer flowed. She was dry heaving, retching pain. She looked older than she was, her face puffy and distorted.

I went to hold her hair, and I remember the sound she made. It was part choke, and gag, and part five year old girl's outraged shout. She knocked my hand away. It was then that I noticed the knife lying on the sink basin.

"Go!" she screamed.

"I'm not leaving."

And she looked at me with such utter desperation and disgust.

"Yes you are! Yes you…I can't…" Her voice trailed off. She closed her eyes and leaned heavily against the side of the tub.

I sat there all night on the tiled bathroom floor, her not letting me hold or touch her, watching her retch over and over, waiting for her to sleep, being the last one that should be with her but knowing I could not leave her alone even long enough to get a phone. I sat there on suicide watch until the woman I loved eventually exhausted herself with her pain and fell asleep, curled on the bathmat.

What have I done? Dear God. Look what you have done.

In my own darkness I too found my way to the bathroom. I rested my hands on the cool damp sink basin and stared bleakly into the mirror. My acne was bad, and I looked wan in the pallid florescent light. My ears seemed unnaturally large. I am not an ugly man, I tried to tell myself. But I was repulsed by my own image. Finally the mirror began to fog. As it did I thought I saw Dave there looking back at me from the mirror the way he had the night he picked a fight, only making eye contact through reflection. Then Dave's image faded, and all I could see was pale white sky.

Anna will be home soon. She was out at a bar. I stayed home. It was often like that. *She will find the note and it must be done by then. It must be done.*

My years fogged before me with the mirror. Time and expectation enveloped me and blurred all vision of myself. The roaring haze descended over me—I was made weak beneath the burden. Oh, to carry the weight of a thousand dates, and smile the practiced laughter of a magistrate, and feel the sunrise setting every time I wake. Shall I run? It is easier to run. But I cannot bear this. I cannot outrun this. My legs are not enough. My legs are gone.

Hush now. Hush. Rest now. You are safe.

My legs had left me on the mountainside with Jack, too. Jack, how did we make it home, with the ground so far below and the clouds so close? Where is that strength? How long can the body endure? Jack, I cannot bear this one moment longer. You said, you told me, that I was made for college. That there were answers for me. But Jack, friend, I am nothing without you. I am all alone. How long have I been hanging from this cliff? It is long past nightfall, and I do not remember if we remembered to bring a flare.

She will be home soon and it must be done by then.

"Will it always be like this, ya think?" Anna said, cinching the belt of her bathrobe.

"I don't know, Anna. I don't think so…" *But there will be days. There will always be days.*

Sitting on the edge of the tub, I slipped the razorblade from its cardboard sheath. Light and thin. I took up the blade. Steel blade. Cold and simple.

"You really believe in this model mental health shit?" Nathan stared at the ceiling with his hands across his chest. "Like there is some perfect mind we must stack up to?"

Was there a me somewhere that was not this? Or had I been duped by therapy? I had lost so much, slaughtered by my whims. I had left Dave and Lindsay and Mara and Nathan, left my whole life to start again, to make it right. And I had ended up here. Maybe this was it. (Mara on the springtime lawn, pulled her knees to her chin, looked down the empty street and said, "I'm afraid of that. I want…something more.") Maybe this was as good as it would ever be. That is the part that wanted to run again, but I understood somehow, finally, that I could not outrun my own darkness.

Razorblades and tickertape parades are just the same.

All it would take is a stroke. Just a stroke. No blood at first. Just the separation of skin. And then the dance of red in clear water, moving out and up and surrounding me as I lean back, and wait.

I recalled all the blood in the first floor men's bathroom. Recalled Dave's reflection in the mirror, the blood falling freely from his broken nose, thinking that perhaps the interplay of blood and water held the answers.

The note is on the coffee table. It must be done before she returns. It must be done soon.

And then all I could see was Lindsay, balled up on the bathmat, choking on her pain and hate. The voices raged, rushing loud, roaring as water. They came quickly now, quick, one on another, like they do.

Look how you have failedthem how they have failedyou they are all is gone. ItMustBeDone. There is no where to be for MeThere is nothing leftThere is only this.

Jack leaned against a thin pine tree and gazed back up the trail. "I wanted to jump in after you." But I am already gone. It is dark, Jack, and I cannot remember if we packed a flare.

I wanted to cry, but was long past the crying place.

"You've changed," she said.

"Of course I've changed. How can I not?" I raged.

"Do you know how many people are living their lives depressed?" Dave said as though in response.

"Is there something more?" Mara and I asked.

This is all there is. And it is not what I meant, not what I meant at all.

I thought briefly and incoherently that the questions and answers were connected somehow. My eyes closed heavily and then labored back open. So tired.

Hush now. Hush.

I remembered that she had commented on the black blue roundness of the night sky. I remembered walking back to campus wishing I had held her hand. I remembered her face occasionally bathed in color and then back to shadow.

On the edge of the tub, in the middle of my night, I lay the thin blade next to me and lit a cigarette to fight the darkness. I lit a cigarette flare and sat for a moment and thought how the lit end was like fireworks. I smiled weakly. I had stopped living. So why kill myself? It was already done.

XXIV

Some people have a long way to fall. My fall was short and swift. Somehow, somewhere I got lost. I truly believed I was an honest man, a good man, but somewhere I lost the ability to value others. And I have no greater proof of it than the loss of my love.

We enter the world naked and pure. Surely, genetics has determined our hair color and nose type, whether we will be short or tall or average height. Moreover, we are even born with embedded predispositions—we may gain weight more easily than others; we might be more vulnerable to alcoholism or have a higher risk of succumbing to depression. These things are surely with us in our inception; we are not clean slates. However, in our beginnings we are limitless. We can be, we can become, we can achieve and rise. We are all potential and all hope.

But somewhere, sometime, it gets muddied. The path becomes difficult, the way unclear, and all that we could have been and could still be is slung together in a mess of pain and elation, expectation and disappointment. That is the reality of growing up. Years add weight—until we are complex, until we are convoluted—and suddenly one day you wake up and realize that the only thing pure in your life is just a few of your many intentions and your four dollar bottled water. How, then, is it possible to reach the ones we love?

"It's time," she said, her blond hair, long and unwashed. Baby cheeks, button nose, even lying here she was fidgety and distracted.

"I've got time," I said. It was an old argument, the one about time. Anna's sense of time was much more practical than mine. I did not think about time as connected to dates, deadlines, and structure. Structure was not my friend. It froze me up, forced me down. "It can never be now," I often stated. *Now* is always merely preparation, perpetual motion of the grandfather clock's pendulum. We ourselves are only recollections of ourselves; only aspirations. You can see how this philosophical approach might not go over well with Anna, particularly when it came to getting to class.

Sun drenched our double bed, her eyes puffy, her skin soft, clammy and warm. She was beyond me. Her mind already past the bed, considering the shower, the coffee, the study, the enormity of things to accomplish in a day. It was often like that. I did not have her present, not even in the morning before it all went astray.

"Get up."

"I'm awake."

"You're not up. You'll go back to sleep. I know you."

The way she said, "I know you" made me realize that she did not know me. She knew the depression. And she believed it to be me. To her, my failure *was* me. How does one explain that away? How could I change Anna's perception when it had been hardened over months by example after example. I could start by getting up.

But it was not just about getting up. For her (for us both perhaps) it was about how I was a failure, a child. And maybe my inability to wake up in the mornings had become less about my depression and more about my need to annoy her, to pay her back for her emotional distance. Maybe I wanted to fuel her frustration. Maybe I had begun to act as the child she saw me to be. Maybe. I could not trust my mind. I had lost my integrity of thought. I had no idea what I was doing, no idea who I was.

"All right, kid. I'll get up."

She was glowing in the light: beauty of form, her hair splayed against the skin of her naked shoulders. But she is not mine, I thought, and I cannot now remember a time when she was.

As I pulled off the sheet and sat on the edge of the bed to break myself from sleep, she said, "Will it always be like this, ya think?"

"What do you mean?"

"I mean this. This bullshit we do every morning." I knew that when she said *we* she meant the "bullshit *you* do every morning."

"God, I hope not," I said looking at her. She needed more though. Her eyes asked. "You mean, will I always be depressed?"

"Yeah, I guess."

"I don't know, Anna. I don't think so."

We were quiet then. The sun was hot through the morning window.

"But I think this will always be a part of me."

Her eyes shaded suddenly, like a shadow thrown across the window. I was struck again by our distance, not just then, but always. Perhaps she did not know me, knew instead the depression as me, but neither did I know her in the sense that no one can know another, in the way that depths are always hidden, in the way that human communication is so wholly inept. Of mouths that confess, eyes that betray, hands that reveal, none is complete.

Anna was my oasis. But as her eyes darkened and she pulled away, she instantaneously became foreign. She had not changed, being essentially herself from one moment to the next, yet I no longer recognized her. I did not deserve her effort, nor perhaps she mine.

I was alone and self-absorbed, and wondered whether love was ever strong enough to break through ego. I wanted to try—to make this connection about my depression with her. I suddenly, desperately, wanted her to understand as much as she could. Maybe we, she and I, could never know each other, but our abrupt and widening distance emboldened me to choose effort and patience.

"I mean, I'm gonna be okay. I'll recover from this. I believe that now," I said, "but it will always be there. A threat, a warning, a voice."

She looked away and then back again, and her eyes were glassy with unspent tears. "What does that mean? I mean, just the way you talk about it, it's...I don't...believe in this."

"Okay." I said, my gut tightening and beginning to tremble.

"It's just not how I work," she said.

"It's not how people work."

"It's not healthy." Her voice was desperate, warming and growing louder with her confession.

"Of course it's not. It's an illness."

"But it's perception. It's the mind."

I stared at her for a moment in silence. Certainly I had never talked with her about my experience of depression, but surely she knew something. Surely she knew better than this. "Alzheimer's is mental. Can people think beyond that?"

Anna got out of bed and put on her robe. She stood on the far side of the room, the bed dividing us.

"That's different. That's medical. Depression is psychological."

"Jesus, babe, it's brain chemicals."

But as I said it, I realized that I did not understand what I was saying. I understood my own experience, but nothing beyond that. I could not fathom the balance of brain chemicals, nor quantify the dark caverns of the soul. She was saying the same things I had said when I had learned about my depression. She had the same doubts, was questioning the same things; she was grieving in the same way.

"Then why do you say it will always be with you? Once the chemicals are adjusted, why won't everything be normal again?" When she closed her robe, she had kept her arms crossed, hugging herself.

"I don't know. It's just a feeling. Depression is not just an illness, it's a part of me. It is me. And isn't."

How could I make her understand that the voices were mine, my voices, my mind telling me life was too heavy, too much? How could she hear that my doubts and anxieties and fears were mine but amplified in an uncontrollable way? There was no way, really. I could try to separate out myself and the depression in a way she could understand—in the way I understood. But the lines were so blurred, my essence was so indistinguishable. I wanted to be angry with Anna, but instead all I felt was shame.

"Okay. Maybe, maybe it's like smoking," I said, trying again for both of our sakes. "My dad used to smoke when I was a kid, you know? He told me it took him ten years after he quit before he stopped thinking of himself as a smoker, ten years before he stopped thinking that someday he might start smoking again. The addiction became a part of his identity."

"Yeah," she said, "it's like you're addicted to depression. It's almost like you don't want to let it go. Like you lean on it."

"Anna, that's not what I meant."

"But it's what *I* mean. I feel like..." She paused as though checking herself but then finding the courage she pushed on. "...like it's an excuse."

She was not looking at me now when she spoke. She spoke to her feet or to the back wall. She spoke as though speaking not to me, but to the idea of me—as if it could be a conversation to have, an accusation to make, with no consequence. "An excuse you use when you screw up. When you can't see something through."

Each word slid out across the room, out and up and around, directed at the idea of me that she must have felt was present somewhere there in our bedroom. As the pain and shaking in my gut moved to my limbs, I closed my eyes and could feel myself outside of myself.

"But I have to let it slide," she said, "because I don't understand what you're going through. I have to trust that you're sick."

With my eyes closed and myself outside of myself, I could hear and feel her move toward me. Not the idea of me, but me. "I'm sorry, baby. It's just that maybe you don't want to get better. Cause it's easier." And somehow she had seen through me and uncovered my deepest fear, the fear that I actually liked being depressed.

"You think I chose this?" I returned and raged. "You think I like having my girlfriend think I'm a lazy, incompetent fuck?"

She drew back. "We're late. I'm going to take a shower," she said.

Bile could have come from her mouth, and I would not have been more repulsed. I sat silently, seething. I felt weaker than I could ever remember feeling. I could not even find the strength to lay down.

My head became a boulder in heft and weight, but I inched it around to look at her, and I could feel each individual tendon and bone in my neck as I did. She stopped in the doorway and turned, looking back, the living room behind her with everything that we owned together, mingled and one.

"Maybe you like being taking care of."

I do not remember the sobbing. I do not remember screaming "stop!" But I must have. "Just stop it!" I did something. I said something. I cannot remember now. In a moment she was next to me. Her voice softened. She was holding me, shushing me in the way that my mother always had, and rocking me.

"Shhh, Waylan. I'm sorry. I'm sorry."

At the time it all seemed disconnected. Her in the doorway dumping all her frustration and confusion and pain on me. And then suddenly holding me, trying to fix what had been broken. It was all jumbled up, the anger and the love. Now I realize that I had forced on her two roles. She had to simultaneously be the mother and the lover, when really all the while she was merely a frightened child.

"I'm sorry," she said. "I just don't know what you need."

"You, Anna. Jesus, just you."

"But I'm here, baby. I'm right here."

"Bullshit." Tears and snot were on my lips, and I spat the word.

"What does that mean?"

"It means," I whispered. "It means," I cried, "that I moved 1500 miles to be with you...and now I can't find you."

"Here, baby." She handed me a box of tissues from our nightstand. I wiped my face and blew my nose. I had stopped crying. Telling her I could not find her was a confession. And calm drew up and over me like a blanket.

Anna kissed me on the forehead. "I'll be right back." And she went to take a shower.

When she returned, her hair was wet. She smelled of coffee and baby powder. Her energy had changed. Perhaps the warm water had made her clean. She clearly had been thinking. I had thought nothing.

She got dressed in silence. She did not look at me as she slid into her khaki shorts. As she stepped into her shoes, half off-balance, rocking her Doc Martins into fit, she smiled at me sympathetically and said,

"I can't be your past, Waylan. I wonder sometimes about the reasons you moved 1500 miles to be with me. But know that I refuse to be what I've been. We can't be who we were. Too much has changed. Too much is different. If you want to be with me for who I am, for who I am becoming, then let's try. But I will not regress. We were kids, and it was beautiful, and I love you for that. But I can't build a relationship on that. I won't build a life on that. You are going to have to figure out why you are here and then decide whether you should be here or not."

Lying there exhausted I had been attacked, sabotaged even. Frustration and anger poured out of me like a spigot wide open.

"How am I supposed to know who you are now? I live with you and don't know. How are you supposed to know who I've become when you don't really want to know? And then you give me, what was that, some sort of ultimatum. What *are* we supposed to build our relationship on when you keep running away from me?"

"I'm not running."

"That's right, you've got your head buried so deep in your books you don't have time to run."

"Don't you dare make me feel guilty for my studies."

"Then don't make me feel guilty for being depressed."

"I need help," I wanted to cry out. "I am begging for it. I'm pleading. But I don't even know what I need. Anything. Something. I am dying. Save my life." But that is too much to ask of anyone. Even Anna.

"I'm going to class. Are you up for it?"

"I'm not going."

"Okay," she said and was gone.

After that the days began to pass mostly in silence as we both withdrew.

It was not a tense silence. It did not grow thick and heavy and bear down on us. It was a peaceful silence, the kind of quiet that develops through the acceptance that the two of us had very little to say to each other. It was resignation. Of course, there was plenty that we could have given each other. We both needed someone to understand. The answer, however, was simultaneously the problem. Silence was easier. And so life became excruciatingly pleasant. Like elevator music. Our relationship did not challenge or inspire, but neither did it disturb.

She always rose early in the morning, made coffee and took a shower, then studied while I dragged myself (or she dragged me) out of bed. I dropped her off at school and picked her up at the end of the day, waiting in the parked car, listening to NPR's "All Things Considered." Then home. Sometimes we would cook dinner together, or we would go out. Then we would study, each with our books in our separate armchairs. I guess she probably went to the coffee shop or the library a lot, especially when I was not feeling the study vibe. I guess I watched a lot of TV. Late night we would have a couple of glasses of boxed Merlot while reading or catching our shows. Then she would go to bed. Most nights I fell asleep on the couch. Our life together was smooth and predictable. It had a rhythm: I was depressed, and she withdrew, and I resented it, and her withdrawal was reconfirmed again and again. We grew more separate emotionally and intellectually, until all we had left was the ease of our cohabitation. The ambiguity kept us both there. Maybe it was our potential that kept us together that year, maybe the memory of our love. Maybe it was our year-long lease.

The night air was hot and viscous. In bed, staring at the ceiling, I knew she was not yet asleep. I turned and touched lightly her naked shoulder. After a minute in silence, she turned as well, but away from me, facing the wall. I withdrew my hand reluctantly and rolled again onto my back. In the dark, her back to me, Anna said, "I can't do this anymore."

There was instantaneous and overwhelming pain in my chest, and I seized slightly. But it passed quickly because, somehow beyond my denial, it was expected. I knew without further explanation what she meant. I knew she was leaving me. I had seen it coming somehow, had hoped even, and yet simultaneously hated her for voicing it. She was right and evil. Not now. Not this way. Not ever. In that darkness, her back a wall I could not scale, her shoulders and legs, my hands and legs, her breasts, and my lips, her flat belly, my aching chest, all sweating and radiating heat yet not touching, I hated her for being smarter than me. I hated her for rejecting me, sure, but more so for knowing, and for having the certainty I lacked. I hated her for losing her.

"Okay," was all I could say.

Our last day together, the day I took Anna to the airport, she was packing her bags, and I entered the room like a hunted man desperate for cover. She stood in the middle of the bedroom as though she had been waiting for me. "It is time," a voice seemed to say in the back of my skull. "It is now."

"Hey," she said, her voice pleased and bright.

"Hey," I returned, but did not know I was saying it.

"What if I should meet you on the street," I thought, but did not say. "Down by the coffee shop and the used books store. What if you were to see me, and I you? What would we be then? How would we act? As friends? As lovers? Strangers? Would you acknowledge me? What would you say? Would there still be words left on your pallet? Still secrets in your heart? Would there be a moment, seeing each other, when both of our hearts cried out for once again our old completion? Perhaps we would stumble over salutations or chat unnaturally and leave the silent screams of unfulfilled dreams unuttered, unarticulated, unresolved. That is most likely, if we should meet someday later by accident or by fate."

"I just wanted to come in and see how you were doing," I said instead, but the voice did not seem to come from me, and I was shocked by its lies.

"Thanks. Yeah, I'm good. Almost finished." She did not say it with annoyance or indifference, nor with sincerity, but instead she stumbled it as though there was something else to be said— something more.

And she looked at me, stared almost. I met her long glance, and in it I saw her heart. It was searching itself. It was trying to remember what had hurt so much. She was trying to reconcile her leaving. In that moment she loved me again and could not recall what had made her stop.

It is time. It is now. As I stood there breathless, holding the door half open, and she looking so beautiful and alone in the middle of the room, that instant held everything. All the history, all the pain, the longing, all the years of love. All was forgotten, then recalled and forgiven.

Anna knelt then, and zipped her suitcase.

"We better get going," she said. "Don't want to be late."

XXV

"Okay. Got to go," she said, after the stewardess called her boarding row.

"Yeah, I..." So many things I should have said.

"What?"

"It's just..."

"Baby, don't."

"Yeah, okay," I said, understanding already it was too late. "Be safe, all right?"

"I love you. I'll call you."

She once looked back over her shoulder and smiled, but then stepped confidently down the corridor, facing only forward. I watched the plane as it sat on the tarmac, tried to decide if I saw her blond hair in one of the windows, though I was unsure whether or not she had a window seat. I watched as the plane taxied, accelerated and lifted off into sky. I watched the plane get small and disappear in the distance, and waited as though waiting for something.

That is not all, of course. I just cannot remember much else. The details are blunted, like trying to make out objects in a dark room—only hints and gestures of form. So I suppose this is largely incomplete; it is mainly lies. But my memory fails me. Memory is malleable and easily distorted. It escapes us over time in the way an old married couple must fill in the details of a story for each other, the years having eroded the minutia from the mind. Yet together they provide a coherent tale, one they could not have recalled alone because memory is solidified in the telling. Memory is remembered when shared. Forgetting, conversely, is a product of silence. Forgetting occurs alone.

In New Orleans, after Anna had boarded her plane and left me for the last time, I went for coffee and beignets at Café Du Monde. I sat outside, and though shaded by the large green awning, was still wet from the afternoon heat. I pulled a handful of paper napkins from the metal dispenser and waved them at the flies circling my damp forehead. The waitress dropped off a scribbled paper tab. As I opened my wallet, a bent and well-worn photograph fell onto the concrete patio.

It was a picture of Jack. I had taken it in the mountains. In it he sits on a rock silhouetted against a white sky, his roman nose umbrellaed by a fishing hat, green pine cascading on all sides. Studying the photo I was struck by his calm, reminded of his self-assuredness. I remembered that I too had held a sort of strength back then. I began to feel as though there was something Jack had said that I needed to remember.

"All I've built up is gone," I thought briefly and without purpose.

So much of the last four years was a blur to me, jumbled and confused, but snippets began to swirl about like flies.

"I'm always your best friend. What we've been doesn't change," Jack said.

"We were kids, and it was beautiful, and I love you for that," Anna said. "But I refuse to be what I've been. We can't be who we were. Too much has changed."

"It's starting over, you know, but it's not," Jack said.

"You can't run from yourself," Mara said.

But I am a runner.

"You must begin to take control," my therapist said.

"The darkness never goes away, Waylan," Lindsay said.

"Make this work," Mara said.

I left cash on the outdoor table and staggered, listless, up the adjacent steps to a line of benches situated along the river. I sat there on the boardwalk and looked out at the great Mississippi, massive artery of America's heart. That river connected St. Paul to New Orleans and had connected two disparate, equally desperate lives, both my own. The Mighty Mississippi bridged myself to myself.

Sitting there, all that I had sent down the Mississippi while in Minnesota poured back to me. All of my love and pain returned to me on the rapids. My sins washed over me again, and I finally felt an overwhelming, crippling sense of shame. I had, of course, blamed my friends for giving up on me. I blamed Nathan and Mara, Lindsay and Dave, and even Jack, for not being strong enough. Blamed them all for not understanding. Mostly I blamed Anna. But there, finally, I realized I had given up on my friends long before they had given up on me. I could blame others, I could blame the disease, but I was alone by my own doing. I had made myself alone.

Alongside the Mississippi that day, all alone, all types of people were there with me: the tourists, the thinkers, lovers, musicians, and drunks. They were all there (all pieces of me.) And I felt somewhere, there, was the answer—to the mystery of New Orleans, to America, to me. New Orleans was not about the tourists as they passed by and smiled, "Isn't that quaint," as an old man played his heart out on the saxophone for handfuls of spare change.

I began to understand, despite what I had believed, that it was not about poverty, depression or death. "This is not death; this is life," New Orleans seemed to say. "This is what we have, and we shall drink and eat and be merry. We will take what you send us down the Mississippi River; we will take on the burdens and destroyed dreams of this nation and make music." No, New Orleans is not about death. New Orleans is about music. The old man on the saxophone that day played to the river and the river danced, and as it passed it seemed to bring him inspiration for each new note. He played, his back bent, his cheeks ballooning to his task, for his soul and for mine. The music raised me up, raised that whole dirty, angry, beautiful town. It was the same music I had wanted to give Jack back on the mountain, a language for which there are no words.

So let me start over. Because this is not so much a lie as it is a love song. Join me again as a young man, with his life still yet before him on the edge of a cliff, and he is told that he is made for college, and he believes it, and there is still time, still hope that he might be right. There is not yet a Minnesota. It exists only as the tundra of growing fear. And no New Orleans, just the lush representation of desperate hope. If I can start again, then it begins with blue morning air rushing through the car windows, the radio turned up loud, while two boys sing all the words to *American Pie*, and it ends with that same pair of boys ragged from a day of hiking opening the door to my grandparent's cabin after dark but still before dinner. And at dinner they share their adventure, already creating memory with their telling, already forming the truth of the experience by sharing it together, playing off each other, reminding each other of the details and pushing each other to new heights of articulation and description until the day takes on mythic proportion, and the whole of their lives together and the whole of their lives yet to come are entangled in the yarn. Potential is on their tongues—hope and fear of possibility exploding in every silent moment, in every gap between breaths.

Or maybe it starts before that, a moment back in high school, when Anna and I had cried and kissed and made love. She wore a white cotton nightgown, and she leaned over, her straight hair made wavy by a day of humidity and tangled by our passion. It bunched and fell about her face. Her eyes shone with old tears, green fading ever so slightly to blue. And she smiled at me. That was it, just a smile, but it was pure and genuine, as though it sprang straight from her depths. It was just a moment, but in that moment I thought, "What I want forever is this."

I tried to tell Nathan these things about Jack and Anna, about the mountain and the nightgown, one day over coffee and cigarettes. We had gone out to discuss my decision to move to New Orleans, and I was trying to explain to him why I had to take the risk.

Nathan sat in a booth staring out the plate-glass window of the St. Clair Broiler, his hands wrapped firmly around his mug for warmth. Finally he said, "Well, some you see 'em lyin', and some you see 'em lyin' dead."

It was a phrase that Nathan had shared before. It was something I never quite understood. He said his grandfather used to say it. Maybe Nathan knew what it meant, maybe not. But he always said it when there was nothing left to say. It came up occasionally in those awkward moments when a conversation had run its course, but more often, most often, it was said when something was too much, like when someone had shared something particularly tragic. It was something to say when things became indescribably sad or when laughter had been so loud and infectious that its diminishment left an uneasy silence. The phrase was a sort of catch-all when the power of life stunted articulation. When nothing felt fair or true, it was an eternal truth.

"Some you see 'em lyin', and some you see 'em lyin' dead," he would say. And everyone would laugh, maybe laugh-cry, or stare off into the distance feeling as though it was somehow all that was left to be said.

Special thanks to the tireless efforts of my editors: Bob and Joyce Coalson, Allan Harley, Pamela Basey and Kyle Wehmann.

Thanks to the help and counsel of Jon Harper, Jackie La Chance, Megan Van Vleet, Catherine Hartzog, Brian Grant, Jason Triplett, Joey Gufreda, Michael Morrow and Jen Reed.

And a thank you to all of my friends and family, and Chuck, who encouraged me during the long years of book writing. *Land Tumbling Backwards* would not have been possible without such support.

Jonathan Coalson has resided in New Orleans, St. Paul, Indianapolis, Raleigh and Flagstaff. His top five favorite things (in order) are a cold Miller Highlife in a bottle, cheese, monkeys dressed like people, the Indiana Pacers, and world peace. Jon currently writes and tends bar in Breckenridge, Colorado.